Seth Carter's Alien ~~Abduction~~ Adoption

by

Fiona Ostler

Kendall —
Thanks for making
this book look so
good. You truly are
a Jedi Master!
w/ love
Fiona

CONTENTS

For my Dad,

Who fell off the mother ship as a baby,
and has always been a Vulcan in human disguise.

Chapter 1
CONTACT

It was the perfect night to get abducted by aliens.

Of course, I had the same thought every night – it's the optimist in me. The sky was perfect, though. The waxing moon was just bright enough to illuminate the dirt road leading to the forest near my house, but not enough to drown out the stars. Although I wasn't exactly sneaking out of my house to stargaze, nor to be abducted by LGMs (Little Green Men), I wouldn't have been opposed to either. I was just meeting my German girlfriend, Meike, for a little pre-vacation make out session...my first one actually.

The trees shot up into the sky like tall spires concealing a dark, mystical world, just like the opening sequence of E.T. I couldn't help the feeling of anticipation welling up inside me as I drew near to the forest's edge, not because I was about to rendezvous with my SHC (Super Hot Chick), but because every time I went to the forest, a sense of wonder would wash over me. I just couldn't help feeling like I was about to make contact with something from another planet. In fact, I had spent so many happy times in the forest wishing to be beamed aboard the mother ship that it was hard to focus on the real reason I was there. Meike and I'd kissed a few times, but never in a long sequence. We'd also been in the forest alone together, but only during the day, and really only to wander around – a German thing, apparently.

When I reached our giant stump, I found that Meike hadn't arrived, so I lay down on the ground to observe the vast canopy of sky and branches above me. The moon and stars through the tree top shadows were so inviting that I longed for the sky to reach out and grab me up into space. It may sound stupid, but to tell the truth, all I ever wanted was to be abducted. I know, it's a pretty lame goal for a normalish fifteen-year-old boy with a good three-point shot and a decent home life, but I couldn't help it. My whole gestalt was about outer space, UFOs, and finding myself a SHAC (Super Hot Alien Chick) to settle down with one day.

It was getting late, and I began to doubt Meike's intentions in inviting me to meet her at the forest at midnight. Her parents didn't like me much. I wasn't sure if it was because I was black, or an American, or not a German, or just because I was a teenage boy with hormones. Whatever the reason, Meike loved to kiss me whenever her mom or dad would enter the room, which always annoyed them, made her happy, and left me feeling like she had an ulterior motive for our relationship. The fact was, Meike was amazing, but although I was captain of my basketball team, I was pretty sure that my space-geek side would inevitably shine through and completely annihilate any cool-guy façade I had managed to maintain in front of her. It really was only a matter of time before she found out the truth about me and moved on.

Before we hooked up, Meike had been the hot but weird German neighbor girl who was a year older than me and didn't really speak English. We didn't have much in common, but I hung out with her whenever I was bored, which was pretty much always, because I was an only child and we lived off base. My Dad was stationed at Ramstein Airbase in Southern Germany. It was our fifth transfer. With all that moving around it really felt like the only constant in my life was the stars.

I heaved a sigh and sat up, taking my notebook and headlamp from my backpack so I could finish an idea I had been working on. In essence, it was a containment chamber that would fuel one of my rocket designs for when I finally went to space. Some of my best ideas came when I was out stargazing.

The crack of a branch told me that Meike had finally arrived. Mechanically and without much discussion, I put away my stuff while she spread out a blanket in the small clearing, and pulled out a tiny radio which began to play a rock ballad about the kind of love that lasts forever. There, under the blazing stars and generous moonlight, Meike pulled me close and kissed me – for real this time – not just to piss her parents off. It surprised me, and I felt my focus shift from my rocket design to the feel of her lips on mine. We kissed more passionately than ever before. Our hands grasped tightly to the backs of one another's shirts and I felt dizzy, caught up in her feminine smell and soft touch. When she broke away, tears were glistening on her creamy cheeks. I held a strand of her jet-black hair between my fingers and stared into her eyes.

"Ich liebe dich, Set," Meike confessed in a whisper.

I loved that she still couldn't pronounce the *th* in my name.

The pause after she declared her love for me was too long. I knew I should have said something back, especially because I wasn't going to see her for two weeks, but I didn't really know how I felt, so I just nodded and tried to kiss her again.

"You vill call me ven I'm gone?" she asked. "Text?"

"Yes," I said, knowing I probably wouldn't.

It was too hard for me to speak or write in German, and even harder for me to read it. Meike always wrote everything *auf Deutsch*, and there was no way I was ever going to ask Mom to translate. Since I attended an American military base school, my German was pretty bad, but Meike's English was surprisingly worse. Most of the Germans I knew could speak English very well, but for some reason, Meike had entirely missed that subject in school. She had studied some eastern–bloc language like Estonian. Luckily, we were able to communicate just fine in basics. I viewed it as excellent training for any future encounter I might have with BEMs (Bug Eyed Monsters), LGMFMs (Little Green Men from Mars), BAHs (Bipedal Alien Humanoids), or SHACs (Super Hot Alien Chicks), because I had developed inference skills that were pretty much off the charts.

After a few more kisses, Meike grabbed my hand and looked up at the sky. I watched her eyes move from one constellation to the next. The symmetry of her face was illuminated in the starlight, and I wished that we had telepathic powers and could understand each other's thoughts. I was almost positive that communication was going to be so much easier up there.

Meike's eyes were bright, still damp with her goodbye tears, even though she really wasn't going to be gone too long. She pointed up at a falling star and I barely caught the end of its dive.

"Make a wish," I told her.

Meike shook her head in confusion, not understanding what I had said. I smiled and wished the same thing that I had wished over every shooting star, every birthday cake, wishbone, and dandelion puff. I wished to have an alien encounter and visit outer space, or OS as I like to call it, and not just as an astronaut. I had thought about it a lot, and I knew that working for NASA would just be plain spooky, and way too iffy – what with the toilet situation on the space shuttles and all. Besides, a lot of astronauts had died trying to get up there, but you never heard of anyone dying from an alien abduction. They'd always lived to tell the tale.

"I wish that I could go to outer space," I said out loud, pointing up to the big dipper.

At that moment, radio static sliced crisply through the music and a small wind chime rang out in whispers across the airwaves. We both jumped. It was unlike anything I had ever experienced – too precise and perfect to be a coincidence. And even though it was pretty creepy, the surge in my stomach was exhilarating. The sound of the chimes rang out in my mind, reverberated through my entire body, and it seemed like all my senses – touch, sight, smell, sound and even that sixth sense, ESP, experienced the static and wind chimes all at once. I don't know exactly why, but my gut feeling was that we were being listened to by real-live aliens, and that they were trying to make contact with me. I can't explain how I knew it. I just did. I could taste alien abduction in the air.

"Vat is?" Meike asked, pointing to the radio and out to the darkness beyond us.

I glanced around, but saw nothing. Yet I knew someone was listening to us from somewhere up there. I shrugged my shoulders and smiled at her. My attempt to calm the situation didn't quite work as well on me, but Meike seemed to relax. She smiled for a moment and then started tearing up again, which was totally beyond me. First of all, I didn't care that we were being separated for two weeks while she went to Spain with her folks, and second of all, we were on the cusp of communicating with actual LGMs. My mind raced for an explanation of my excitement, but I knew it was pointless to even try. She wouldn't have understood, whether I spoke perfect German or not. Nobody I knew wanted to be abducted, so I ignored her sobs and focused on the static and wind chimes whispering through the speakers, waiting desperately for something more to come of it.

She placed her hand on mine, but I slipped it out of her grasp to play with the tuner on the radio. The music began to tune back in. Then she put her hand on my shoulder in an attempt to pull me back to her. I shrugged her off and picked up the radio, shaking it for all I was worth.

Once Meike understood that I was too preoccupied to continue kissing, she stood up, brushed herself off, and began walking home. Eventually, when nothing else happened, I gathered up the blanket with the radio and followed after her. When we got to her door, she grabbed her things and walked inside without saying a word.

So I had blown it with Meike, which was inevitable, really, but I didn't care. My mind reeled with possibilities as I crossed the street and headed for home. The birds were already chirping, although the sky was still dark. I crept through the front entryway and was about to climb up the stairs when I heard a chair scrape against the kitchen floor. Dad walked out into the hallway to meet me.

"Where have you been, Seth?" he asked, directing me into the kitchen. He sat me down and took up his seat on the other side of the table again. A collection of rolls and pastries from our bakery was set out on the table. I took a chocolate covered croissant out of the box.

"I went to the forest," I said.

"With Meike?" he asked.

"Yeah, she was there," I said, trying to shrug off the fact that I'd sneaked out of the house in the middle of the night...to be with a girl...without permission.

"She's a nice girl." He said as if it were a question.

"Yup."

"Did you...," Dad's face contorted as he struggled to find the words.

"Nope. Don't worry, Sir. I blew it...like I think she dumped me, but it was in German, so I don't really know what happened."

"You blew it, huh?" Dad shifted his shoulders.

He took a bite from his buttered roll and leaned back into his chair, staring at me contemplatively. While Mom would have grounded my butt for an eternity for staying out all night, Dad just chewed and swallowed.

I bit into my croissant, dying to tell him about my almost LGMFM encounter. I was trying to figure out if I should tell him about the wish I had made on the falling star and the static and wind chime that rang out almost as if in response, but instead, I asked,

"How did you know you wanted to marry Mom?"

He flashed me his typical Lando Calrissian smile. "You'll just know."

He must have thought I was all broken up and stuff about Meike dumping me, and he tried to reassure me with another smile, but I guess the look on my face told him that I needed more. It inspired him to launch into some weird pep talk, which, oddly enough, answered the real question in my head: *Do you think that I will ever get to be abducted by aliens?*

"Seth," he said, leaning back in his chair, "Don't worry about any failure tonight. You're a smart boy who always makes good decisions. When it comes down to the important stuff, just go with your gut. You'll know what to do. Trust yourself. So, tonight, it didn't go the way you wanted it to. It's probably not time for you to get tied up in all that kind of stuff anyway. When the time comes, you'll be able to do all the right things. You just dream big and reach for the stars, and know you're gonna make it, kiddo."

"Thanks, Dad," I said, relieved that he understood. But, then, I realized that he really didn't.

I wanted him to know what had just happened to me. It was so beyond cool, and, despite my better judgment, I felt like I could trust him. I don't know why, because Dad practically went through the roof whenever I'd talk about wanting to go to OS. The whole idea of getting abducted was too far-fetched for someone like my Lieutenant-Colonel father who was completely grounded in reality. Unfortunately, he was being so chill and I was so desperate to talk that before I knew it, I blurted out the whole story – static, wind chimes, and Meike getting annoyed and leaving – and all.

"I think if I go out there a few more times... at night probably ... I may be able to make contact again," I concluded.

He said nothing.

"I know they were there, Dad...listening!"

I could see the wheels in his head turning like we were playing a game of chess and he wasn't sure which move to make.

"I know the static and wind chimes was their invitation."

His right eyebrow rose slightly, but he remained silent. We stared at one another for several seconds and then he suddenly nodded to the stairs, dismissing me.

"Yes, Sir," I said, saluting as I stood, trying to ease the tension. It didn't, and Dad remained stoic and silent like a statue. I high-tailed it up to my room, all the while trying to decide when my next venture out to the forest would be, and whether or not Dad would try to stop me.

I fell asleep to the sound of wind chimes tinkling from the eves outside my window and I drifted quickly into dreams. Somewhere in those moments, the chimes sang a promise to me that I would be picked up soon.

When I awoke from my morning nap, the movers had already arrived. Dad informed me that he'd just been given an emergency transfer to Nellis Air Force Base, Nevada.

Chapter 2

VEGAS

The move back to the States took a little less than three days. Mom and I were furious when we first found out. We hadn't been consulted at all, and there hadn't been time to say goodbye to any of our friends. I will admit that a small part of me was relieved; it was kind of nice to escape having to see Meike ever again. But the rest of me was pretty angry.

My main problem was that I couldn't figure out whether or not the transfer was a routine inevitability, or a direct result of my telling Dad what had happened in the forest. I was pretty sure that if I'd gone back to the same spot, I would have figured out a way to get abducted, but then, within hours, all my hopes were ripped from my grasp. To top it off, Dad basically stopped talking about anything real to me after that night, and my parents started fighting. Mom was ticked about having to live in Las Vegas, of all places, and it looked as if she would never forgive him.

We had to stay in a motel near Nellis during the weeks it took our stuff to catch up with us. At least there was a pool, and Dad was issued a car, but our packing job had been so rushed that we had missed a lot of essentials. We had to go to the store about ten times in the first few days, rebuying things we already owned, that were still somewhere en route.

There wasn't a school on the base, and Mom couldn't

convince Dad to pay for a private one, so I was enrolled in public high school – my first time ever. Despite my best efforts to prepare, my first day started out pretty crazy. I found myself sitting in my new clothes at the motel table, staring at my breakfast of Pop-Tarts and wondering if my shirt really was in style. Not that it mattered in my whole grand scheme of wishing to get abducted, but I had learned that it was always a good idea to at least try to fit in.

Mom sat on one of the motel's queen beds, completely entranced with the morning news. With each new story she muttered darkly to herself about how crazy Vegas was. "Just what have we gotten ourselves into," she asked no one in particular and rolled her eyes.

Dad walked out of the bathroom dressed in his uniform. "You ready, Seth?" he asked.

It was still early, and we could have finished the newscast, but I could tell he was eager to get out of range of mom's bad mood.

"Yes, Sir" I said, taking the hint.

"Just look at this crazy!" Mom interrupted us. Her distinctively silky-soft voice had adopted a new hard edge, and a scowl had replaced her usual smile. "Look at this congressman, Sam!" She pointed to the screen. "He's just been caught in his hotel room with a prostitute and a bunch of drugs, claiming that he doesn't even how he got there. Claims he's happily married and would never do something like that to his family. And there've been stories like this all morning long!"

"What are you going to do today, Marla?" Dad asked, ignoring her outburst.

"What can I do?" She asked slapping her hands on her thighs as she dropped them in defeat. "Don't have a car, don't have a house, don't have a job, and don't have any friends. Maybe I'll take a bus into town and gamble our life savings away, and when you ask me what I was thinking, I'll just say I don't remember. I guess what happens in Vegas stays in Vegas, right?" She gestured at the T.V. The congressman was all over his public apology.

Dad walked me quickly over to the door, "Just please don't watch the news all day, Marla. It's making you unhappy."

"It's not the only thing that's making me unhappy!" she yelled after him.

"Bye, Mom," I called over my shoulder as Dad ushered me out into the glaring daylight, Pop-Tart still in hand. The pool in the center of the of the motel courtyard glistened in the morning sun.

We drove in silence on the freeway. I looked out the window at the scenery – basically either discarded dead plants or colorful plastic. Vegas was an enormous playland in the middle of a barren wasteland and I began missing Germany's lush green forests and ancient architecture. During my fifteen years of life, we had been stationed in Virginia, Guam, Japan, England, and Germany. I wasn't exactly accustomed to desert.

"You doin' alright?" Dad asked finally.

"Yup," I lied. A midyear transfer to a new school was going to be rough, even for an Air Force brat, but I had a secret. Aside from never having to face Meike again, the only other thing that had made me feel better about moving was the fact that only a hundred miles away from Nellis was Groom Lake Air Force Base, otherwise known as Area 51. It was my own personal Mecca – a shrine for extraterrestrial enthusiasts – and I had wanted to go there ever since I had heard about it from Jeff Jones in the third grade. I was going to get out there as soon as I could finagle a way.

"You nervous?"

"Nope," I answered.

"What you thinking about?" Dad tried a third route into a conversation.

"Groom Lake," I answered, just to see what he would do.

Dad's hands clenched the steering wheel and his eyes looked like they were going to bust right out of his head in agitation. "They will shoot you on sight if you set one unauthorized foot on Groom Lake Air Force Base! Do you hear me? And don't you even think about snoopin' around there and hopin' to find somethin' like the time you snuck off to Stonehenge to get abducted. They will blow your brains out at Groom Lake. There is nothing out there, Seth! No aliens…nothing! It's just a test site – you understand?"

"Yup," I shrugged my shoulders and tried to remain calm, but inside I was about to orbit the Earth. Usually, Dad ignored the subject of Area 51 altogether, but the fact that he wasn't trying to do his usual change-the-subject routine – he was actually breaking into a sweat, even threatening me – was an excellent sign. Dad had the MC (military clearance) to find out what they were covering up out there. Maybe he already knew. I guessed by the perspiration glistening on his brow and his determined concentration on the road ahead of us that something really was hidden out there in the desert, and it was only a matter of time until he cracked and told me about it, especially if he was scared about me getting my head blown off. As annoying as our move was, we were stationed at Nellis. Nellis equated to Area 51 in my book, and that meant aliens.

"Shot on sight," Dad warned again and changed lanes.

It was a good thing he did, because out of nowhere a pickup truck swerved into the space where our car had been, sped past us, and crashed into the car ahead of it. At the moment of impact everything around us seemed to slow down. Dad maneuvered perfectly through the collision, but as our car jerked to the left, my head slammed into the side of the passenger door.

It felt like I had blacked out for half a second. When I came to, I looked up to see the rogue truck plow into four more cars before crashing into the median. The attacked cars had ricocheted all around us, but we never collided with them. Dad had driven through the out-of-control traffic as if he were flying a jet in a dog fight. I had tried to keep my eyes on the cars around us – linking them to the screeching tires and sounds of crunching metal blaring in my ears – but eventually had to close them just to breathe, and then there was silence.

"Seth, are you alright?" Dad asked. It was eerie how calm he sounded. I opened my eyes and saw that he had come to a stop near the wreckage of the pickup truck. I could only nod. I was so sick to my stomach I was positive that I was going to puke and tried as hard as I could to get ahold of myself.

Dad unbuckled his seat belt and instructed me to stay in the car, then he jumped out and ran over to the wreckage. The driver's body had been thrown ten feet from his truck, which had caught on fire. Dad stooped over to examine it and I was freaked out that the guy might be dead. I didn't really want to watch, but I couldn't help it. I was so dazed from the concussion I must have gotten from hitting my head that I began to hallucinate.

In my hallucination, I thought I saw a large being of green light with jet black eyes rip itself out of the man's lifeless body the way I would expect a ghost or apparition to leave a dead corpse. At first glance, it actually looked like an alien you would buy at a truck stop or specialty store, but as the thing sailed in lazy circles over the dead body, I realized it was something much more menacing than a LGM. It was a demon, and right as I thought the word, it turned and leered at me as if to say, *you're next.* I blinked a few times, trying to clear my head, but then Dad approached the demon and flashed his Air Force personnel badge, of all things. I expected the thing to tear Dad into shreds, but instead, it vanished.

I tried to get up from my seat but I almost passed out. It felt like my brain was still rattling around in my skull from all of Dad's defensive driving, so I closed my eyes and tried to chillax my mind. We had just survived the worst traffic accident I had ever witnessed and as the terror of the moment caught up with me I found that my body was shaking in response. I was in shock.

In Germany, accidents, though rare, were always terrible because the cars drove so quickly on the Autobahn. If a car crashed, the accident was almost always fatal, and the traffic jam it caused would last for hours. Once, while we waiting for such an accident to clear up, I designed a freeway system in my head that would prevent such traumatic events from happening. It would deliver each car safely to its destination at a very high speed, kind of like how a car wash controls the driving and moves the cars along while preventing them from crashing into the cars ahead. It was during moments like these that I wished our world were more advanced.

When I opened my eyes back up, I was already starting to feel better. Dad was checking on the drivers in the other crashed cars.

I could hear the sirens. I glanced back and saw a huge buildup of cars, but somehow a few ambulances, two police cars and an Air Force-issued sedan, identical to ours, managed to appear on the scene. A tall, black woman with long, braided extensions stepped out of the sedan and walked over to my father. She was so beautiful – almost like a movie star – and it took me off guard to see her speaking so casually with him in the middle of all the nightmare wreckage. Somehow, Dad talking to her was even more out of place than watching him dismissing the lime-green fire demon my mind had conjured up.

About that time, I felt my heart rate return to normal. I wanted to get out of the car to join them, but Dad glanced over at me and motioned for me to stay put. The woman looked over as well and waved, a huge smile on her beautiful face. It was weird how fast she got there and also that she was so happy. And also, what was an Air Force employee doing in the middle of an accident scene anyway?

Nothing was adding up, and I figured that I must have hit my head hard enough that my logic was off. I pulled out my journal and tried to sketch a picture of the monster tearing itself out of the body. It was pathetic that aliens had become a subconscious mirage in my new desert home. Only this alien was dangerous and menacing – not at all like the E.T. I had wished to encounter as a boy. I got stuck on sketching its eyes: two dark black holes in the middle of a fusion of green static and felt my heart began to race again. I shut my book and focused on breathing steadily for some moments.

When Dad finished speaking with the police officers on

the scene, he returned to the car.

"Did they want me to give them a report, too?" I asked, as he buckled up.

"They have our information," he answered, calmly, "If they need a statement, they'll contact you."

"Is the driver dead?"

"Uh," Dad was thinking, but seemed distracted. "Uh… yes, I think so."

"And the people he hit?"

"Only one other casualty," Dad muttered. "Everyone else will be fine."

I felt numb as I glanced around, seriously doubting it. Stretchers full of victims were being loaded into the ambulances. Two people dead. I felt sick and helpless. There was nothing I could do except be grateful I was alive and hope that the others would be alright.

"Who was that woman?" I asked.

"She's my assistant," Dad answered, nonchalantly, putting the key into the ignition.

"Does Mom know?"

"Know what?"

"That you have an assistant who looks like that?"

Dad looked over at me and shook his head, "Nope."

I nodded and looked down at my watch.

"We have just enough time to get you to school… if you're up to it," Dad offered.

I didn't know what I was up to doing by that point. I didn't want to tell Dad about the strange thing I had seen – that I'd hit my head so hard that I was actually seeing monster-type extraterrestrials. Truthfully, I was amazed we were alive and not on the way to the hospital. I didn't really want to go to school, but I didn't want to go back to the motel and spend another day watching the news with Mom and eating stashed doughnuts from the continental breakfast. All I could say was, "Yeah, okay."

Dad started the car and we drove slowly away from the wreck. Once we were back up to freeway speed, Dad sighed and said, "Promise me one thing, Seth."

"What?"

"Don't tell Mom about the accident, okay?"

"Why?" I asked.

"Just...don't."

Chapter 3

NELSON

Central High School was a red–brick building sprawling out over an entire city block. It reminded me of a giant castle, complete with granite gargoyles positioned on the roof, watching the students of all shapes, varieties, and sizes that streamed into the foreboding building like a massive ant colony. A lump formed in my throat. I tried reminding myself that all I had to do was keep my mouth shut about OS, play some good basketball, and I would have friends in no time, but it was no good. I really should have gone to the hospital to get checked out instead of meeting my new peers with a head injury.

Beam me out of here. I wished.

The crowd tightened in around me as we approached the front doors and bottleneck a few feet in front of the entrance where I stood. Since I was taller than most of the other students and was able look ahead to the cause of the jam. A makeshift security scan checkpoint blocked the entryway. Every student had to walk through the metal detectors and pass by the staff members who rummaged through their backpacks for contraband items. I thought of the Swiss Army knife I always carried with me, realizing that it probably hadn't been okay to carry a knife to school at Ramstein either, but they hadn't had a metal detector, so I never really thought about it before.

I looked around for a good place to stash my knife,

deciding that it would be better to hide it somewhere and recover it later than allow it to get lost in the abyss of confiscated items on the tables ahead. Ignoring the growing panic in my gut, I dug in my heels and searched for an escape route when someone bumped into me, knocking the backpack off my shoulder and onto the ground.

"Oh, hey, sorry, dude!" a boy said half to me and half into his cell phone. "Well then tell them no."

"Excuse me?" I said.

The boy pointed to his phone.

"Oh."

The boy was white, like, pale-pasty-not-enough-sun white. His blond hair looked as if he had actually gone into a salon to get some professional highlights done. He was at least a foot shorter than I was and it looked as if he had never worked out a day in his life. He wasn't fat, but he didn't have any muscles either.

"Call me later," he said, slamming his phone shut, then bent over to pick up my backpack.

"Hey, sorry I bumped into you," he said, handing it to me.

"It's cool," I said, wondering why it was even a big deal to him. He had already apologized twice.

The boy smiled.

"What?" I asked.

"Nothing," he said, "it's just… you're new, right?"

"Yeah," I said. "How did you know?"

"Yearbook staff. I know almost everybody here at Central."

"Oh."

"And you're AF, right?"

He meant Air Force. I nodded. "Yeah."

The boy nodded in return. "Haircut."

I looked around. With the exception of Pasty-Highlight Boy, almost every guy wore his hair loose and long. It looked like it was 1969 and I was stuck with a short military cut. Mom was worried I was going to stand out like an Oreo in a glass of milk at public school, what with my military background and all, but I felt more like a Marine in the middle of Woodstock.

"My dad would flip if I grew my hair out," the boy said.

I wanted to ask why his dad didn't flip over salon highlights, but he began walking the opposite direction of the double doors and motioned for me to follow.

"We're stationed at Nellis, too," he announced, once I'd caught up.

"Where are you going?" I asked.

"Out to my car. Well, technically, my sister's car. I'm a freshman, so... you know, but she can drive since she's seventeen. Anyway, we're not allowed to have cell phones anymore."

He waved his phone at me. I thought about the cell in my pocket and wondered if I had anything else in my backpack that was considered illegal. I followed him out to the parking lot.

"So is this your very first day at Central?" the boy asked, stopping in front of a badly beat-up, rusted old car. I couldn't find one section on the surface that wasn't damaged somehow.

"Yeah," I said, trying to conceal my smile, "first day at public school."

"You've always been on base?" he asked, ignoring how funny I thought his family's car looked.

"We've always lived overseas, except for Langley, but I was three when we left. I started school in Guam..."

"Wow! Okay, so always overseas, huh?" he said, cutting me off. "Well, this is The Dent." He slapped the roof of the car. "All of my sibs have crashed it somehow. This summer will be my turn to do some damage. You should hear it backfire – it's totally boss."

I smiled out of courtesy.

"Do you have anything you want to stow in here before we head back?" he asked, opening the trunk.

At first, I thought it was some sort of trick, a way to steal stuff from the new kid. But the earnest – almost helpful – look on the boy's face convinced me to trust him. I pulled my knife and cell phone out of my pockets. Then, I opened my backpack and grabbed my portable video games and walkie talkies. A couple of my friends and I used walkie talkies at school in Germany, but pulling them out in front of this kid made me feel silly, almost as if I were a grown boy still playing with action figures.

I didn't have long to feel awkward, however, as highlight kid grabbed a receiver out of my hands. "Nice," he said, turning it over and examining it. I realized then that I didn't even know his name.

"Uh, what's your name?" I asked, feeling really stupid.

"Nelson White," the boy answered. "You?"

"Seth Carter," I said, stifling another smile. Nelson was as *white* as they came.

"Well, Seth, I'll be your friend and show you the ropes until you find your own peeps."

"My peeps?" I asked.

"With all due respect," Nelson began, "I know that we're both AF, and I'm letting you stash your stuff in my car, and we'll probably eat lunch together, and I'll get my sister to give you a ride home after school, but that doesn't mean that we have to get along, or that we have to be best friends or anything. You won't owe me anything for helping you out. And you can choose a different best friend if you want. I mean, don't feel obligated to me or anything. I'm just helping you out as a fellow Air Force brat."

"Okay, but you sound like a girl," I joked as we threw our stuff in the trunk and headed back toward the school.

Nelson and I got through the check point and metal detectors without being stopped or questioned – probably the haircuts. We looked like total geeks compared with the other kids around us. All we needed were matchy-matchy calculator watches. Several students had to spit out gum and throw away food and there was a pile of confiscated electronic devices on a table behind the guards. It shocked me that they were still trying to get through the doors with contraband items so late in the school year. Didn't they already know it would get taken?

As if reading my mind, Nelson announced, "This is all new. Last month, one of our students did a drive by shooting and almost killed someone. He swears he doesn't know anything about it or how it happened. Whatever... you know? Anyway, now the administration is so worried about gang-related incidents that they set up a security detail along with a whole bunch of restrictions... dumb stuff, like no cell phones or gum, or electronic devices, with the exception of calculators. They're even talking about having a dress code with uniforms and stuff."

I couldn't help wondering in that moment if SHACs dug uniforms like I did. When I became interested in girls, I started daydreaming about my soul mate in OS. In all my dreams, she wore a uniform, you know, like the SHCs wear in almost every sci fi show I had ever watched. My favorite was definitely a form-fitting, little white number, with a utility belt and matching boots. It was too much to hope that the school administration would settle on spandex, though.

A large, Polynesian man ushered us quickly away from the tables to keep the traffic moving, breaking me out of my jumpsuit fantasy.

"That's Mr. Talafale'uluakiola, but most people call him Mr. T because they can't pronounce his name," Nelson informed me. "He teaches science. He's pretty boss. Science fair's in a couple of weeks, by the way."

I was elated to discover I hadn't missed it. I glanced down at my schedule and noticed I had Mr. T's Honors Earth Science class for 6th period – right before the ominous Drama class I had been forced to register for. Nelson read my schedule over my arm and discovered that we had those last two classes together.

I wasn't surprised at all that he was taking Drama I, but shuddered at the thought of having to take it myself. There hadn't been any other elective classes open, so I was stuck with it. I hoped my teacher wasn't really going to make me do a skit or a reading or something idiotic like that. Of one thing I was certain: there was no way I was ever going to wear a black turtle neck like the theatre geeks at Ramstein. I wasn't super into clothes, but that was one look I could definitely do without. It was right up there with tucking t-shirts into sweatpants, and wearing socks with sandals.

As Nelson chattered on about sharing the same lunch, a really long-haired boy walking by reached out and slammed his head into the locker next to us. The kid didn't even stop, though several of his friends who were laughing their heads off glanced back for Nelson's reaction. Nelson, however, didn't miss a beat as his head crashed hard against the metal door. He just kept on talking as if nothing had happened. When the bell rang, he walked away, calling out happily, "See you later, Seth." I was pretty sure his nose was bleeding.

I shook myself in an attempt to see if I was hallucinating again. I wasn't. As I watched my new friend make his way down the hall, I suddenly realized that Nelson was what you might call a "mirage nerd." At first glance, you think he's just a normal kid, but the closer you get, the more you realize the truth: your new friend is a total and complete geek.

There were some things that should have clued me in, like the highlights and the weird talking as he tried to define our relationship, but subconsciously, I must not have wanted to accept the truth. My first friend at public school in America was the kind of kid that got his head slammed into a locker without even flinching. He was used to it, had probably grown up with it all his life. I was so disoriented by the car accident that I hadn't even seen it coming.

Chapter 4

ROXY

As Nelson disappeared from view, I glanced down at my schedule. My first class was history on the third floor. I heaved my backpack back onto my shoulder and started up the stairs. By the time I found the room, the bell had already rung. I headed straight for the teacher, Mr. Rackley, a white-haired man who looked as if he should have retired years earlier. He signed me into his class and selected a seat for me at the back of the room. Some volunteer mom who was giving career counseling to the class passed out a note card to each of us and instructed us to write down the top three things we wanted to do once we graduated. I stared at the card and wondered if I could be completely honest or if we had to share our answers with the group.

I scrawled "Professional Basket Ball Player" in spot number one. "Civil Engineer" was my second choice. Then I hesitated. I really wanted to be in the FBI or CIA or NSA or any other kind of military or government intelligence agency that would give me real answers about UFOs and LGMs, but I knew I'd get laughed at if I admitted it. I finally settled on "Air Force Academy and Fighter Pilot" for my third written choice, because I was positive that writing "Space Soldier" would get my own head slammed into a locker.

The mom asked about our choices and suggested universities or trade schools to the kids who shared their

picks. The boy sitting next to me was trying to read my
card. He had hair as short as mine and had written "AF" as
his first choice.

"Your dad a pilot, too?" he asked.

"Something like that," I answered.

"Miguel," he said, nodding in my direction.

"Seth." I nodded back.

Miguel glanced quickly over my answers, then wrote
"Professional Soccer Player" in his number two spot. Most
of the other kids were talking with their friends or staring
out the window. No one was really listening to the woman
at the front of the class examine some brainy girl's list and
encourage her to apply for Harvard. I glanced up at the
board, where she had written *YOU CAN BE ANYTHING
YOU WANT TO BE!* in big letters.

Space soldier it is! I smiled to myself.

"So, did your Dad just get transferred?" Miguel asked,
hitting my shoulder to get my attention again.

"Yeah," I answered.

"But it's, like, only a few months till school's out,"
he realized.

"Yeah."

"That sucks."

"Yup."

"My parents always wait till summer," Miguel said.

I had no comment.

"So, where'd you transfer from?"

"Ramstein."

"That's in Germany, right?"

"Yeah."

"Man, you're lucky!" Miguel said, "I've never been
overseas."

"Mr. Gomez," Mr. Rackley said, peering at us over his
glasses, "please pay attention to the presentation."

"Sorry, sir," Miguel said with a bright, toothy grin.

When the bell rang, Miguel fell into step beside me,
bombarding me with questions about Europe and filling me
in on his story. His family had been all over the U.S., but
only at Nellis for a year. He didn't like Vegas very much.

"It's like everyone here expects you to be in a gang if you aren't white," he mumbled. "But I just want to fly jets, you know?"

I didn't know, but I nodded and said, "I know."

I just want to fly UFOs, dude, I thought.

Nelson found us in the hallway. He and Miguel gave each other some sort of knuckles salute and I realized they were already friends. I was about to ask if all the AF kids stuck together at Central when another boy with a buzz approached us.

"Is this the new guy?" he asked.

"Yup," Nelson said. "Seth, this is Koa. His mom is also stationed at Nellis, and they live on the base. They're from Hawaii."

"Hey Seth," Koa nodded casually.

I nodded, "Koa."

And just like that, I was part of a group. At lunch we all met up to eat together, which was great, because I hate eating alone.

"We playin' soccer or football today?" Miguel asked while chewing his ham and cheese sandwich.

"Or volleyball, guys?" Koa interjected.

"It's football today," Nelson stated.

Koa groaned. "Oh, not football!"

"I'm sorry, but I think it's my turn to pick," Nelson insisted. "We've played soccer every day this week. I know it's been a while since we played volleyball, but if you remember, Koa, you picked soccer yesterday, so it's my turn today, and I choose football."

"Well, what if our new friend, Seth here, wants us to play basketball?" Miguel asked.

"Not basketball!"

"Come on," Koa said, "We gotta play a game with Hoops, here!"

"It's football today."

"Hey, the Gringo is taking over the plans again!" Miguel joked.

"Who are you calling a Gringo?" Nelson asked, a little too defensively.

"Come on, Haole," Koa said with a smile, "Miguel's only joking."

"Yeah, Cracker," I added. "Lighten up."

"Good one," Koa said giving me the knuckles salute they all used.

We all laughed, except for Nelson, who put the contents of his lunch back on his tray. "I guess you think all those racial slurs are acceptable because I'm white, but what if I started calling you…" Nelson looked at each of us and shrugged. "Forget it. Excuse me, gentlemen, but I'm going to sit with my own kind."

Nelson got up and walked away slowly. Too slowly, in fact. I could tell he was waiting for one of us to stop him, and Miguel finally gave in. "Oh, come on, Gringo! We're only messing with you. We didn't mean it rude! You know we're your own kind."

I think Nelson would have come back at that moment if we hadn't burst out laughing again. It was a good thing his Dad was in the Air Force and he had short hair like the rest of us, because I saw no way he would have had any friends otherwise. Especially if he was going to act like a moody five-year-old girl every time he got upset.

"You need to get a sense of humor, Haole," Koa called over to Nelson.

"Yeah, come on back, Cracka'!" I called, stifling another laugh. It was then that I remembered my stuff was in the trunk of "Cracker's" car, and I wondered if I would ever see it again.

Nelson shook his head and joined a group of white girls across the way.

"He'll be back," Koa said, "Don't worry. No one else will hang out with him."

The moment he sat down, the girls at Nelson's table got up and walked away. Nelson pretended he didn't notice. Miguel waved at him to join us, but then started laughing again.

"So you guys wanna play basketball today after school?" Koa said loudly enough for Nelson to hear.

"Sure," I said. "Where?"

"There's a park by the 7-11 on Lancaster. Do you know it?" Miguel asked.

It was just down the road from our motel. I said so and quickly found out that everyone but Koa lived off-base in a neighborhood adjacent to where we were staying. Miguel offered to pick me up and walk over to the park with me. We spent the rest of lunch talking about some of the HCs at Central.

After finishing his food, Nelson deposited his tray and came back to join us. "I'm only here to show Seth to his next class."

"Sure, sure," Miguel said.

I was happy to find out that the four of us were in Mr. T's class. Koa, Nelson, Miguel, and I all sat together at a table in the back and planned out our science fair project. They were leaning heavily on doing something based on cleaner jet fuel. When I told them I thought we should focus on a new jet engine design altogether they put me in charge of the whole thing.

Then, tragically, it was the last period of the day. Nelson was positively giddy as we walked into Drama together. The room was set up amphitheater style with three large platforms surrounding the stage in a half-circle. We took a seat on the middle step and an obnoxious, red-headed girl sat down next to us and began telling me how perfect it was that I was taking Drama because there weren't enough boys to partner up with for the love scenes. As I glanced around, I was surprised to find that girls outnumbered guys three to one and I got the immediate impression that if you wanted to pick up chicks fast, being a heterosexual male in that kind of setting would certainly help.

The assigned performance was weeks away, but the last thing I wanted to do was a love scene in front of everybody. I asked Ms. Hunter if I could do a monologue, and she said she would think about it. I stuck my nose into a text book for the rest of the class and tried my best to keep under the radar.

On the way out to the parking lot after school, two HCs whistled as we passed by. We stopped when one of them asked Nelson who his new friend was. Then Nelson introduced me, and I realized they were talking about me. One of the girls even gave me her number right then and there.

"Wow! You already got digits!" Nelson exclaimed as we walked over to the Dent. None of the girls overseas had been so forward. In fact, none of the kids I had gone to school with had ever been so open and welcoming. It was weird – nice, but weird nonetheless – and it worried me that I might stop wanting to be abducted so much if I actually fit in somewhere.

"I tell you, Seth, chicks dig us fly boys." Nelson added, looking back at the girl who had hit on me.

"I'm not the one who flies," I mumbled.

"You've flown before, though, right?"

"Yeah, Dad's taken me up a few times."

"Me too. It's boss!"

I tried to picture Nelson flying anything and smiled.

"Yeah...chicks just dig us fly boys," he repeated.

It was obnoxious. "I'm not the one that flies," I said again.

"Yeah, but they don't know that, Dude!" Nelson was giddy. "It's like they expect us to be as boss as our dads are!"

I wondered if Nelson's dad really was "boss." I figured it could go one of two ways. Either Nelson's dad was awesome, like the soldier from *Transformers,* or he was a complete wanna-be like Nelson and filled the tankers for real Air Force fighter pilots. I was trying to picture the man who actually fathered a boy like Nelson White, when suddenly I stopped dead in my tracks. The girl sitting in the driver's seat of Nelson's beat-up family car was a super-model disguised as a teenager.

"Roxy, this is my new friend, Seth. Seth, this is my sister, Roxy," Nelson introduced us as he climbed into the back seat. "She's a junior."

"Hi," I managed to say without letting my voice crack, annoyed that Nelson hadn't told me his sister was an SHC – in fact, she was a SSHC (Super Super Hot Chick). I was taken completely off guard.

"Hey there," Roxy said, flashing me a dazzling smile.

"You're tall, Seth," Nelson said, "so you can have the front seat."

I was just standing outside of the car, staring at Roxy with my mouth wide open. Quickly, I hopped into the seat, buckled up, and tried my best to keep my eyes on the road and off Roxy, who was seriously like some sort of Swedish swimsuit model. Her highlights were just like Nelson's, only her hair was longer. In fact, everything about Roxy was longer: lashes, nails, and legs all seemed to flow out of her tan, size-nothing frame. Her voice was earthier than I expected, and she was calm and collected, not like Nelson at all. It suddenly seemed possible that Nelson's dad was cool after all.

When Roxy dropped me off in the motel parking lot, she asked, "So, you wanna ride in the morning, Seth?"

"Uh, sure," I stammered. "Thanks..., Roxy."

"See you at seven-thirty, then," she said, popping the trunk so I could retrieve my stuff.

"Bye, Seth," Nelson called out. He was crammed in the backseat and I wondered if he minded that he would have to sit back there in the morning as well.

"Bye," I said. "And thanks for the ride."

"See you at the park," Nelson reminded me.

"Cool," I said.

I took one last look at Roxy. Our eyes locked and she smiled at me, then winked. My heart thudded against my chest. It seemed that Earth was offering me a really good reason to not try to get abducted. After my awesome first day at school, Roxy White was its ultimate argument.

She revved the motor as she stepped on the gas. The Dent drove away, leaving me coughing in a cloud of white exhaust.

I spent the next few moments wondering how Roxy White would stack up against a SHAC. I was pretty sure she could hold her own, with or without the skin-tight white uniform, leather utility belt, and matching boots.

Chapter 5

ROSA

Mom was still sitting in front of the TV in her bathrobe when I got into the motel room. I began telling her about my day, but she only nodded vaguely, her eyes still glued to the screen. It was weird. We usually explored our new home together, eager to discover all the strange and exciting things about the places we were transferred to. And she always grilled me about the first day of school. This was the first time she had refused to engage.

I sat down at the small kitchenette table next to the microwave and mini fridge and worked on my Math homework.

When Miguel showed up at our door to pick me up an hour later, Mom hadn't moved or spoken. The news had come on again, which was featuring a story about the accident on the freeway that morning. I kept waiting for Dad and me to appear on the footage, but we must have left before the news crew had arrived. Dad's assistant had still been there, though, smiling as if nothing horrible had happened at all.

"So, can I go?" I asked.

"What?" Mom said, tearing her eyes away from the screen.

"Can I go to the park with my friends?"

Miguel smiled his toothy grin at her and said, "Don't worry Mrs. Carter. It's just down the street, and this neighborhood is real safe. We'll be back before dinner."

"Fine," she said and turned back to the newscast, the cloud of depression encircling her once more.

I sent Miguel out the door and turned back to talk to her. Mom was completely lost, and I wondered if I should leave her since Dad wasn't due back for a few hours.

"Hey, Mom?"

"What?" Her voice was tired.

"I love you."

"Oh, I love you too, baby."

She smiled – her first since we'd left Germany.

"It's gonna be alright," I said, trying to focus on my new friends, and not on the newscast. Apparently more people had died than Dad had realized.

"Do you want me to stay?" I asked, hoping she wouldn't say yes.

"No, you go," she said, getting up off the bed. "Have fun with your new friends." She turned off the television and stretched. "I'll make dinner or... something."

"Mom, I know this place sucks. It's dirty, and there's all that weird stuff on the news, but I've already met some pretty cool friends today. I know you will too – we just need to get into a house and get settled, and I know that you'll love it here. We always find good and bad wherever we go – remember?"

She sighed, but didn't answer.

"Mom, you know it's gotta be bad when the son has to give his parent the pep talk, but here goes," I launched in with everything I had, half joking, but really hoping it would work, "Buckaroo... remember how bad it sucked in Japan at first... everyone kept trying to feed us squid and we had to eat on the floor? Nobody showed their emotions and we kept thinking everyone hated us because we were loud Americans? You bawled your eyes out when we left Okinawa, and now nobody will eat your squid when we have people over for dinner."

She kind of smiled, so I kept going, "Or how ticked off we were at the hot and cold water taps in England?

She cracked a genuine smile then, and said, "You

couldn't understand why a first world country wouldn't just connect the water lines together with a pipe so that they'd have warm water."

"And now we buy English chocolate whenever we can find a British specialty store, and you still write to your book club and you all send each other those knitting patterns and recipes," I added, hoping that the thought of friends would help, but it backfired. Her eyes glazed over becoming distant as her smile drifted back into the pained grimace she wore just moments earlier.

When she glanced back at me she forced a smile. "I know, Seth." She breathed again. "I'll get used to it – just shut up and get your butt over to the park."

"Yes, Ma'am."

I kissed her on the cheek and then ducked out the door. Miguel was waiting in the courtyard. We walked the couple of blocks over to the park together.

I was happy to find that Roxy had driven Nelson over so she could sunbathe while we played. She wore a pair of rhinestone-studded sunglasses which made it difficult to see if she was looking at me or not, but it felt like she was. She had set up a radio on a blanket and was already basking in the sun. A stack of fashion magazines and a pedicure kit soon came out of her zebra-striped bag, but she really spent the majority of the time on her cell phone.

Miguel's twin sister, Rosa, had joined us along with three of his older brothers and two of his younger sisters. I recognized Rosa from Drama, and I was pretty sure I had seen all of his brothers in the halls. When I mentioned it, Koa told me it was typical to have at least one of the Gomez kids in every class. There were seven kids in Miguel's family, which completely blew my mind. Considering the stress my parents had with only one kid, I could not comprehend the nuthouse that must have been Casa Gomez.

Miguel's two younger sisters, Maria and Anna, were in middle school. Miguel and his twin, Rosa, were freshmen like me. Juan was a sophomore, Hector was a junior, and Enrique was just about to graduate and go to the Air Force Academy. All of Miguel's siblings looked alike, with dark curly hair, big bright brown eyes shadowed by thick, heavy, black lashes, and bright, toothy, frequent smiles. They were all good-looking too, and fast. I guessed they had to be fast with so many kids in one family.

If Miguel's family hadn't shown up, there wouldn't have been much of a game. Koa and Nelson weren't great, and Roxy was just there to work on her tan. The Gomez kids were all athletic, and had played together a lot. They were like a flock of birds, even when they were on opposing teams they could read each others' moves.

During the first game, I tried hard not to stare at Roxy too much, although the distraction evened things out. I was, by far, the best basketball player in our group. Koa, Nelson, Miguel, and Rosa played on my team. The rest of Miguel's family made up the opposing side. We thrashed them quickly, so the next round I was given all the girls and, ironically, Nelson, who was practically a girl. We won anyway.

"How about next game it's Seth against everyone else?" Maria teased. I glanced down at her. Her chest was heaving and sweat glistened from her face. She was about a foot and a half shorter than me and I had tripped over her several times on the court.

"Very funny," Miguel said.

"He'll still win," Anna frowned, tossing her hair. "He's, like, good."

"We could play soccer," Hector suggested. "See how Seth does with that?"

"Basketball today and football tomorrow," Nelson gasped between cool-down breaths. "Seth got to choose today because he is the new guy, but it really is my turn to choose, so..."

I tried to picture Nelson playing football and shuddered. You had to give him credit for his enthusiasm, but I had never seen a worse athlete in all my life. He was one of those cheerleader-types who yelled his head off, though his performance wasn't too much to get excited about.

"Is Nelson any good at football?" I asked Miguel's twin sister, Rosa, under my breath. She was standing next to me, barely winded, with a massive smile on her face.

"No," she whispered back, "but I think he likes to be in control of something or else we'd just play soccer all the time. You think you're good at basketball – you should see Miguel play soccer."

She grinned at me. I could tell she hadn't meant to be offensive, that she genuinely liked me, but I didn't like what she had said. It wasn't like I was going around acting like I was a professional basketball player, but she assumed I had an ego. It annoyed me that Rosa thought so little of me when all I could think was how pretty her eyelashes were. I liked the way she moved, too. She played basketball like some figure skater gliding gracefully on the ice. I looked down at my sneakers and tried hard to think of something else to say.

She walked away before I could think of anything so I called out to the group, "I'm pretty tired. Think I'll sit this one out."

Roxy waved and perked up as I approached her blanket, although she was still yakking into her cell phone. I lay down on the ground, next to the radio. She was listening to a political talk show, of all things. I thought it was strange that Roxy listened to the same stuff my dad liked.

"I think I'll sit this one out, too," I heard Miguel saying as the others divided themselves into teams. He walked over to me and plopped down. After that, everyone decided to come over to the blanket for a rest. Roxy ended her call and moved her stuff around to make room for everybody. Hector plopped down next to her. At first, I assumed it was because they were both juniors, but when he started rubbing her back, I realized there might be something between them. Roxy was giggling at Hector, but kept looking over at me while he flirted with her. I hoped nobody noticed that I had been staring at Roxy earlier, especially Hector.

"So," Roxy said, "has anyone asked anyone to Prom yet?"

"Koa is going with Cami," Nelson said, "And you know I asked Melissa, but she hasn't gotten back to me. Is a month too long to wait for an answer?"

Roxy rolled her eyes and directed her attention on Juan

and Enrique. They both shrugged.

"So Foxy Roxy, you wanna go with me?" Hector asked, and kissed Roxy's hand like he was Zorro. After he kissed it, he held onto it and started massaging her palm. It was kind of smooth, but pissed me off.

"Oh, sure, Hector," Roxy answered, still looking at me, "thanks."

Roxy's face sported a smile, but her cheeks went red. I was confused. Roxy and Hector were holding hands. They were going to Prom together. He was rubbing her back... a lot. So why did she keep looking at me and smiling? It made me uncomfortable, and I hoped no one else caught onto her weird signals – if they were signals at all.

"Are you going to Prom?" Rosa asked. I hadn't noticed her sit down next to me. Her brown eyes sparkled and her teeth were white against her smooth toffee skin. Thick black curls spiraled in a frame around her flushed face.

"I didn't really know about it," I mumbled, trying not to meet her gaze again. I didn't mind dancing. I did, however, mind having my father drive me anywhere with a date. Prom was pretty much off my radar until I had a license, and so was dating. Luckily, I didn't have to explain my lack of Prom-enthusiasm to anyone. Roxy and Hector were discussing their plans, Nelson was trying to get a group of us to go to up to the lake, and Koa and Miguel and his brothers were talking about girls at Central.

"Yeah," Koa said, "I barely know Cami. I'm surprised she said yes."

"See guys," Nelson said, "It doesn't matter if you don't know the girl you like... just ask."

"Doesn't matter for a guy like Koa," Juan corrected.

"Burn!" Maria piped in.

"So Seth, do you like Vegas?" Rosa leaned over to me.

"Yeah," I said, "it's pretty cool."

"It's about to get hotter," she teased and began to play with a fraying edge of the blanket between her fingers. Her hands were small and delicate, and her nails were unpolished but neatly trimmed. I liked the way Rosa seemed like a graceful tomboy. She cared about the way she looked, but not too much. It wasn't her life. I glanced over at Roxy who was giggling as Hector whispered in her ear. Tearing my eyes away from the two of them, I looked back at Rosa.

"Do you all still get together and play when it gets warmer?" I asked her.

"Only at night. It gets too hot during the day. Usually, we'll go swim, or go down to the lake… also at night. The temperature is perfect in the evenings. We just stay inside during the day and play at night. You'll see."

"Night games… cool," I said, spinning the basketball on my finger. For some reason I was trying to impress Rosa, but I almost spun the ball into her face. "Which lake?"

"Lake Mead," Rosa dodged the ball and grasped it tightly between her hands.

"What else do you do for fun around here?"

"Oh," she scrunched up her nose, "just like, this, and dances and stuff. Video games. I like to read."

She didn't give the ball back to me, although I grabbed at it a few times.

"What do you read?" I asked.

"Science fiction books," Rosa answered. "I know, I'm a geek. I just finished the last book in the *Martian Dust* series."

I wanted to reach over and kiss her.

"Oh." I smiled, "I loved it."

"Wasn't it awesome?" she said. "I loved how the Wrilth Robots entered the battle in the end. They totally kicked everyone's butt! I didn't even think about the possibility that they would help!"

"My favorite was when the space ship touched down for the first time and then they found Derek's clone," I added, my voice almost cracking with excitement. "I wish I could fly a spacecraft like that… it was amazing. I just want to go to outer space."

The radio on the blanket suddenly went silent, and then instead of an angry caller rambling on about politics, static cut through the airwaves. When the wind chimes sounded, chills tingled down my spine. No one seemed to notice the static or chimes whispering in the air, but I knew instinctively that they were listening again – almost like they had tracked me down and were trying to see if I was serious about abduction. I could hear, taste, smell, and almost touch the LGMFM vibes circling thickly around me.

Suddenly, I became so possessed by the idea that I actually had a chance to tell them what I wanted that I began to speak directly to the radio,

"I've always wanted to be abducted by aliens."

More chimes and static seemed to blast out of the speakers. Rosa nodded, listening attentively, but the odd noises didn't even catch her attention like they had mine. The pause was too long, and the caller's voice returned, complaining about a recent bill that had been passed in Congress. The wind chimes sounded faintly over the cacophony of talk radio and the group's gossip about Central.

"I would go right now, this second, if given the chance," I directed my voice to the speakers.

Static crackled back into the airwaves and into my ears. I could barely make out the tinkle of chimes, but they were still there. Years of wishing and waiting suddenly tore up through me and out of my mouth.

"Come and get me!" I shouted. "This is Seth Carter! I know you're listening. Come and get me right now!"

Everyone in the group stopped talking and stared. Roxy removed her sunglasses and slowly grabbed at her radio. When she found the switch, she turned it off and tossed it back into her bag. I began to study the seam on my jeans.

"Dude, Seth, are you all right?" Nelson asked, passing me a water bottle. "That last game get a little too intense for ya, huh?"

"Uh, yeah," I said, twisting the lid off, "thanks."

Nelson would turn out to be the kind of kid that could get someone out of an awkward moment. I was in his territory – totally embarrassing myself in front of the group – and he had just thrown me a life preserver. After a minute, I looked up to survey the damage.

Rosa's wide-eyed, expectant look suggested she may have understood everything I said, the whole build-up of my feelings, and acting like I was possessed. I had yelled at the LGMs to come for me, but another glance told me Rosa was probably the only one in our group who thought I was serious. Everyone else just laughed it off as I drank down my water. I hoped Rosa would just drop it and we could talk some more about night sports, but once everyone was back to their conversations, she leaned over and whispered, "Hey, Seth, do you really believe in UFO landings and aliens and all that stuff?"

"Yeah," I said, "Do you?"

"No," she said. "If all those sightings really were aliens from outer space, don't you think we would know about them by now? I mean, seriously, think about it. If a spaceship could reach Earth – that would take some pretty intense technology, don't you think? A species that advanced isn't about to hide themselves from us. Why would they? If there was intelligent life out there we would have been enslaved or enlightened by now, right?"

"What if they have a good reason to keep us in the dark?" I suggested.

"A good reason…" Rosa repeated flatly.

I looked around to make sure no one was listening and said, "What if there's a reason they only abduct a few people and leave the rest of us alone to wonder what's going on?"

"Like, what kind of a good reason?" Rosa's eyes twinkled as she looked deeper into mine. I felt completely energized as we huddled in closer to talk. No girl had ever wanted to go into alien abduction theories before.

"Maybe there's a code… some interstellar decree of the universe they have to live by?" I offered.

"Nah." She shook her head. "As if they could get that kind of cooperation from every inhabited planet out there. We can't even get our own planet to get along. Just look at the United Nations. Most countries vote with the U.S. less than thirty percent of the time."

"What are you guys talking about?" We both jumped as

Nelson barged into the conversation.

"You ever been to Area 51?" I asked quickly. It was out of my mouth before I could even think about what I was saying.

All the conversations around us stopped again. I felt like such an idiot. Roxy pretty much looked like she would not be picking me up the next morning – or any other morning.

"You want to go to area 51?" Koa asked.

"Groom Lake Air Force Base, baby!" Nelson was practically bouncing up and down. "Although, I think they just changed the base's name again, to throw everyone off the scent."

"Are you kidding?" Roxy whined. "What is it with freshmen boys and Area 41?"

"Uh… it's Area 51" I corrected, trying to read the rest of the group. It was worse than I thought; they were all staring at me like I was nuts. I tried as casually as possible to ask, "Anyone here ever been?"

"No, but I've always wanted to check it out!" Nelson said. "We should go! It would be totally boss!"

"There's nothing there!" Roxy was exasperated. "It's just an old air base in the middle of nowhere. They do government testing, but Dad says there have never been any real aliens associated with it."

"Yeah, Roxy, but think about it; maybe it's a cover up and there really is something hidden out there," Nelson squeaked, then asked a question that completely sideswiped me, "Haven't you ever wanted to get abducted by aliens?"

I couldn't believe Nelson had actually asked his sister that question; in fact, it completely creeped me out. LGM abduction was my quest, and I did not want to share it with a complete geek like Nelson.

"It's like Nelson fell off the mother ship anyway," Koa laughed.

I was about to be sick. I was the one that fell off the MS – not Nelson. When I was six, I was convinced I'd been left on Earth as a baby, and that one day, my real alien family would realize their mistake and come back to Earth to rescue me. Unfortunately, I soon learned enough about my own biology to count that theory out. Besides, I looked exactly like my dad, and I was pretty sure he wasn't a BAH (Bipedal Alien Humanoid).

"Yeah... Nelson's just trying to get back to his kind," Hector added.

"Or he just wants to get probed," Enrique joked.

"Eww!" Roxy said. "That's just sick and wrong on so many levels... not to mention gross!"

"It could be cool," Rosa came to our defense. "Uh, not the probed part, but what if you got to see outer space, and not like an stupid astronaut would, but like, Captain Kirk?"

"Yeah," I said, not able to help myself, and happy that Rosa understood my whole astronaut aversion, "There is a huge difference between orbiting the Earth and what happens on Star Trek. The Enterprise always seems to be able to come out on top, but once a space shuttle explodes, that's it... just, game over. Getting abducted is the only way to go to outer space, fly a space ship, and live to talk about it."

Everyone was staring at me again. Rosa giggled and hit my shoulder as if I were kidding, but I was being completely serious. I don't know why they were only looking at me. Rosa was the one who brought up Star Trek, and it didn't sound like she was joking either.

Nelson perked up. "So, Mom held me back a year because I was a late bloomer. Technically, I should be a sophomore, but anyway, I get my license in a few months. Maybe I could drive us out there."

"My dad says they'll shoot us on sight if we actually step onto the base without permission," I said, trying my best to discourage him.

"Well, we could do a perimeter scan," Nelson offered. "Just check it out, for now. I've got a few pair of binoculars – you guys all in?"

"I don't believe this," Roxy rolled her eyes and stopped smiling at me altogether.

Miguel and his brothers got up to leave. They were laughing and making UFO sound effects.

"We gotta get home for dinner," Miguel said, stretching out his arms and legs. "See you tomorrow, Seth?"

"Yeah," I said giving him knuckles, grateful that he was still speaking to me after witnessing my geeky side unleashed. "See you, Bro."

"Seth, don't you need to get home, too?" Rosa asked.

Her brothers started cat calling and chanting, "Ooohhh—Rosa has a crush on Seth."

Rosa blushed, but I knew that wasn't the reason she wanted me to walk home with her. She just wanted to talk aliens some more. We had just had a sci-fi encounter of the first kind, which was rare for sci-fi nerds, and it felt like we both just wanted to continue the discussion.

"Yeah, okay," I said, looking at my watch, "I'll walk with you guys."

I went over to say goodbye to Nelson and Koa. Koa nodded to me, waved to everyone else, then took off on his skateboard. Nelson went to give me what seemed to be a hug, but I dodged it and we ended up giving each other an almost high five instead. The boy was just clueless when it came to being one of the guys. I was pretty sure that if Nelson stopped trying so hard, he would almost seem normal. Perhaps it was years of getting his head slammed into lockers that made him so absurdly eager to have friends, but it really came off as lurpy.

"So, you're coming to the lake with us?" Nelson asked. "We'll cook something on my portable grill, listen to some boss tunes, and just relax."

"I guess," I said, as Roxy flashed me a big smile and nodded happily. She tilted her head to the left and her hair cascaded over her shoulder like a sunlit waterfall. Maybe she had forgiven me and I wouldn't have to ride into school with Dad in the morning.

"And I'm serious about our road trip out to Groom Lake," Nelson added with a wink. "You just tell me where and when, brother. As soon as I can drive us, we are so there."

I just smiled this time. Something inside of me desperately wanted to do all my snooping out at Area 51 on my own, even if it meant a four-hour bus ride on some random Saturday. There was no way I was going to let Nelson White butt in on my dream, but I didn't know how I was going to distract him. Just like a dog that heard his master talking about a walk, I was pretty sure Nelson wouldn't stop scratching at the Area 51 door until we went.

"Oh, and you know what, Seth?" Nelson interrupted my thoughts, "You should probably go with us to Prom. It would be so boss! Koa and I are renting a limo—there's plenty of room. I think it would be fun. We could have a sleepover the night before and plan and stuff."

"I don't really know anyone..." I began, trying really hard not to laugh at the sleepover suggestion and fighting the idea that Nelson might be a bit slow, mentally.

"Take Rosa," Nelson said, nodding over at her. Rosa blushed, Miguel rolled his eyes, and I looked down at my sneakers again.

"I'll think about it," I managed, and began walking toward the motel. Miguel joined me.

"You don't have to ask Rosa," he muttered so no one else could hear. "She won't be offended or anything... she's cool."

"Okay," I said, not sure what to say. "Thanks."

I nodded at Miguel. It was funny, him trying to defend his sister's honor. She was saying goodbye to Roxy, who kept pointing over to me. Her cheeks were flushed, and not from playing basketball. I felt bad that Nelson had embarrassed her in front of everyone and wondered how long it would take for her to get back to normal around me again.

Luckily, the awkwardness only lasted for about two seconds. I walked behind the rest of the Gomez kids, and Rosa slowed down so I could catch up to her. We spent a few moments in silence, then I broke the ice,

"So, I'm taking it as a personal challenge to convince you that there are alien life forms out there."

Rosa smiled and nodded, "Well, the way you were yelling into Roxy's radio almost had me convinced."

"Really?" I asked.

"No."

"Oh."

"But do you really think someone was listening to you, or something?" she asked.

Her tone wasn't necessarily sarcastic, so I explained, "Didn't you hear the static and the wind chimes?"

"I guess," she said. "So, that's supposed to mean something?"

"Someone is listening to me," I said. "Every time I mention something about space around a radio, I hear static and wind chimes."

"Every time?" she asked. "How many times is *every time?*"

"Like two," I admitted.

"Oh, I can see why you think a BEM is really listening," she laughed. "You're such a geek."

I loved that she used Bug Eyed Monster terminology. "And you're…so…" I couldn't think of anything to say.

"Skeptical?" she offered and stopped to look up at me. I stared down into her big brown eyes. They were sparkling with mischief.

"No," I said, "you're…beautiful."

It was out of my mouth before I had time to think. Rosa squeaked out a laugh of surprise, and then blushed again. Shaking her head she asked, "Are you messing with me, Seth Carter?"

"No," I said, realizing that I really meant it. She wasn't hot like Roxy, but she was beautiful in a sort of sweet, intelligent, funny way, and her confidence was completely unnerving, but refreshing.

"Oh," Rosa smiled and started walking again. Her eyebrows wrinkled up and her face flushed. I wished I had said something else – maybe actually asked her to go to Prom with me, but I wasn't about to get attached to someone right before I took off for OS – even if she *could* speak sci-fi. That would be a stupid thing to do, especially because I was convinced, by that point that the BEMs were following me.

I spent the rest of the walk listening to Rosa talk about some of the places her family had been stationed, nodding and smiling, but not really listening because I was thinking about the contrast between Roxy and Rosa. They were night and day different, and yet, I was attracted to both of them. In the end, I decide to focus on Roxy because she was safe and already attached to Hector. Crushing on someone like Roxy who flirted, but didn't really mean anything by it, was superficial and easy. But if I fell for Rosa, I would never want to leave again, and leaving was all I was ever going to do.

Chapter 6
SURPRISE

The following weeks passed and I quickly fell into a comfortable routine. It was too comfortable, in fact. The gang had taken over my life, especially my spare time. Instead of trying to make contact again, I had spent the month it took for our stuff to arrive from Germany working on our science fair project, trying to avoid doing a "love scene" in Drama, and playing games at the park with everybody after school. Trying to figure out whether or not to do something about Rosa or Roxy occupied a lot of my time as well. Only when our stuff arrived and we began to unpack did I recognize I'd been majorly sidetracked.

Our new house was located in the same neighborhood where Nelson and Miguel lived. Nelson spent Saturday morning helping me set up my room, and I was amused by the continual look of shock on his face as we unloaded box after box of my books.

"Have you really read these, Seth?" he asked, admiring the collection amassing on the bookshelf nearest to the closet.

"Yup," I said. He had technically become my best friend because I spent the most time with him. But I had made it a habit of keeping my responses to one-word answers and having him actually going through my stuff was just creepy. Nobody had ever gone through my stuff before, not even Meike. I wasn't going to let him in on the real me.

Nelson pulled out a huge volume on rocket engines from a box and hefted up onto the shelf, then sighed, "Figures."

"What?"

"You just whipped out that rocket for the science fair last week. Did you come up with that design by yourself?"

"Yeah."

"Dang."

"What?"

"Man! I thought you stole it off the internet or something," he admitted and sighed. "I guess that explains the look on Mr. Talafale'uluakiola's face as you explained how it worked to the class."

I tried hard not to laugh. I loved the look Nelson got on his face whenever he said Mr. T's name. He could rattle it off without any problems and every time he did, I wondered how many hours he had spent alone, practicing. It was his way of showing off.

"You really knew what you were doing, then?" he continued his investigation.

"I guess."

"So, when Mr. Talafale'uluakiola pulled the rest of the science faculty over to check our project out, and you stumped them all completely…that was for real?"

I couldn't help smiling. "Has anyone ever told you that you ask too many questions?"

"All the time."

I kept working quietly, hoping he would just let it go.

He cleared his throat and exclaimed, "Man! I thought you were making it all up! I really thought you were B.S.'ing – and our teachers didn't really know enough to call your bluff. But you've actually studied this stuff! You get it."

"I guess," I said. I focused on hooking up my computer, hoping he would just stop.

It wasn't as if I were a genius or anything. I hadn't launched myself into OS. I had built a facsimile of one of my rocket ideas, but I hadn't been able to fuel it properly, and it certainly wasn't built to scale. What I really needed in my life was a genius engineer buddy to build my design ideas. I glanced over at Nelson, who was the farthest thing from a genius engineer buddy, and wondered why the universe sent me a slap-happy cheerleader for a best friend instead.

We had just begun putting up an exact replica of the summer night sky in the northern hemisphere with my glow in the dark stars when the revelation of what I really was finally dawned on Nelson in full force.

Out of nowhere he yelled, "You're a space nerd!"

"I'm sorry?" I tried to deflect the attack.

"Seth, with all due respect, I get called a nerd all the time, but I really don't *know* anything and get teased mercilessly, anyway, but you... you're a *real* nerd... and nobody messes with you! How do you get them to leave you alone?"

I wanted to argue that you could be a classified as a "nerd" or "geek" even if you were an idiot, but didn't see how it would help me get the rest of my constellations up before dinner, so I said something about getting picked on at other schools and how the Nellis gang was so nice to take me in. Instead of calming down, Nelson whipped out his cell phone and said something about needing to make a call. I cringed, inwardly, but decided not to panic. The rest of the gang already knew what I was since our first basketball game, and if that hadn't tipped them off, the science fair certainly should have. Everyone was still willing to hang with me, though, so what could Nelson possibly tell them that they didn't already know?

He returned to my room in moments. "Come on. I have a surprise for you. We're going out."

After asking mom if I could take a break, to which she probably agreed because Nelson had been so helpful with everything, we were outside and waiting on the front porch.

"What's going on?" I asked.

Nelson shook his head. "Uh-uh. It's a surprise."

A few moments later, Roxy showed up in The Dent, sporting her Rhinestone-studded sunglasses and looking very amused. The car backfired as she parked, which almost calmed my queasy stomach. It was nice to see a flaw in her perfection.

As we walked over, Nelson announced happily, "Okay! I'll tell you! So, Roxy's taking us to Area 51 right now! Tuh-dah!"

Worry washed over me as I registered the massive smirk on Roxy's face. Even if her car was a piece of crap, she still had a car to drive. We were the freshmen nerds begging her to take us somewhere... and not just anywhere... to space-nerd mecca.

"How did you get her to agree?" I asked Nelson.

"He's doing my dishes for a month," Roxy cut in. "Now get in – it's gonna take a while to get out there."

I was speechless. I didn't know what was worse, the fact that Roxy was going to come along and witness me in all my geek-glory, or that I was going to owe Nelson the equivalent of a life debt for doing chores to get me out to Area 51. It took some doing on my part, but I convinced Nelson to let me have the back seat. I didn't want to have to talk on the drive, and wanted to sit behind Roxy so I could watch her in the rear-view mirror.

We stopped for gas and fountain drinks and then took off out into the desert northwest of Vegas. I had a pretty good view of Roxy's face, so I fixed my attention on that and the rock music she played as we drove – anything to help me focus on being a teenage boy instead of a space nerd. She and Nelson sang along to the music, which made me relax more about being accused of being a geek. They were like a couple of Disney Kids – highlighted, happy, and singing with everything they had. Nelson closed his eyes and Roxy drummed the steering wheel.

I had dreamed about driving out to Area 51 for years, but the trek out there was long, slow, bumpy, and, frankly, a lot less wonderful than I had imagined. We didn't see anything but dust and dry brush for miles as we drove the deserted roads. Things did begin to pick up when we made it to the Extraterrestrial Highway. All the construction and barricades helped foster my excitement because I couldn't help wondering if they were deliberately trying to discourage people like us from doing exactly what we were doing. My optimistic side told me we were onto something.

As we came closer, I realized that the road wasn't going to take us to the base, but rather in a direction that paralleled it from a safe distance. Deserted landscape surrounded Groom Lake for miles and the mountain range nearby, where people on the internet had boasted of hiding and spying, now seemed to be a part of the base itself. It was completely off limits. Roxy finally pulled over to the shoulder, even though the gates and the guard shack were a few miles in from the main road.

"What are you doing? They'll see us?" Nelson yelled out in a shrill falsetto girl's voice, vocally capturing the panic I felt.

"It's a free country," Roxie answered, popping the trunk. "It's not like we turned onto any private roads."

By the time Nelson and I calmed down and decided to join her, Roxy had already set up three lawn chairs and her radio was stationed to her talk show. I was surprised that she could pick up anything. I grabbed the center seat and took a swig of my drink. Nelson handed a pair of binoculars to me and Roxy and then surveyed the base through his own.

I could see several test-site looking areas and bunkers near landing strips. There were even satellites and what looked to be a rocket pad surrounded by a man-made rock bed. The view from the binoculars was amazing. When I mentioned it, Nelson proudly informed me that they were super Hi-Tech military-issued from his dad.

We sipped, watched, and waited, none of us saying a word. Through the binoculars I could even see the guard watching us from his shack. He was talking on his phone. I half-expected the county sheriff to show up and arrest us, or, at the very least, fine us for driving a car like "The Dent," just to get us out of the way. A sign next to the guard shack read, **No Trespassing. Use of Lethal Force Authorized Beyond This Point.**

Shot on sight! Dad's voice echoed in my head as I noted

other signs instructing visitors not to take photos or even dream about loitering.

Nelson took a few loud sips of his drink and observed, "Looks like a few Humvees and an Apache out there on the helipad."

Not to be out done, I pointed out the row of F-22's, and the F-117 that glistened in the sun at the far end of the main runway next to a dried-up salt lake bed, just past the last, nondescript building.

"Stealth attack aircraft are so boss!" Nelson exclaimed after I pointed out the F-117.

"I designed a stealth helicopter," I blurted out, completely forgetting Roxy was there. "Wanna see it?"

"Oh, yes, definitely," Nelson encouraged. "Only, I think they already have one."

"No way," I said.

"Uh, contraire…What do you think they used to take out… uh…" He paused, then said, "Never mind."

I couldn't tell if he were serious or if he really knew something.

I whipped out my notebook and flipped through my designs, explaining why mine were superior, even if the military had come up with one. We viewed the pages silently together. Every once in a while, Nelson said something was "cool" or "boss," and then he'd take an enthusiastic sip of his drink. I wasn't able to explain the details in full to him, but at least he appreciated my artwork and was kind enough to look interested for most of the sketches.

I had almost been able to keep my nerd in check in front of Roxy, but going through my designs, it was unleashed. I completely lost all social filters. In fact, Nelson and I had become so wrapped up in my stealth line of attack, bomber, and fighter aircraft designs that we didn't notice the guard walk right up to us, an M-16 hanging off his right shoulder.

"May I help you?" he asked, interrupting our conversation.

I was a bit startled, but didn't miss a beat. "Are we too early for the air show?"

The guard shook his head and said, "You must be Seth.

I was told you'd be the smart alec."

He handed me a piece of paper. It was a typed message that read,

Seth,

Get your butt home immediately!

   - Dad

Nelson, who had read the note over my arm, whispered, "It's like your dad has eyes in the back of his head!"

"Yeah, pretty much," I agreed.

I was pissed.

The guard was already walking back to his shack, but even with his back to us, I could tell he was laughing.

Roxy obediently began packing up our stuff while Nelson finished the last few sips of his drink. I tossed my chair in the trunk and then stared at the base for a few moments. Longing burned inside of my throat and I pushed back the frustration I felt at the way my father kept managing to hold me back. Three questions rattled around in my head: How did he know? Why did he care? What was he hiding?

I grabbed Roxy's radio up off the ground, hoping they were there, but as I talked into the speakers about abduction and OS, the radio program rambled on as usual. This time, static and wind chimes did not interrupt its regular transmissions as I'd anticipated, and my heart sank. I had lost their signal, or, perhaps, they had given up on me.

"Come on, Seth," Roxy said, patting my shoulder. "Time to go home."

We drove back to Vegas in silence – no air drums and singing this time, just silence. Even Nelson didn't have much to say, and, unfortunately, he seemed just as disappointed at not finding anything out there at Groom Lake as I was. I didn't want it to mean anything to him. It was my dream, not his.

Toward the end of the drive, Nelson began to perk up and make further plans for Prom. It made me feel better that he was focusing on something different. I tried to keep myself from being angry so that I could confront Dad in a

SETH CARTER'S ALIEN <del>ABDUCTION</del> ADOPTION

calm way once I got home. I wanted to know how he had known I'd gone out there.

When I walked through the back door, I found Mom and Dad sitting at the new dining room table they had bought specifically to enhance our family meals, only they were arguing. Since moving to Vegas, fighting had become their only way of communicating.

Mom hadn't yet been able to locate or unpack the kitchen boxes so dinner was pizza on paper towels. I sat down and stared at my allotted slice, sausage and mushroom, completely defeated, as I listened to them go on and on. Mom was freaking out because the pizza delivery guy had mentioned the new security checkpoints at all the doors of Central. We'd been able to keep it a secret from her for a month.

"This place is nuts!" she shrieked. "All the doors have metal detectors!"

"I think every school should," Dad countered, calmly. "We can't ever be too careful these days. You never know who's going to go berserk. Besides, Seth should get used to security check points if he's going to join..."

Mom cut Dad off, "Don't you dare, Samuel!"

I took a bite of my pizza and chewed, waiting for Dad to look at me, but he was deliberately avoiding my gaze. Mom passed me a water bottle, kindness flashing across her face as she took a moment to look at me, then she turned back to Dad and her face became hard once more.

"Marla," Dad said, "Seth has some good friends here... they play games in the park almost every day, and his friend, Nelson, helped us unpack. He even has a ride to school and back..."

"Oh yeah, real great friends. This whole neighborhood's stationed at Nellis."

"At least he has some friends. Isn't that what you're always worried about – Seth having good friends?"

He wasn't mentioning that my friends had just taken me out to Area 51 or how he had put an end to our little venture. When he did look at me, I raised my eyebrows as if to call him on his intervention. He shook his head slightly.

"I don't want all his friends to be Air Force buddies, Sam!" Mom answered his last question, oblivious to our hidden communication, "I just know they'll convince him to join up once they all graduate!" She whispered it, although I was sitting right there, and it was more than obvious I could hear everything she was saying.

"Have you ever wondered if Seth might really want to join the Air Force?" Dad asked.

Mom countered, "What if he turns out like you? Stationed all over the world. Never bringing his wife and kids home to visit the grandparents... to visit us!"

"You want to visit your folks?"

Dad was calling Mom's bluff. She hated her family and rarely called or spoke to any of them.

"Yeah, maybe," she said, and I swear the look on her face was basically suggesting that anything would have been better than Vegas.

"Well then, I'll take you to see them!" Dad bellowed. "Will that make you happy? Seeing our parents? Taking Seth to visit my mother?"

Mom grew very quiet. Dad rarely mentioned his mom. From what I knew, Dad's father abandoned them when he was twelve. He never talked about it. I think Dad's parents must have fought a lot, and that's probably why things ended. Mom once told me that no one liked Grandma Carter because she was one of the most bitter, toxic women alive. Mom also told me that I should avoid going to the Air Force Academy at all costs because Grandma Carter lives in Colorado Springs and I'd have to visit her regularly if I ended up there.

"Have you ever wondered if Seth is like your dad?" Mom changed the direction of her argument. "What if he takes off and disappears, just like your father did. We'll never see him again!"

"That's the most asinine thing I've ever heard!" Dad muttered, then declared, "Seth's nothing like that man! He's not going to become my father just because we moved to Vegas."

The edge of determination in that assertion sent chills through me. The truth was, I *was* like my Grandpa Carter – restless and needing to wander – not just itching to abandon my family, as he had done, but wanting to abandon Earth altogether. Yes, it was selfish of me to want to get abducted. I knew that. But weren't most everyone's dreams selfish? After his note at Groom Lake, I was positive Dad was trying to stop my abduction goals, which made me so angry I needed to leave the table.

I rose from my seat and asked to be excused.

Neither one of my folks answered. They were too busy pretending I wasn't there, anyway, so I took my water bottle and pizza and headed for the stairs.

I couldn't stand how casual Dad was about our transfer to Nellis, especially because it had made Mom so sad. I knew he wanted us to be happy in Vegas, but he wasn't addressing or validating any of her concerns like he usually did. And it wasn't like he was about to address any of mine.

That night, Dad slept on the couch, and the next day, he avoided Mom and me as much as he could. I finished setting up my computer and arranging my room. I could hear Mom throwing things around downstairs as she unpacked boxes. Around noon, Dad came home with a few big-ticket items to appease us. Mine was a bike.

"You sure you don't want to keep saving for the car you're gonna buy me when I turn sixteen?" I joked when he gave it to me, but inside, I was grateful for anything that would get me around.

"You keep pulling crazy stunts like yesterday and this might be your only transportation ever," he warned.

"How did you know?" I ventured.

"Seth, just don't." He shook his head mournfully. For a split second, I thought he might actually explain what was going on, but a frantic, almost fearful look flashed across his face and then vanished. He disappeared for the rest of the day.

Mom went therapy shopping that afternoon, and I unpacked the rest of my boxes. Each one was full of books and paraphernalia that represented my life-long search for more intelligent life in the universe. As I unpacked, it dawned on me that I had lost my focus because I had become so interested in my new friends. I had tried as hard as I could not to geek out at the science fair or bring up OS anymore, just so they'd like me. I had settled down into my new groove so easily that I had almost forgotten my primary objective.

I hadn't heard from my BEMs since the park with Rosa. They hadn't connected with me at Area 51. Had they had lost interest in me? Was it because I had stopped actively searching for them? It had been over a month.

As soon as I finished connecting my computer to the internet, I began a new search for my LGMs. This time I googled *alien abduction wind chimes,* hoping to discover something that would get me back on their trail.

Links popped up on the screen. There was a nice-looking, green alien head wind chime available on EBay, although not really anything connected to what I was looking for. But then, one entry caught my eye near the bottom of the screen. Some woman had written a short article about surviving an alien abduction, only, she called it an "alien adoption." Chills ran up and down my spine as I scanned the sentence, *We call it abduction, they call it adoption.* Were the aliens trying to adopt me? Was that what they were doing?

The woman's name was Connie Jenkins. Connie said she was adopted by the aliens when she was eighteen, right after the Great Depression, which would have made her, like, a hundred years old, but her photo looked as if she were mid-sixties. The main thing she remembered was the wind chimes which she had heard periodically the month before she was taken. The best part was that Connie heard the wind chimes through her radio. She said it was a signal from the aliens – a way to make contact with her before she was adopted.

I read through the comments people had left after Connie's article, which were pretty rude, actually. Mostly, people were ticked off because she wrote about something they had never heard of before, like wind chimes and adoptions. They probably wanted to read about all the cliché garbage they learned from Hollywood, like crop circles and mutilated cows. They thought Connie was lying because her description was so different from the usual abduction stories. The only thing she seemed to have in common with the rest of the abductees was the fact that she had some sort of amnesia and couldn't remember any of the time she had spent in OS.

It was the only link that had anything to do with my own strange occurrences, however, so I decided to go with it. The article mentioned that Connie Jenkins was living in an old folks' home called "The Good Life Living Center." I googled it and discovered there was a nursing home with the same name just down the street from our house.

"No way," I said out loud to my computer screen.

What were the odds that the one woman on Earth who could answer my questions lived only six blocks away? My whole body erupted with goose bumps as I realized I could probably find her and maybe even talk to her about it. Unfortunately, it was already late and I was pretty sure that visiting hours were over.

Chapter 7

WIND CHIMES

That night I had a particularly awesome dream about OS. Meike and I flew up to the Moon in my rocket, and then she was suddenly clad in black shiny leather to match her black shiny hair, and riding on the back of my Special Edition Lunar Harley Davidson motorcycle. We sailed over the floor of the Tycho Brahe Crater, her arms wrapped tightly around my chest. She turned into Roxy for a brief moment, and then became Rosa. When we stopped, I leaned in to kiss Rosa, who then turned into the alien wind chime I had seen for sale on eBay.

I mulled it over in my head while I showered and dressed. As I headed down for breakfast, I decided that my subconscious was choosing to go with the SHACs instead of hooking up with an SHC like Roxy on Earth. Despite Dad's efforts to keep me in reality, I knew I needed to get abducted. It was time to focus on my dreams.

Mom was at the kitchen counter trying to find a spoon in one of the moving boxes so I didn't have to eat with my fingers.

"Do you want some O.J.?" she asked over her shoulder as she opened another box.

"Sure," I said, staring blankly at our dining room table, trying to figure out what to do next. I'd go visit Connie Jenkins, the woman I found on the internet that morning since she was my only lead. I felt a surge of excitement well up inside of me at the thought. Despite the disappointment that Area 51 had been, I still felt like my old self, and was happy about the prospect of continuing my search for intelligent life in the universe.

Mom set the orange juice carton down on the table in front of me and I turned to stare at it instead. There weren't any glasses. Mom was still frantically searching for a spoon, so I took a swig from the carton when I was sure she wasn't looking.

"Seth Carter!" she wailed over her shoulder, losing her usual composure, "You best not be drinking straight outta that container! Get off your butt and help me find a glass!"

I walked over and decided the Tupperware she was rummaging through would work just fine. I poured some juice into one of the round, plastic bowls and took it back to my seat. Then I sipped the milk in my cereal bowl as loudly as possible.

"And don't slurp your cereal!" Mom scolded, opening up the next box. She usually didn't freak out over little things.

I grabbed a fist full of soggy crunch and crammed it into my mouth. Milk splashed all over the table and my chin.

"Yes, Ma'am," I said with my mouth full of food. I don't know why I was being so obnoxious – probably because she was fighting with Dad so much.

Mom sighed, took a deep breath, and yelled, "Samuel! Breakfast!"

Dad walked briskly into the kitchen. He looked as sharp as ever in his uniform. A light blue shirt was neatly tucked into navy pants. His shoes were polished and every step he took was assertive. Dad had definitely found his calling in life. I wished that I could find such a good fit for myself. I seriously doubted it would ever be with the Air Force, though.

Mom was still preoccupied with her boxes and Dad was glancing through some papers, so I quickly texted Roxy that I didn't need a ride that morning. If I was going to visit Connie Jenkins instead of going to class I was going to need to do it without Nelson tagging along. He was definitely a tagger, and I was positive he would have followed me all the way to the rest home if I had ridden to school with him.

"Hey, Dad, can I get a ride in today?" I asked.

"Sure," he said.

"You want breakfast, Sam?" Mom asked.

Dad took one look at my bowl of cold, soggy cereal and winced.

"You want to grab a breakfast burrito on the way to school, Seth?" Dad asked under his breath. Although he was deliberately slamming Mom, I was happy to see that he was cool with me.

"I heard that," Mom said over her shoulder as she threw the silverware she had just found into a drawer. I wondered if I should bother getting a spoon from Mom or if Dad really was really going to get us some fast food.

"He's already having breakfast," Mom declared. "Doesn't need to have some crappy, processed burrito on the way."

Dad examined the list of ingredients on the side of the cereal box, then said, "I'm sorry, crappy, processed what, Honey?"

Mom shut the silverware drawer and turned around to face Dad. The look on her face was pure exasperation. Dad set the cereal box back down on the table and headed for the door.

"See you tonight," he mumbled, then looked at me and added, "we better hurry if we're going to get you some real breakfast."

I sat there, frozen, not really knowing what to do. If I finished my cereal, I would have taken Mom's side. If I hurried out the door, I would have chosen Dad. It was an agonizing moment. Mom had already turned on the radio and was listening to a morning program as she continued her search through the boxes. Even though she was preoccupied, I knew she'd still be upset if I didn't finish my breakfast. Then, mercifully, the phone rang. When she turned away to answer, I took my bowl to the sink and made a break for the door.

On the way, I grabbed my backpack, which was on the kitchen counter next to the radio. Something urged me to give it another go, so I whispered, "Alien adoption." Static began to burst out of the speakers instead of the commercials. I couldn't help smiling as the faint sound of wind chimes tinkled in the background. Suddenly, the wind chimes on my back porch rang out as well as if to echo the thought that this was my destiny. They were back.

"Listen, I want to be adopted," I said as loudly as I dared. "I want you to come get me, please."

There was more static, and then a distant voice clearly said, "We'll come for you, Seth."

"Seth Carter! You find that radio station right now!" my mom barked from the other side of the counter, a hand covering the phone's mouthpiece. I jumped – not so much because of her shriek, although it startled me, but, really because I had just heard an alien's voice. My stomach churned and my heart raced. Someone had actually answered, which freaked me out, but was super-cool at the same time.

After catching my breath, I stepped away from the radio and the static dissolved back into Mom's show. For a split second, I wondered if my mind was playing tricks on me – because I was so desperate to make contact – like it had the morning of the accident when I had imagined Dad talking to the fiery green demon. I was, quite possibly, becoming delusional. I blinked a few times and then slapped myself in the face as hard as I could. It hurt, so I knew I was awake, which meant that a voice had just promised to come for me; it actually knew my name.

Dad was waiting for me in his new SUV. I must have still been in shock because when I plopped down on the passenger seat, he said, "What's wrong, Seth? You look like you just saw a ghost."

Or an alien, I thought.

My mind was racing. An alien had just talked to me. They were coming to get me. They knew my name. I had so many questions I didn't even know where to begin. I was even more determined to skip school and go directly to Connie Jenkins—that is, if she were living in that exact home…or still living at all. We passed a large group of condominiums at that moment. A sign flashed "The Good Life Living Center" in bright pink neon letters. It was too coincidental. I just knew it was the same place from the article and that I would find Connie there. Chills ran up and down my spine and a smile erupted on my face.

"Seth?" Dad asked.

"Uh, yeah?"

"I've been talking to you… what's up?"

I wondered how long it would take me to get back to the retirement home if I walked. The drive to Central wasn't too far—maybe three miles. I started looked for bus stops and bus numbers. The number twenty-five came through our neighborhood.

My dad cleared his throat and inhaled, as if he were about to start talking. Typically, he listened to the radio as we drove. I turned it on, hoping that it would sidetrack him.

"You in a funk or something, Son?" Dad asked, turning down the volume.

It was bad that I was planning to miss school, but perhaps I could be back before lunch—only miss a few classes. If I took the bus, it would definitely be faster.

"Son," Dad paused until I looked up and over to him, "do you need to talk?"

"Just thinking," I said.

"About this morning?"

Not really. No.

I didn't really care much that my parents were fighting. They would eventually work it out. What *I* needed to work out was where the nearest bus stop to school might be and if the number twenty-five passed it.

"I guess your mom and I need to work on the fighting," Dad sighed. "I want you to know that I love your mother. I'm crazy about her."

I decided that if I could catch a bus right after dad dropped me off, I could probably make it to see Connie in less than an hour. I felt in my pocket to see if I had enough change for bus fare.

Dad turned on the air conditioning full blast, even though it wasn't that hot, and drummed his fingers on the steering wheel.

"Look, Son," he said, "I know it's tough. I know you are probably having a hard time finding any kind of faith in stability or love and marriage or women..."

I tuned in. "I like girls," I said.

"Oh yeah?" Dad asked.

"Nelson's sister, Roxy's, cool," I offered.

"I'm not talking about thinking that cute girls are cute," Dad said, "Roxy White is pretty obvious, Seth. I'm talking about your possible inability to form loving and committed relationships with women because your mother and I haven't been getting along lately."

I had no idea what Dad was talking about so I just nodded, hoping he would stop soon. Dad slammed on the brakes right at that moment because we were about to run a red light. He came to a halt in the middle of the crosswalk and a mom jogged her stroller around our front bumper, shooting a dirty look at him.

"Err...sorry," Dad muttered mechanically. He turned his focus to me, "Just want to know what you're thinking about, Seth...what you need from us."

"I don't know what I need," I answered, truthfully.

I just want to go to outer space. I thought.

Static replaced the news report playing on the station and Dad's temper suddenly escalated, which caught me off guard, because I had no idea why he practically punched a hole through the radio as he angrily turned it off.

"What did you just say, boy?" he demanded.

"What?" I asked, completely flummoxed.

"You still want to go to outer space?" he repeated.

"Did I say that out loud?"

There was no way I did—no way I would say something like that to my father ever again.

"Yes! You just said you want to go to outer space."

There was an awkward pause. I was so sure it had only been a thought. After our last emergency transfer and the note at Groom Lake, I knew I couldn't trust him.

But a second later I heard myself explain, "I'm trying to get abducted by aliens right now."

What is in the water here? I thought, waiting to see if Dad heard that as well. In a flash of silly paranoia, I wondered if the Air Force had developed a truth serum and if I had been slipped some at breakfast.

Dad pondered a moment, and then said something that almost made me crap my pants, "Seth, look, I know you've always loved looking at the stars – ever since you were a little boy – it's probably in your blood – but, trust me, son, you don't want to go there. Space is a cold, dark place full of crazy, unfriendly things. It's best just to stay here on Earth. I'm warning you. Stay on Earth."

I didn't know what to say to that. What was I going to do? Argue? I just nodded and tried to push back the feelings of rage. I spent the rest of the drive counting prime numbers sequentially to keep myself from giving anything else away.

One awkward goodbye as Dad dropped me off, and one twenty-minute bus ride later, I was in the lobby of The Good Life Living Center. The receptionist, a young girl who looked to be just out of high school, was on the phone when I approached the main desk. She was giggling and held a finger up at me, signaling that she'd only be a minute. I fiddled with the chain attached to the pen on the desk as I waited.

The girl turned her back on me. "I know. Yeah… I know. Seriously, right? I know. I know…. Yeah…. I know! Uh-huh…"

A minute later she said, "Hold on," into the receiver and turned back around.

"Yes?" she asked me.

"Uh, Connie Jenkins, please?" I stammered.

She checked a chart and said, "Room 145L. Please sign the log," then went back to her phone call. "I know!"

I quickly signed "Nelson White" into the log and wrote down Connie's room number. Two minutes later I was outside of room 145L and knocking on the door. There was no answer. I knocked again. There was still no answer, so I knocked a final time.

"Who is it?" a soft voice asked on the other side.

"It's Seth Carter." I answered as if she knew who I was. I figured that if Connie Jenkins did have amnesia, she wouldn't know if she knew me or not and perhaps she'd answer.

Several chains rattled on the other side of the door, and in a few seconds it opened to reveal a confused, old, white lady. I recognized her from the picture in the article. Connie Jenkins was a medium-build-looking hippie type with frizzy grey hair and an enormous backside. She frowned the moment she looked at me and said, "I don't know you."

The door began to close again, but I jammed my foot against it. "Please Ma'am, I'm doing a report for school and I need to talk to…"

"Get out," she said.

"I just wanted to speak with you for a moment…" I begged.

"GET OUT!"

"I'm doing a report on alien abductions…"

"Leave now, young man, or I will call security!"

"Please, Mrs. Jenkins, I hear static in every radio—and wind chimes…"

There was a slight pause, then, "Ha! That's what they all say!" Then Connie Jenkins actually stuck her tongue out at me and rammed the door against my foot again. The door began to budge its way closed. My foot throbbed. I couldn't believe she wasn't going to let me in. Everything that day seemed so providential.

Connie was about to slam the door against my foot again when I managed to say, "Today, a voice in the radio told me they are coming for me."

Connie's frown melted into a smile. She held the door wide open and beckoned me. "Come in, come in. No sense in your standing out there all day."

"Uh, thanks," I said and walked into her room.

The prominent color on the walls and furniture was white. Several well-selected plants were placed in perfect locations around the room. The room was neat and tidy with very few belongings; in one glance I could tell that everything she owned had a place and a purpose. After seeing her room, I wouldn't have been surprised to find out that she was a feng shui interior designer. I passed by a bathroom and a small kitchen on my way in. Next to her bed was a semi-dining room with chairs that suggested a sitting room.

"Sit down, ah…oh, what's your name again?"

"Seth."

"Well, Seth, please have a seat," Connie said warmly, indicating the white leather chair opposite the brown trunk at the foot of her fluffy white bed. Connie sat on the trunk and pulled the glasses hanging around her neck up onto her nose. "You better tell me what happened."

I quickly summed up all three static and wind chime experiences: the forest in Germany, the park with Rosa, and my mother's kitchen that morning.

"And this morning is the first time you actually heard them speak back to you?" she asked, leaning in toward me.

"Yes, Ma'am," I said, scooting my chair closer to her.

"That is very interesting," Connie smiled and peered at me over her reading glasses, "very interesting."

I felt like I was being examined by a psychologist who needed to be examined herself. While she stared at me, she tapped her fingers on her knee caps and hummed a little tune like Yoda did in Empire.

"What should I do?" I asked, growing impatient.

"Well, do you want to go with them?" Connie asked.

"I think so."

"You know you will never be able to come back," she whispered. "Never ever."

"I didn't know that," I said, my stomach sinking. "But it makes sense, I guess. Why would they come all that way to get someone who would want to come right back again?"

Connie nodded. "As I said in my article, which I assume brought you to me, it is an adoption, not an abduction. Someone there wants to keep you for good. They'll explain that part to you, and ask you if you are willing to say goodbye to earth life forever. They will make a pact with you, and if you agree to it, then off you go. Of course, if you chicken out at the last minute, they will wipe your memory and send you on your way."

"How do you know all this?" I asked.

"I've been able to piece together a few things—mostly from right before I was taken," Connie got the words out slowly. A sad and distant look spread across her face, almost as if she were a little girl reminiscing about a favorite lost toy. "I don't know much about where I went or why I had to come back."

"Have you asked through the radio?" I asked.

"That doesn't work anymore," Connie looked out the window. "Not for me, anyway. But how exciting for you! When do you go?"

"I don't know—they didn't tell me," I said.

"No," she rose abruptly and stood over me. "They wouldn't."

Her expression melted from a happy dream-like state into fear and anger. She looked me square in the eyes and said, "Seth, trust me. You don't want to go to space. Space is a cold, dark place full of crazy, unfriendly things. It's best just to stay here on Earth. I'm warning you. Stay on Earth."

I blinked a few times, feeling nauseated. "My dad just said that exact thing to me this morning."

"He did? Well, he's right. Want a cookie?" Connie asked, walking into her kitchenette. She brought back a large, enamel bunny jar and pulled off its ears. I reached my hand in and pulled out a few Oreos. Connie sat back down without taking any cookies for herself, and smiled expectantly at me. For a split second I wondered if they were poisoned; I didn't know why, but I bit into one anyway. The only way I was going to get any information out of Connie was if I trusted her, and if she trusted me in return. I chewed, swallowed, and waited.

"I don't remember much," she sighed, returning to her calmer self.

"What do you remember?"

Connie's gaze returned to the window and the lost toy she couldn't find. Her hair was all over the place. It looked like wild thoughts shooting out of her brain. The only things that seemed sane about her were her smile and how neatly she kept her apartment.

"I was born somewhere around the turn of the 20th century," she said. "I know how old I should be. I don't know why time moved forward while I was up there. All I know is that I'm an ancient woman stuck in a younger body that has been diagnosed with Alzheimer's and dementia. I remember wind chimes, radio static, a voice, and a promise never to come back to Earth. A space ship... and then something horrible happened and I ended up here. That's it, Seth. But I'm not supposed to be here. And I am not supposed to look like this!"

"Like what?" I asked.

"Haggard!" the woman breathed heavily. "Seth, I would have taken much better care of myself than this!"

I glanced around the room and had to agree. She didn't belong in the room she was living in.

"It's almost as if someone ruined my body for me," she continued. "I shouldn't be this fat! My face shouldn't look like I've been on a continual beer binge and smoking since I was five! I'm an alcoholic and I don't remember ever drinking a drop!"

"Okay...," I said, thinking about every person on the news claiming they didn't know what happened to them when they did something terrible. "So..."

"That's it," she said, "Space is no good. It used me up and spat me out. It's warmer here anyway... better."

"How do you know this?" I asked.

"I just know," she said and stared out the window again.

I looked at my watch. The bus to take me back to Central before lunch would be leaving in ten minutes. There were so many questions I wanted to ask Connie, but knew she didn't have the answers to them. I finished my last Oreo and stood.

"I better go. Thanks for talking with me."

"Be careful, Seth," Connie said taking my hand in hers. "And be sure. You will never be able to come back. I'm positive about that."

"But you did," I said.

"I don't know why. Something must have happened… you just be sure if you choose to go."

"I'll be sure," I said, and walked to the door.

"Seth," she called after me, and I turned back around to face her. Tears were streaming down her cheeks and she hesitated for a moment, grappling with emotion. "Please come and get me. If you make it … if you end up going, please ask them to come back for me. That is, if it's safe. You'll have to see if it is safe first, and then come back and get me."

"I will. I promise."

Chapter 8

MONOLOGUE

I arrived back to school right after lunch had begun. Koa, Nelson, and Miguel were sitting at our table, but for once Rosa had joined them. I sat down next to Miguel, who nodded to me and pushed the other half of his sandwich in my direction. Nelson was talking about how boss a heavy metal boy band would be – especially if they played tag team guitar solos. He was angry that grunge had come along and ruined the hard rock party. There wasn't any room for me to merge into the traffic of conversation so I mouthed a "thank you" to Miguel, who just nodded again and smiled his white, toothy grin. I stole a glance at Rosa, who flashed an identical smile at me and kicked me in the leg.

"And that's the reason, Koa, plain and simple," Nelson stated, then turned to me, "Hi Seth. Missed you, like, all morning long. Where have you been?"

"Doctor's appointment," I said. Everyone seemed satisfied except for Rosa. She had stopped smiling and touching my leg and her beautiful brows contorted like dark branches on a leafless winter tree. Then her nose wrinkled up a bit and she pursed her lips. I cleared my throat and sniffed.

What? I motioned to Rosa with a shrug of my shoulders.

She cleared her throat, tilted her head to the side, and raised one eyebrow in a look which basically said, *I know you're lying.*

I dished the look right back at her and she rolled her eyes and smiled, scrunching up her nose once more.

"So...," Nelson interrupted our nonverbal communications.

I glanced around at the gang. They were all staring at me and Rosa.

"So we're finally going to the lake on Friday night – you down, Seth?" Nelson chose his next topic of conversation. He'd been talking about it ever since I'd arrived.

I watched him as he shoved a lump of his protein bar into the side of his mouth so he could talk. He chewed, swallowed part of it, and then swigged the rest of it down with Gatorade. I remembered, suddenly, that he'd been eating some greasy school lunch the day before and wondered about his change in menu. Then I noticed he was wearing a sweat suit. I glanced under the table at his sneakers, which were also brand new.

"You getting in shape or something?" I gestured to the Gatorade.

"So check it," Koa said – his voice breaking into a giggle, "Nelson's on a diet." Nelson's white face turned bright red, "I just need to lose a few."

"You're such a girl," I joked.

"What? I'm a girl because I want to take care of myself?" Nelson's voice rose and then he snapped. "Just because you're tall and athletic doesn't mean you can look down on the rest of us who aren't."

"I think that you need to eat a little chocolate and you'll feel better," Miguel told him. "Rosa always gets irritable when she diets."

Rosa's head snapped in Miguel's direction, but she looked mortified instead of angry.

"Anyone else here ever been on a diet?" I asked. There was silence. Then I said, "I rest my case. Nelson, guys don't diet—not till they are old—like thirty."

Nelson practically tripped over his new shoes as he bolted from the table. This time, as he left, Rosa went with him. They sat down at a table on the other side of the cafeteria, far away from us. Miguel, Koa, and I looked at each other and then burst out laughing.

For the month I'd been there, something stupid always seemed to upset Nelson during our lunch conversations, but by the end of the day we were back to being friends. I was sorry I had offended Rosa, though. I couldn't understand how anyone who was as beautiful as she was would need to go on a diet. Then, Roxy walked by in her size-nothing white Capri pants, and it all became clear. Suddenly, I even understood why Nelson was on a diet; his sister was made for stardom and fame, and he was a geek with a slight paunch.

"Hey guys," Roxy said. Hector was following her, which made me want to punch him in the gut. "Have you seen Nelson?"

"Over there," Miguel said, pointing out Nelson with his lips.

"You still need a ride home today, Seth?" She put her hand on my shoulder when she asked. "Missed you this morning."

"Uh... sure," I said. "Okay."

"Good," she smiled with a slight wink. "And I have room in my car if you want to go to the lake with us."

"Cool," I said.

Roxy floated away in a smoke cloud of lights, camera, and action, as Hector followed protectively behind, looking more like a watchdog than a boyfriend. The only thing that kept me from completely ripping him to shreds in my mind was the fact that he was Miguel's brother, and actually pretty cool. Besides, Hector didn't know that I had the hots for Roxy, although it was pretty obvious that most boys at Central did. I watched Roxy's body as she walked for a moment and then shook my head back into focus and found Koa staring at her as well.

"Dude, Roxy's just hot!" he announced. "How did Nelson ever end up with a sister like her?"

"Would you say that Nelson's dad is more like Nelson or Roxy?" I asked.

"Roxy," Koa and Miguel answered in unison.

I nodded. *Transformer Dude.*

"Are you guys going to the lake?" I asked.

"Hector's planning on going, so we might tag along," Miguel said, not really clarifying who "we" meant. Just then the bell rang and I headed for my next class. Out of the corner of my eye, I could see Nelson jostling his way through the crowd to reach me.

"So," he began as if nothing had happened, "Roxy says you're getting a ride home with us. I think we'll be playing football at the lake. It's my turn to pick, and I love football—or maybe ultimate frisbee. That's always fun."

Nelson was yapping at my side like a little puppy dog trying to keep pace with a long-legged master. On the way to class, his head was slammed into a locker twice. Not surprisingly, Nelson just kept on walking and talking both times. I began to wonder if I should do something to try to protect him, and finally asked, "Does that bother you, dude?"

"When I let it." Nelson's smile was awkward, almost pleading with me to drop the subject and never bring it up again. Then he changed course. "So, you're coming to Prom with us, right?"

It was only a week away, and I hadn't asked anyone, or even agreed to go. As far as I knew, the girl Nelson had asked still hadn't answered him either. It had been over two months since he invited her. I was beginning to wonder if he would show up to her house that night only to find that she was going with someone else.

Before I had time to think of an excuse, however, Rosa sneaked up on my other side while we walked, and whispered, "I need to talk to you in Drama. I saw your Dad drop you off on the corner this morning." Then she disappeared down another hallway.

Nelson was still talking Prom plans. I stuck with the familiar routine of smile and nod. A third bully slammed Nelson's head into a locker as he passed by, and Nelson went into a list of restaurant options to choose from, "Or maybe we could make dinner for our dates."

I thought about my visit with Connie Jenkins. She had

asked me to come back and get her, and I had promised that I would. If space was a cold, dark, place full of terrible things like she and my dad both said it was, I didn't know why she wanted to get back so badly. I decided that space must be like Earth. It was full of both terrible and wonderful things. Maybe the wonderful outweighed the terrible. My only question was: was the thing coming to get me the wonderful or the terrible? I really hoped my gut would know the difference.

Rosa was already in Drama when we arrived. I sat down on the third step next to her, but didn't look her in the eye. I was still trying to think of a way to cover up the lie I had told at lunch. The best comeback I had was that it wasn't really any of her business and to butt out, thank you very much.

Ms. Hunter walked over to us. "Seth... yes... I've considered your request and finally found just the monologue for you."

It had only taken her a month to get back to me. I'd been sure she had forgotten, since most of the kids had already performed their scenes. I didn't know how I was expecting to get a grade in the class if I didn't perform as well, but part of my plan was to blame her for forgetting to give me a project before it was too late.

Ms. Hunter continued, "It's from a new ethnic play, if you will, a friend of mine just produced in New York—off Broadway—but has had strong reviews for its tenacious ability to make us look at how each of us feels about the equality of men...oh and women...didn't see you there, Rosa."

I rolled my eyes and braced myself for the inevitable, carefully worded explanation, which would be so filled with political correctness that Ms. Hunter would be patting herself on the back for months because of it. I hated the way white people sometimes tried not to sound racist when they spoke to me. One truly cool thing about Nelson was that he treated me like his friend – not his "black" friend. In fact, I was the one who played the race card by calling him Cracka'; he just called me Seth.

When Ms. Hunter finally finished her breakdown of the play, she passed me the script and sighed.

"Thanks," I said, taking the pages from her.

"Rosa, since you have already performed your scene for the class and don't have much to do, would you mind helping Seth work this into shape? Maybe help him with his blocking and memorization? He needs to perform this next week."

"Sure." Rosa smiled.

Ms. Hunter nodded and then walked over to another group of students. I looked down at the script in my hands and for the first time in my life, I wanted to burst into tears. I had no idea how to act, or memorize, or block –whatever the crap that was.

"So why did you lie?" Rosa demanded as soon as Ms. Hunter was out of earshot.

I was about to ask her what she was talking about, but she gave me that 'don't even try it' look that Mom was so good at. All of a sudden, I felt the need to tell someone about Connie. Besides, at that point, I would have done anything to avoid talking about the monologue lying in my hands.

"I went to see someone…who's been abducted before. She heard wind chimes and static too."

"How'd you find her …in a chat-room?" Rosa asked, looking up at me. I had at least a foot on her, even sitting down. She was so little that I wanted to tell her she really didn't need to diet, but somehow knew it would be a bad idea to bring up our lunch-time conversation again.

Instead, I answered her question, "I googled wind chimes along with alien abductions and she had a link."

Rosa breathed out heavily and shook her head. Brown-black curls bounced around her shoulders. The aerial view I had of her eyelashes was amazing.

"Whatever, Carter!" she smiled, playfully. I liked how she called me by my last name. Meike sometimes called me Carter when she got frustrated by not being able to pronounce my first name correctly.

"You don't believe me?" I asked.

"I believe you," she said. "You went to go see some crack pot you found on the internet. Pretty typical of the dumb teenagers I know. I wish everyone would just get a clue and meet real people their own age, instead of desperate, middle-aged ones on-line."

"Okay..." I said, deciding that working on my assignment actually would be better than a verbal flogging, "So, you gonna help me with this thing or what?"

At that point, anything would be better than having Rosa scrutinize the logic of my choices. I passed her the script. While she read over it, I looked around the class. Groups of kids were talking and joking around. It didn't look like anyone was really working on getting ready to perform, which was basically how it had been since day one.

Three girls surrounded Nelson. He was having the time of his life until Ms. Hunter walked over and sent two of them away. Nelson was stuck working with the overzealous redhead who had wanted to do a "love scene" my first day in class. They began reading through their scene together. Poor Nelson was trapped – he obviously hadn't anticipated having to work with her.

"Okay, I think I've got a few good ideas," Rosa interrupted my thoughts. "Why don't you come over to my house on Saturday and I'll help you block this..."

"Block?" I questioned.

"Figure out your movement while you say theses lines," Rosa explained. "And you'll need to wear a suit when you do this."

"Why?" I asked.

Rosa passed the script back, "This guy, Jamal, has just taken the afternoon off from his job on Wall Street to visit his old friends in the 'hood."

"Okay," I said.

She went on, but while she spoke I heard her explain more to me than just my character's psychology, "Jamal is now rich and wealthy. He drives a fancy car...has a fancy watch. His friends hate him for changing, for leaving them behind in the ghetto. He can never go back to the way

SETH CARTER'S ALIEN ~~ABDUCTION~~ ADOPTION

things were. Once you leave... there's just no coming back. Once you go beyond your little world... there's no being happy with what you had."

"Sure," I said, thinking about what Connie had said about never being able to come back to Earth if I chose to be adopted. "Got it."

Chapter 9
LAKE MEAD

I decided to go to the lake with everybody that Friday night. Thankfully, they came for me before either of my parents got home. I left a note explaining where I'd gone, and that I would be fed and home before curfew.

Nelson sat in the back seat of his father's Jeep next to Koa, while I rode shotgun next to Roxy. She explained that we had to go off-road to get to the beach, since Lake Mead was manmade, which was why they got to borrow the Jeep, which was, unfortunately, also very much like the Dent.

The perfume she had on was amazing. She was amazing. I spent most of the drive wondering why a girl like Roxy was driving a bunch of freshmen boys to the lake instead of bringing along a few girlfriends, but the longer I thought about it, the more I decided that no girl in her right mind would ever want to be friends with someone like Roxy. She was an inferiority complex just waiting to happen.

Since Lake Mead was behind Hoover Dam, as soon as we passed the turnoff for it, Nelson started in on the dam jokes.

"Hey Seth, what did the fish say when he swam into the wall?"

"I don't know—what?" I said.

"Dam!" Nelson howled.

He went on and on about the dam tours and all the dam

lines, breaking out every so often in a chant of "Hooooo-ver DAM!" that Roxy, surprisingly enough, joined in on. I glanced back at Koa a couple of times to find him giving me a look indicating that he also thought the White family was nuts. I just nodded and smiled. Unfortunately, Nelson thought I was smiling at his jokes, which made me laugh, and encouraged him to keep going.

The upside was that Roxy blasted her rock music and drove the Jeep like it was a bullet bike. The adrenalin in the air was intoxicating, right up until the moments that Nelson opened up his big mouth and drenched everything in the cold shower of his idiocy. It was like I was on a date with a gorgeous daredevil who just happened to bring along her nerdiest living relative.

We left the main road and bounced down the wash to the lake shore. Nelson kept opening his mouth and doing an annoying bumpy noise sound, which drove me nuts, but made Roxy gun the engine and take it faster. One more glance back at Koa convinced me that he was right with me. How on earth did someone like Roxy have a brother like Nelson?

When we arrived at our spot, I discovered to my relief that only Miguel's older brothers had come. Rosa, Anna, and Maria had stayed home for a girls' night with their mom and aunt. I hadn't really spoken to Rosa after she called me an idiot for going to see someone off the internet – who was the real deal I might add. Although she was still planning on helping me with my monologue the next day, I was relieved that she was absent from our lake excursion. The less time she got to psycho-analyze me, the better.

Another reason it was good Rosa hadn't come that night was that she was far too perceptive and inquisitive. I had decided to come to the lake with everyone in order to talk with the alien I had heard on mom's radio earlier that week. After my little chat with Dad on the way to school, there was no way I was going to try anything at home. The lake venue was perfect. There was a small transistor radio in my jacket pocket, and as soon as I could find a quiet place alone, I was going to attempt to make contact again. I didn't need some girl who didn't believe in LGMs following me around and endangering the mission.

In fact, my full intention before getting into Roxy's Jeep was to get abducted that very night. I had brought along my backpack filled with things I couldn't leave behind on earth and even worn my favorite jeans and brought along my Swiss Army knife, just in case. I figured it was pretty much the best time to leave, since it would not only allow me to realize my earliest childhood fantasy, but also help me avoid public suicide by performing my monologue for Drama class. I just didn't need Rosa's eyelashes to convince me otherwise.

Only a bunch of bored teenagers would have found it cool to hang out at Lake Mead, I thought as I walked around the dry desert shores and inhaled the stench. But at least I was able to see the stars again. I had felt cut off from them since moving to Vegas because the light pollution blocked them out, but there, they were visible. It was nice to have them back, even though they weren't shining as brilliantly as I would have liked, they made me long to leave more than ever.

"Seth?" a voice called to me. It was Nelson and, unfortunately, he was holding up a football.

"Sure," I said, walking over to him.

Hector and Roxy sat in lawn chairs next to the portable grill while the rest of us played a game of touch football, which was Nelson's choice because he didn't like the idea of anyone tackling him. Nelson was worse at football than he was at basketball. Miguel was probably the fastest out of all of us, and if he was able to catch the ball, he could easily score a touchdown before anyone tagged him. Enrique and Juan couldn't catch worth anything. Koa and I were the only ones who really could hold onto the ball without fumbling. In fact, Koa never missed a pass.

After my team lost, mainly because of Nelson, I excused myself to take a leak. I was surprised when Nelson didn't offer to come along with me. Girls were always going off to the bathroom together in herds, and I just assumed he'd want to do the same.

I grabbed my jacket and backpack, and headed off to find a secluded spot. When I could no longer hear my friends' voices, I pulled the radio from my pocket and flipped it on.

"This is Seth Carter," I began. I was just about to say that I wanted to be adopted, but the static beat me to it, and the chimes rang out clearly.

Then the voice cut in, "When do you want us to come for you, Seth?"

"Would now be alright?" I asked hopefully.

There was a funny noise that sounded like it might be a chuckle on the other end, and then the voice said, "Can't right now – how about sometime next week?"

I envisioned a 3' 2" slimy green life form penciling "abduct Seth Carter" onto its calendar.

"Great," I said.

"Seth," the voice became serious, "I must explain that you'll never be able to come back to Earth. You won't be able to see your family or friends again. Are you sure that this is what you want?"

"Yes," I said even though I wasn't. On one hand, I really liked my new friends, but on the other, Vegas was just crazy. Mom and Dad were fighting a lot, which was really making my life miserable. Then, there were all the things going on in the news. Not to mention the fact that Rosa, the only girl I had ever been able to talk to, was so skeptical of my OS theories. It would have been nice to jettison my problems, no matter how small they really were and leave it all behind.

Almost as if the voice on the other end had heard the debate going on in my head, it answered, "Whether you know it or not, you've got a pretty good life."

"With all due respect, I know what I've got, and I know what I want," I tried to convince the voice, or, perhaps, myself.

Everything suddenly became unstable, almost as if the ground were shaking beneath my feet. Several conflicting thoughts fought their way to the front of my mind. Was I ready to leave? Did I like Roxy, or did I really like Rosa? She felt so real – like the super hot alien chick I'd been wishing on stars for all my life – the one who could read my mind and knew me to the core. Maybe it was just hormonal. Maybe Mom and Dad would stop fighting and fall back in love. Maybe we wouldn't get transferred to some other place like Guam in the middle of my Junior year and we'd stay at Nellis with my friends. Was I running away? What if the voice on the other side of the radio was the bad guy? Was he the one that Connie wanted to return to, or the one that spat her out and marooned her on Earth without any memories?

"Why can't I ever come back? I asked.

"You can't come back because we have a much better life for you, one that we aren't ready to share with everyone on your planet … just a chosen few," the voice explained. "I've been watching you for a long time and you're a perfect fit for us, Seth. I think that we might be a good fit for you, as long as you are really happy to say goodbye to your life on Earth."

There was a pause, and when I didn't have anything to say the voice continued, "Seth, I won't lie, we need you – your designs…"

"You know about my designs?"

"Like I say, we've been listening. You have a mind we could use, and I want you to come join us, but I don't want you to come unless you are ready to stay for good, alright?"

There was no way to understand or describe the emotion I felt the moment the voice had told me they needed me. It was something that every part of me wanted desperately to hear. No one had ever really needed me before. A lump caught up in the back of my throat. I felt like I was about to go home for the first time in my life.

"Why don't you think it over this weekend, and get back to me on this radio on Sunday," the voice said. "We've got you locked in, and I will always be able to talk to you. We have a direct line now, so don't worry if you need to take some time. It's a big choice." The voice was so soothing and understanding. It felt almost as if it were giving me a hug over intergalactic radio waves.

"Is it worth it?" I asked.

"It was for me," the voice answered.

"Never come back?"

"Right. But you will be able to boldly go where very few earthlings have ever gone before."

That hooked me. All of my questions would be answered, and I would be able to explore the Galaxy—maybe the Universe—and not as a flimsy astronaut, but as Captain James Tiberius Kirk.

"I'll let you know on Sun...,"

"Hey, Seth, do you mind if I come and take a leak with you?" Nelson barged in. I couldn't believe I didn't hear him coming.

"YES! I DO MIND!" I yelled. The static left the radio and the wind chimes were gone.

"Uh, sorry," Nelson said, glancing nervously at my radio. "You're not really peeing, are you?"

"No," I said.

"The radio thing again?" he asked. "Listen Seth, I don't know what's up with that, but maybe you should get some help or something. Hey, I'm as open-minded as the next guy, but really, what is up with you? Do you want to talk about it? You know, talking about things is what got me through Jr. High and the last two transfers my Dad made. This one really sucks because I got stuck with the whole nerd thing here in Vegas, and for some reason, that I don't understand, Roxy is super popular and I'm not."

I turned my back in an attempt to drown out Nelson, and tried to listen for anything else the alien may have been trying to say, but he was gone. All I heard was Elton John harmonizing with the surrounding crickets and the thumping heart of a teenage boy who was about to have his greatest wish come true.

Chapter 10

PRACTICE

I arrived at Rosa's house Saturday afternoon completely worn out. I'd been up most of the night repacking my backpack. I felt stupid for wanting to bring along comfort items, but I just wasn't certain of what I was going to encounter in space. I included a change of clothes, along with shoes and socks, my swiss army knife and my walkie talkies, extra batteries, my journal of designs since the Alien on the radio seemed interested in them, some photographs I had put into an album, and for some weird reason I included my passport – half hoping the aliens would stamp it for me. Even though I didn't know if I could recharge them, I also packed my cell phone and iPod, and included a small grooming bag with a comb and deodorant and my toothbrush and paste. It felt stupid to pack them because I was sure that aliens must have entertainment and hygiene issues and most likely had comparable items wherever I was going, but I reasoned that it was my way of saying goodbye to Earth life.

I had barely fallen asleep when Mom woke me up to help her deep clean the house, and then Dad insisted I help him in the yard before I left for Rosa's. After consuming the last of the caffeinated cola in the fridge, I showered and dressed. I barely remembered to grab my monologue and Sunday suit as I headed out the door. It was awkward cycling over to Rosa's with the suit still fresh in the dry cleaning plastic, but I didn't really want to wear it the whole time I was there.

The Gomez' residence was a tan, stucco home, similar to mine. Several palm trees, rocks, and yucca plants landscaped their front yard. Juan and Hector were out washing the family SUV. They both nodded as I approached, but busted up laughing once I passed.

Miguel opened the door, not even trying to suppress his smirk.

"Sorry, Seth," he said shaking his head. "I can't help it."

I shot him a side smile and nodded as I followed him into the living room. I'd be laughing at me too, if I were Miguel.

"Rosa said she was going to help you practice and then you'd perform for us," Anna smiled up at me from the living room floor. She and Maria were playing a game of chess.

"Nice uh…suit," Maria said, pointing to the hanged items I was carrying.

I nodded and followed Miguel past the girls and down a hallway. The smell wafting through the doorway of the kitchen hit my nostrils. My mouth salivated and my stomach growled in response. I realized I had skipped breakfast and lunch.

"Hi, Seth," called Mrs. Gomez from the front of the stove as we entered the kitchen. Although she had wrinkles and plump curves that came with age and babies, Miguel's mom was beautiful in the same way that Rosa was. "I'm Julia. It's nice to finally meet you."

I took her hand and shook it firmly.

"Are you hungry?" she asked.

"Yes Ma'am," I said following Miguel as he sat at the counter on a chunky dark-brown barstool—the kind you'd find at second hand stores right out of the 1970's. Mrs. Gomez took my suit and hung it on a hook by the cupboards, then passed us plates full of homemade Mexi-American goodness. My first bite was the perfect combination of black beans, seasoned rice, salsa, guacamole, sour cream, homemade tortilla, and cumin-spiced chicken with a hint of lime in the aftertaste. I don't know who coined the phrase, but food is definitely the way to a man's heart and I hoped there was a cook like Julia Gomez in outer space.

Rosa eventually appeared, taking up residence on the stool next to me and picked at the food Mrs. Gomez placed in front of her. Miguel snorted suddenly, and his mom shot him a disapproving look. I looked over and found that Miguel's toothy grin was much larger than usual. It was all he could do to restrain himself from laughing.

"What?" I asked, though I pretty much knew what.

"Just weird," Miguel snickered. "You working on homework with Rosa."

"She's helping me with my monologue," I tried.

"It's cool, dude, whatever," Miguel shrugged.

Rosa stood up to leave, obviously bothered as well. It was pretty evident that her brothers had been teasing her about inviting me over. I finished my last bite and stood.

"Well, Mrs. Gomez," I said, "that was delicious. Now, if you don't mind, I'm going to take Rosa into her bedroom and make out with her."

"You do that, Seth," Mrs. Gomez chuckled, and took my plate.

"He's kidding," Rosa said to Miguel whose jaw had just dropped onto the counter. "Mom got it. I don't know why you're so slow! Dude! It's just an assignment!"

I took my suit off the hook on the cupboard, grabbed onto Rosa's hand, and led her from the kitchen to play out the joke. As we got out of sight, she silently slid her hand out of mine and moved past me, directing me down the hallway and into her room.

A bunk bed and a lone twin bed by the window suggested that all three girls shared. I realized they had been given the Master Bedroom with an adjacent bathroom. All the bedding was matching-home-made pink and purple fluff with white lace trim. Each pillow had a name on it. Rosa, apparently, had the twin bed, Anna had the top bunk, and Maria had the bottom. Several posters of teenage rock stars were plastered on the walls. A poster of planets rotating around the sun hung next to Rosa's bed.

Her nightstand was covered with books. *Dune* and *Ender's Game* were the two I recognized by cover design from the doorway.

I turned to face Rosa. She was anxious – almost annoyed that I was studying her book pile – and I got the feeling I was invading her private space, just like Nelson had invaded mine. When I smiled to put her at ease, she shook her head and slumped down onto her bed. I took the folded wad of script from my suit coat pocket.

"Oh, just a second," Rosa said, "I've gotta get something. You change while I'm gone." With that, she bolted from the room, closing the door behind her. I quickly put on my suit and then sat down on her bed, reading over the script as I waited. After a few moments, Rosa knocked and entered with a basketball which she tossed to me.

"You want to play basketball?" I asked, palming it.

"No," she said. "It's a prop—something that will tie you back to your brothers. I think you should hold this... dribble it, and twirl it on your fingers as you beg them to talk to you. You know, show them what you were like growing up with them. Remind them that you used to play basketball and stuff."

"Okay..."

"It will also help you with your nervous energy," she explained. "I never know where to put my hands when I'm performing, so I like to hold onto a prop or something. I noticed you were fiddling with the basketball at the park. I think it will help you relax."

"Thanks," I said, awed by how insightful she was, "That's really cool."

We worked on blocking and running my monologue for two whole hours. The best part about Rosa was that she helped me get all the cheesy, emotional lines to sound normal, even believable and the basketball did help me calm down. I played Jamal like he was hurt that his friends hated him for being successful, but was hiding the hurt behind his focus on the ball. Every time it got too intense I would dribble or spin the ball on my fingers. At the end I bounced the ball once and left it bouncing up and down as

I walked off the stage. The ball finally lost momentum and died – like the character's relationship with his friends had.

When I was ready, I performed it for the whole Gomez family. They all clapped instead of laughing when I finished. Miguel slapped me on the back and said, "Well, I about peed my pants laughing when Rosa told me about this, but you really did good. I'm surprised!"

"Thanks," I said. "But, Rosa was the one that's good. She makes acting look like breathing."

"No," Rosa said, "You were… good, Seth."

She was lying. I pretty much sucked. Everyone was just too nice to let me know the truth.

I changed back into my normal clothes as soon as I got the chance and then ended up staying for dinner, which was excellent. I was invited to play games with the family, which was a blast. As hard as I tried to fight against it, I kept picturing myself hanging out with the Gomez family after school and on the weekends. I kept seeing myself at Prom with Rosa. I saw myself on graduation day with Nelson, Koa, and Miguel taking pictures, and then all going off to the Air Force Academy together.

Everything was so confusing. My attachment to my new friends was much too deep for the short period of time I had known them. I could envision the rest of my high school and college life with them. Pretty much the only thing that was really holding me back from telling the alien to come and get me was Rosa, Miguel, Koa, and Nelson… in that order. The more I thought about them, the more confused I became. The more I tried to think about leaving forever, the more my heart actually ached. It had never ached when we had been transferred before.

Rosa and I ended up sitting outside on the back porch eating popsicles and moon gazing. Of course we couldn't see any stars because of the Vegas light pollution, and the moon was pink because of all the other pollution, but it was perfect, anyway, and I loved being there with her, listening to the crickets and enjoying the quiet evening.

Rosa stared at me, not in an 'I'm into you' way, but more as if I had something growing out of my head. Her gaze was fixed hard and her brows were knotted up in thought.

"What?" I asked finally.

"I'm trying to figure out who you are," she answered, truthfully.

"Meaning?"

"You play basketball, but that's not really you. You're also really smart and yet so clueless when it comes to girls..."

"Thank you."

"You're welcome." She smiled, and continued, "And then there's the whole space obsession thing."

"Weird?"

"Not normal... but for you, it kinda works."

"Thank you."

"So, when do you have to leave?" she asked and licked her Popsicle. It was like she had taken a pick-axe and crashed it down onto my inability to speak to anyone about the possibility of being adopted by real aliens. I had wanted to tell someone goodbye, but avoided confiding in Nelson at the lake. In that one moment it was like Hoover Dam itself burst and the whole story tumbled out. I even mentioned what the voice had said about never coming back to Earth and having to leave my friends and family behind forever.

"So, they said that they'd come pick me up next week," I finished. Only then did my mind register the look of horror on Rosa's face.

"Seth, when I asked you when you were leaving, I was talking about when you had to go home," she said slowly, "... like, tonight."

"Ohhh."

She looked at me like there were green zits all over my face and yellow foam oozing out of my ears.

"You're such a jerk," Rosa muttered, then cursed in Spanish.

"What...why?"

"I don't know whether to believe you or to kick you in the balls!"

I flinched involuntarily at the thought. "What does that mean?"

Her face was hard, but her eyes were sad. I braced myself for an attempted foot to the groin maneuver. It never came. Instead, actual tears glistened in Rosa's eyes.

"Uh, sorry," I murmured.

Rosa shrugged my apology off like an unwanted sweater on a cold night.

"I can ask them to come get me after I perform my monologue," I suggested.

"You're such a jerk!" Rosa said again. "You actually think that some alien is really going to come for you! I thought you were all right, Seth, but you're just another crazy butthead who's messing with me! Well, I don't think you're funny at all, and I'm sick of your stupid jokes."

"Wait—are you mad because I didn't ask you to the Prom?" I asked.

Rosa's eyes flashed wildly with anger. "Uh... NO! As if I would even want to go to Prom with an idiot!"

"Okay...," I said bluntly. I turned away from her and started walking into the house.

"That's it?" Rosa called after me.

I wasn't going to start fighting with her; she could rot for all I cared.

"Seth, I'm sorry."

I went through the house and retrieved my script. Mr. and Mrs. Gomez were snuggling together on the couch and watching a movie. Mr. Gomez stood up and ushered me to the door. He was shorter than Rosa, but his smile was larger than the world. He slicked his black hair back with his hand and then took my hand and shook it. I saluted and walked out the door.

"Thanks for the food Mrs. G," I called on my way out.

"See you soon," she called back.

Not likely, I thought.

Rosa was standing in front of my bicycle with her hands on her hips.

"Why are you leaving?" she asked, her voice was softer. I could tell she was sorry, so I rubbed it in.

"You called me an idiot, Rosa."

"Oh," she smiled, "that."

I rolled my eyes and tried to get past her. She grabbed onto my arm and pulled at me.

"Look, Seth, I'm sorry. It's just kind of hard to believe that anyone would ever want to leave and never come back."

I didn't know how to explain a whole lifetime of abduction obsession. If she didn't get it, she just didn't get it.

"My parents are fighting a lot, okay? They yell at each other," I said trying to avoid the alien abduction angle, and focusing in on my family drama instead. "I don't like it."

The expression of confusion on her face melted into understanding, and she nodded.

"Sorry I yelled at you," she said.

She loosened her grip, and I reached past her to unlock my bike from the fence post. I started walking slowly because I didn't want to get so far ahead that she wouldn't be able to catch me if she wanted to keep talking. Rosa caught up to me only seconds later, the way Nelson did in the hallway at school, half-jogging to keep up with my long strides.

I smiled when she picked up her apology where she left off, "And also I think I'm a little confused because, well, we get along so well, and I helped you with this monologue... and I just need to get my head in the right place. I know you like Roxy. It's okay. I don't expect you to take me to Prom, Seth. I'd just really like to be your friend, that's all."

I stopped and turned to face her. We studied each other silently for a long time. I nodded, finally, and said, "Rosa, I accept your apology. I'm a bit confused, too. I have no idea what to do with you. I am leaving forever sometime next week."

"You really believe that this voice... this static and wind chimes you keep hearing are from outer space? What if it's really some genius freak dude playing a hoax on you? Some child predator...now, I know that *they* exist."

Okay. I had never thought about the possibility that

some random dude was messing with me, like some sadistic predator stalking little girls on the internet. I hated that Rosa even mentioned it, because for the first time doubt entered into my mind as to whether or not I would really be able to go to outer space. I had had complete faith that the voice on the end was an alien.

"I'll make a deal with you," I said, composing myself quickly. "I'll bet you a date to Prom that this isn't a hoax. If it is, then after I beat the crap out of my stalker, I'll show up on your doorstep and take you to Prom next Friday. If it isn't…"

"If it isn't?" she asked.

"I guess you'll just stay home that night." I smiled.

"You're such a jerk," she smiled back, turned around, heading for home, then called over her shoulder, "I'll see you on my doorstep next Friday night!"

Instead of getting onto my bike and riding, I ended up walking it the whole way home. I was too stunned to think about anything else. I tried as hard as I could to work out in my head if the alien was for real or a chat-room stalker.

When I walked up to the garage, I found Mom inside, packing her car with anything and everything she could fit inside of it. She was a mess. Mascara and tears left mudslides down her cheeks. As she saw me approach, she dropped the box she was holding and crumpled to the ground, crying even harder than before. I went to her and put my arms around her. She knelt and embraced me. Her chest shuddered against mine between sobs.

"I'm so sorry," she could barely get the words out. "I'm leaving. I'm going to leave your father. I just can't take it anymore. We're getting a divorce."

"Mom, please don't do this," I said. Emotion welled up in my throat, but I choked it back down. I didn't want to cry – I was too angry for that. She must have known that if she was leaving Dad, she was leaving me as well, but she didn't acknowledge it.

"I love you, Baby," Mom said. "No mother could be prouder of her son, so tall and smart and handsome."

My face got lost in her hair as she hugged me one last time.

"I'll call you," she promised, then picked up her box and went to her car. I followed, watching in silence as my mother turned her back on me. I waited for her to look at me, hoping that she might change her mind and stay.

She backed her car out of the driveway and vanished in less than thirty seconds and I was left alone in the shadow my house cast on the driveway's pavement. I must have waited for her to come back for ten minutes, but she never did.

Numbly, I walked into the house, not really sure what to do next. My mother had just left us and I hadn't even seen it coming. Sixteen years of marriage had just been annihilated by a couple bad months.

Mom had left a letter for Dad explaining everything, which was better than me having to explain it to him myself. I was hurt that she hadn't left a note for me. But then, the more I thought about what had just happened, the more my hurt turned into anger. We had spent the morning cleaning so that she wouldn't be leaving a messy house. She had tried leaving when nobody was around and hadn't really planned to say goodbye to me at all. She was being completely selfish.

I walked up to my room and climbed into my bed without changing into PJs or brushing my teeth. In the empty darkness I fought back angry tears mixed with memories of happier times before we moved to Vegas. I knew Mom was angry, but I couldn't believe she would just leave instead of trying to fight for us to be the way we used to be. She had abandoned us without any discussion. She hadn't even asked me if I wanted to go with her. Somewhere in the middle of my desperate analysis of the situation, I fell asleep. Dad didn't wake me when he got home.

Chapter 11

BOONE

It was easy to tell that Dad had received Mom's note the next morning because he was already banging around the house when I woke up and he spent most of the day avoiding me. When we did bump into one another in the kitchen, he didn't mention Mom at all, but I could tell he had been crying. We made small talk about needing to go to the store for some bread and he asked me if I had any homework.

That afternoon, he went out to the garage and hung up a punching bag in the spot where Mom had parked her car. I watched Dad box out all his emotions from the kitchen window for a few moments, then, without really thinking anything through, I went upstairs, grabbed my backpack, and put it on.

Mom leaving us had just cinched it; I was ready to commit forever.

Dad didn't look at me as I retrieved my bike from the hooks in the rafters, although I was pretty sure he noticed me walk into the garage.

"Goodbye, Dad," I said, but he didn't stop wailing on the punching bag and he wouldn't turn around. I hated him for it. He wasn't the only one who was hurting. Mom had left me, too. I wondered if he would have said something to me if he'd known I was planning on leaving for good, but he just ignored me, so I turned my back on him and rode off as fast as I could down the street.

On the way to nowhere in particular, I passed Rosa's house, Connie's retirement home, and the park where my friends and I usually played sports after school. Eventually, I lost myself in a foreign neighborhood to the east of my own. House after house flashed past me. I wondered who lived in each one and if they all had happy home lives. I shook off another painful memory of Mom backing out of the driveway, turned a corner, and found myself heading for an undeveloped, weedy cul-de-sac with a barren plot at the far end of the street. When I reached it, I dropped my bike at the edge of the sidewalk and walked over to the middle of the field. It was perfect; the landscape was as abandoned as I felt at that moment.

I pulled the radio out of my pocket and turned it on. The Beatles sang, *she loves you… yeah, yeah, yeah.*

"Are you there?" I whispered into the speaker. "It's Seth."

"Hey Seth, I read you loud and clear," the voice replaced the music immediately. I had never really listened to the alien's tone before, but for some reason, in that moment, I thought it sounded a little like my Dad's, deep and resonant. Perhaps I was just wishing he had said something to me before I left home.

"I'm good to leave," I said, shaking off the thought of my father, broken and silent, unable to reach out to me in the garage. "I want to go… forever, like you said I should."

"Alright," the voice said. "How 'bout now? Are you ready to go now?"

"Yeah, but…"

"I'm in the neighborhood running an errand," the voice explained. "It would be no trouble at all."

"Yeah, okay," I decided, wondering what kind of errands he was talking about. For a split second, I half-wished I'd left a note.

In hind sight, I probably should have been more weirded out by the whole thing—especially after Rosa's hoax theory, but something assured me that everything was going to be alright. My gut decided the alien coming for me was a good guy, and maybe part of me was so angry I just didn't care what happened to me. Some kids do drugs, some join gangs… I was trying to get abducted by aliens.

In seconds, a solid-black obsidian-colored vehicle pulled up to the curb in front of my abandoned bicycle. It looked like the automobile version of a stealth bomber – only the polished, volcanic-looking metal had more of a mother-of-pearl luster to it, just like a black-beetle's wings. A well-built BAH got out of the vehicle. I was shocked because the closer he came the more he looked human. Actually, he looked very much like my dad. Ironically, his suit was close-fitting white spandex, which accentuated his muscles, stood out starkly against his dark skin, and was exactly the uniform I was hoping for all my life. It was almost as if the aliens had read my mind.

The alien wore sunglasses that reflected the same violet and cobalt-blue shimmer as his car, and a wide smile spread across his face as he strode toward me.

"Hey Seth," he called, jogging the last few steps. It was the same voice from the radio. We shook hands. "I'm Boone. I'm here to adopt you, son. You ready to go?"

I probably should have said something like, "You drive a car?" Or maybe, "Why do you look more human than BEM?" But what came out of my mouth was a nonchalant, "Yeah, I'm ready."

"You sure?"

"Can I have a thirty-day trial?"

"I'd love to say yes, but I don't know where we will be in thirty days," Boone chuckled and pulled out a flat, black rectangle from his pocket. "Sign here. Just a thumbprint'll be fine."

I looked down at the object in his human-looking hand. A screen the size of a paperback book displayed an agreement in fine print. I read through it. "I, Seth, agree to be adopted by the Cillian Base Community, CBC, under the custodial care of Boone. The CBC will provide all necessities, basic or otherwise, training, and education. In return, I pledge my allegiance to the CBC and promise to live all charter laws present and future. I will stay with the CBC indefinitely and will not return to my former life on Earth."

There was a space at the bottom for my thumbprint. Without even reviewing the agreement again, or asking the clarifying questions that should have surfaced in my head, I pressed my thumb down on the screen.

"Scanning," a female voice said. "Seth Carter, male, earthling, fifteen, no criminal record, no drug or alcohol addiction, no sexually transmitted disease, no pre-existing conditions, blood count normal, heart rate and blood pressure normal, no psychological or learning disability, ... one moment please."

Boone smiled at me, "Relax, Seth, I know you'll pass."

"Did it just scan all those things?" I asked.

"Yup," Boone smiled. "You'll be amazed what we can do, Son... what you're gonna do."

The rectangle beeped, "Adoption confirmed. Congratulations, Seth. Welcome to the CBC."

Boone tapped on his rectangle and a small vial of green liquid appeared in my hands by what seemed to be teleportation. I about geeked out, but tried my best to keep calm, cool, and collected.

"Drink it," he instructed, pointing to the vile. I drained the liquid without even considering that it might be something harmful. It had no distinct taste and was neither pleasant or unpleasant.

"Alright, we are good to go," Boone smiled and took my arm as we walked over to his vehicle.

"What was that?" I finally thought to ask.

"Don't worry, we all have to drink it," Boone smiled, "It prevents us from... oh, you know...betraying the group. Even under torture, hypnosis, or any other kind of method, if you are about to give away any of our secrets to an enemy, your brain will sweep your mind of any memory of your life with the CBC. It protects both you and our community."

I wondered if that was what happened to Connie Jenkins. "Who's the enemy?"

"Depends on the day or the situation," Boone smiled. "But don't worry about that now, Seth. We usually don't have to deal with anyone we don't want to."

"Okay," I said, a bit bewildered.

Boone stopped and turned to me. "You bringin' that backpack?"

"Yeah, is that okay?" I stammered.

He waved his rectangle over it as a light flashed quickly through its contents. A beep sounded and the voice said, "No harmful items included."

"I guess you're taking it," Boone smiled as he read through an itemized list on the rectangle's screen. "If you're sure it won't mess you up."

I clung to my pack as we turned and walked the last few steps.

"Activate," Boone ordered into his black rectangle and the doors of his space craft opened. I half expected smoke to billow out, but instead was hit with some sort of smooth, disco-funk music. I sat down in the white leather bucket seat on the passenger side, placing my backpack on the floor next to me, although I wanted to carry it in my lap to make sure it didn't go anywhere. Boone got in the driver's seat and the doors hissed shut.

From the outside, the space craft seemed compact, like a sports car, but once I was inside, it felt more like the size of a small bus. There weren't any seat belts, which instantly made me feel vulnerable, because I was pretty sure that we'd be traveling faster than the usual 65 mph. The console had a recognizable steering mechanism, but the rest of it was covered in screens similar to the rectangular device Boone carried with him as opposed to the silver and white lit-up buttons I was expecting.

"Hey Sistah—you ready?" Boone asked.

"Voice command affirmative," a lady's voice answered in a deep soothing tone—just like the one Mom used when she wanted something.

"Take us to Base," Boone commanded.

"Sure thing, Sugar," Sistah said. "Preparing space launch. Fluxing and converting space craft. Estimated arrival to Earth Moon Base in forty-five minutes."

"We're going to the Moon?" I asked, completely unable

to hide my geeky excitement. I realized it was probably a pit stop on the way to the rest of the wonders of the galaxy, but I had wanted to visit the moon for years.

"Yeah, we're set up there right now," Boone smiled. "But don't get used to it. We won't stay there long. We actually just came to adopt you and pick up a few other things."

"Oh." I was completely captivated by the thought of them making a special visit to adopt me by setting up camp on the moon. The moon was two hundred forty thousand miles away. I tried to figure out how fast we would have to go to make it there in forty-five minutes.

"We'd have to go over three hundred thousand miles an hour to make it to the Moon in forty-five minutes," I realized out loud.

"That fast, huh?" Boone smiled.

"And we'll have to hit three thousand miles in order to reach escape velocity from earth's orbit!"

"Got it covered, Son," Boone smiled. "Don't worry about a thing. Just sit back and enjoy the ride."

Adrenaline surged through me, and it was a good thing none of my peers were around to witness my absolute and overwhelming geek out. Tingles and goose bumps erupted all over my body simultaneously. If I had been a dog, I would defiantly have been salivating, barking, and trying to stick my head out the spaceship's window by that point.

We rolled forward slowly, and then Sistah turned around and accelerated at top speed out of the cul-de-sac. Boone swiveled in his chair to watch my reaction.

It looked as if we were about to crash into the houses ahead of us but right before the moment of impact, we were sucked up into a conduit of light that swept us into a white, tunnel-like current. It was almost as if we were traveling in some sort of transparent channel, like the deposit tubes in the bank's drive up window, and Boone's craft was the little black capsule patrons sent their transactions in. We were catapulted on an upward angle to the sky until we hit the right trajectory and were propelled straight forward like a rock out of a sling shot. That's when we really began to move. I could barely catch the wisps of cloud and atmosphere that flew past us as we sailed higher into the sky.

"I wish you could see the look on your face, Seth," Boone said with a loud chuckle. "It's priceless."

I swiveled in my chair to face Boone, and he removed his sun glasses. The resemblance to my own father was uncanny. I wondered if they did that on purpose—to make me feel more at home. Boone slumped forward toward me, his arms resting on his knees. I wanted to match his relaxed posture, but my fingers locked themselves around the edges of my armrest, which only made Boone chuckle more. My back was rigid against the leather seat and I felt the beginnings of motion sickness.

Suddenly the light in the tunnel dimmed as the blackness of space enveloped us. Chills washed over me as I realized we had just left Earth's atmosphere.

"I'm in space!" I said, stupidly, wishing that we were moving slower so that I could catch a view. There was nothing I could have said to express how I felt at that moment. I was actually in outer space, and not as an astronaut, and much cooler than Captain Kirk. It should have been one of the most exhilarating moments of my life, but I felt as if I was about to pass out.

"You need to try to relax," Boone observed. "Maybe try taking a nap. Space-lag is the worst."

"Um, there's no way I'm going to sleep right now, sir."

"Suit yourself," Boone chuckled, then added, "Hey Sistah, how 'bout a few beverages for me and Seth here?"

A light appeared in my hand which turned into a bottle of chilled cream soda. The lid was already off and smoke rose from the brown glass rim.

"That was one of the reasons I was in the neighborhood. Just had to pick up a case of this stuff," Boone said. He clinked his bottle against mine and took a long pull on his drink. "Ahhh…. Now that's good and smooth. Pretty much the only thing I miss now is cream soda."

I took a swig. It only then registered what he had said. I swallowed and quickly said, "I'm sorry, sir, but are you from Earth?"

"Yes."

"But why did you get to come back?"

"Just to pick you up, Seth. A few of the humans on our base wanted to adopt other humans, so we set up operations on the Moon. I felt that I would be a better instructor for an earthling adoptee than for a human from anywhere else. I've been listening to you from across the galaxy for a long time, son. Just knew you wouldn't be a waste."

I was trying to wrap my mind around the idea of humans from other planets as opposed to humans from Earth, but the hum of the engine was finding its way into my joints which relaxed me and my eyelids grew unavoidably heavy. I took a swig of my drink in an attempt to wake myself up, but found that I couldn't open my eyes. A yawn escaped my mouth, then another.

"It's space travel, Seth," Boone explained. "You'll get used to it, but for now, I'm afraid all you're gonna want to do is sleep."

"I can't seem to open my eyes," I said, my voice slurred and disappointed.

"I'll keep talking," Boone said, "Where was I... well, I'm a base engineer for the CBC. We travel around in companies of about forty family-type units."

"What kind of craft is Sistah?" I asked, "Do you call her a car or FS or what?"

"FS?" he asked.

"Flying Saucer" I slurred.

Boone chuckled and said, "Actually Sistah's a car, plane, submarine, moon-buggy, space ship ... you name it, which is why I just call her Sistah. Her model number is 2035 of the CBC spacecraft, but if you want to get really technical you could call her an ATV."

He laughed at his own joke. I wanted to laugh with him, but was incapable of anything beyond zoning.

"I think you just lost me," I said, drifting away.

"No worries," Boone said, removing the drink from my limp fingers. "You've got plenty of time to catch onto this."

Everything else Boone said became a sea of jumbled phrases sloshing around in my head. He instructed Sistah to recline my seat and I felt the warmth of a blanket around my shoulders.

SETH CARTER'S ALIEN ~~ABDUCTION~~ ADOPTION

Chapter 12

ROSCO

When I came to, I found myself buck-naked, lying on an examination table. Surrounding me on all sides were your typical LGMs. They were holding all kinds of contraptions and spoke in a gurgled clicking language. One of them took my hand and wiped it with a warm cloth. I cringed, waiting for my skin to start burning off or a giant probe to appear. Then, the LGM holding my hand morphed into the lime-green demon man thing that I had conjured up in my head at the accident scene. Only, instead of coming out of my body, like it seemed to have done with the driver, it was trying to get into it. A green, hissing hand crackled as it slowly broke its way into my flesh. I could feel it trying to slip and rip through my cells, and while it didn't hurt, it began to make me nauseated. In seconds, I lost the ability to move on my own; the creature controlled my actions. I wanted to vomit, but I could do nothing to alleviate the rush of sick welling up inside. He and I screamed. His were sounds of triumph and sadistic domination while mine were screams of panic at my complete loss of control.

"Enough!" I yelled and shook myself awake. In the silence, I began to breathe again.

Dad and Connie had both warned me of unfriendly things in Space, but that dream was the first time I was consciously affected by their warning. For the first time in my life I was afraid of Space. I concentrated on breathing slowly to help calm myself down, then opened my eyes.

I lay in a dimly lit room, not my bed at home, but somewhere new yet familiar at the same time. For a split second, I thought I was back in Connie Jenkin's apartment at the Good Life Living Center. The walls around me were white and lush green plants hung from the ceiling, but the farthest wall from me was transparent, and beyond it, I could see a view of moon rock formations set against drab gray craters. Just beyond that, I could see pinprick stars delicately illuminating the velvety blackness of space.

My mind raced as I tried to remember what had happened after Boone had picked me up, but all I could remember was falling asleep in Sistah. I tried to sit up and orient myself, but my head was spinning. Then, I heard a rustle from the floor below me, and I realized that whatever made the noise had been licking my hand.

I stood up to inspect the source of the sound. The blanket I was lying under slipped, and I discovered I really was buck-naked. Gathering the blanket around me, I bent down and found a creature so odd that I laughed out loud. It looked like the unlikely love child of a Komodo Dragon and a Persian cat. When I pulled my hand out of reach, it shifted its overweight, gecko body and began licking at a wild white mane. Furry paws popped out like boots on the end of each of its scaly legs. Two yellow eyes peered out from a fat, fluffy face. It was definitely a biological improbability on Earth. I guessed it was a pet, though, because it seemed domesticated. It coughed out some sort of gurgle-whinny salutation, and began to lick my toes, which just creeped me out.

I looked back up at the transparent wall to see if I could figure out what side of the Moon we were on. The Earth wasn't a part of my view, so I reasoned we were on the dark side.

"I'm on the Moon," I said to the thing licking my toes. "I made it."

The beast stopped licking then wandered off in a sort of spazzy waddle through a large doorway and out into the darkness beyond. I got up to follow when I noticed my backpack lying on a white, table-looking platform. I dressed quickly, glad I had the foresight to bring along an extra change of clothes, and walked out of the room carrying my backpack along with me.

I hurried down the darkened hallway toward a light at the other end. When I arrived I found a room that could best be described as a breakfast nook at the Apple computer store. With the exception of a few green plants, everything came in a nice, sterile, white plastic. Boone was already sitting in the nook consulting his black rectangle. I cleared my throat. He smiled widely and motioned me over, although he remained engrossed in whatever was on his screen.

Slipping my backpack off my shoulder and onto the ground, I sat down across from him, bracing myself for a cold, uninviting seat. But instead of the toilet bowl in the middle of the night I was expecting, the seat formed itself ergonomically around my body and a heated massage commenced while soft meditation music played quietly in the background. It was like I was test driving an Audi with heated seats in the middle of a snow storm. I took a deep, refreshing breath. The plants gave the room a homey, oxygenated feel. There were no transparent walls showing moon-rock formations or stars in the breakfast nook.

My stomach, which had been growling, suddenly stopped. I felt it, and found it was hard and expanding.

"You're being fed as you sit there," Boone explained, not glancing up from his rectangle.

"I'm sorry, what?"

He pushed a few buttons and set it down, finally looking at me. "This seat is transporting the exact serving size and perfectly balanced nutritional supplement into your body. At the same time, it is exporting all excess waste from your intestinal tract and bladder."

My buttocks puckered in response to his explanation of the warm sensation I felt inside.

"Weird," I said.

"But very cool," Boone answered. "You'll never overeat, or be malnourished again. There will be no upset stomach, food poisoning, or germs transferred into your body through food or drink."

"So what you are saying is that my food is being beamed aboard my stomach right now?"

"Yup," Boone said. "It takes a while… don't want to eat too quickly. Just sit back and relax."

"And my crap…"

"Yup," Boone interrupted me, "don't ask."

"Weird." I began to see why cream soda was so important to him.

There was a lull in the conversation, so I asked, "Why did I wake up naked?"

"We needed to decontaminate you and your clothes," Boone said, waving his rectangle. "You want to try out some CBC clothes?"

"No," I said, which surprised me, because I had always wanted a uniform. I guess I just wasn't ready to give up my jeans.

"Have it your way," Boone said with a half-chuckle and pushed a few buttons on his rectangle. My clothes instantly felt just-out-of-the-dryer clean. My feet, hair and skin were suddenly squeaky. I inspected my fingernails which were manicure-perfect. When I ran my tongue over my teeth, a smooth glide replaced the shag I had going on when I woke up, and as much as I hated to admit it, my GI track felt wonderful after having my food beamed aboard. I felt that just-been-swimming sensation of perfect balance.

The animal that had licked my toes came bounding into the room. It stretched out on the floor and a light began to teleport its breakfast into its tummy as well.

Boone stood up and walked over to it, knelt, and began scratching its ears. "This is Seth, Rosco."

Rosco gurgled up at me.

I nodded, "Rosco."

Boone cleared his throat and said, "Rosco's a Boska beast. He's crazy, but you'll get used to him. I picked him up when we were living on Tralis Four in the Minart Galaxy."

Rosco clicked and gurgled happily on the floor, which

made the hair on my arm stand on end. Boone stood again and pushed a few more buttons on his black rectangle. I immediately felt deodorant under my pits.

"Thanks," I muttered, feeling a little violated.

"You bet," Boone said.

"So, what happens if you lose that thing?" I asked, pointing to the rectangle.

"I'll get a new one," Boone answered, sitting back down across from me. "It's called a Brain, by the way."

"When do I get a Brain?"

"You'll get a Brain when you are ready," he said.

"How do you know which buttons to push?" I asked, ignoring his smirk.

"It's really just mind transference," Boone said. "You push one of a few personalized buttons – self-care, habitat, hygiene, entertainment, nourishment, communication, etc – and then think your command simply and specifically. The Brain does whatever you want. The buttons are just for shortcuts and clarification, but for the most part, it's guided by thought transference. If you lose your Brain, you simply take the next new one, put your thumbprint up to it and it will automatically set up the way your previous one was set up. It's amazing what is locked in our minds, even if we don't remember it's there. You'll get used to it."

Boone went back to consulting his Brain as I finished having my food transported. The whole time we "ate," I couldn't decide what was a worse way to eat in Space – astronaut-style with dehydrated pellets or the beaming thing. I didn't even want to debate the toilet situations in my mind.

After breakfast, Boone announced he was going to take me on a tour and then over to CBC orientation.

I grabbed for my backpack, but felt Boone's disapproving gaze before he said, "You can leave it, Seth. It'll be safe."

"Yeah…," I said, dropping it back on the floor.

Boone escorted me out the door and through the halls, Rosco tagging along excitedly at our heels. Every so it often stopped in front of me as we went. Each time I tripped over the little beast, I thought of playing basket-ball with Maria Gomez, who had a similar habit of getting right in my path, and my first wave of homesickness crashed down hard on the desolate beach of my raw emotions.

We went from room to room, all decked out with the same sterile white with green plants, or translucent walls showing off our moon surroundings. The base was massive and seemed under-populated for the space it took up. We passed a group of CBC members with delicate Asian-like faces and physiques, and skin that had a sea-green hue. They nodded pleasantly, but, unfortunately, no introductions were made. Each wore a white spandex suit like Boone.

"Not everyone here speaks English," Boone informed me. "In fact, it's really not a popular form of communication, which is sometimes useful if you want to talk without being understood."

"Is there a universal language?" I asked.

"Nothing yet," Boone said. "But we get by."

We turned a corner and found a tiny person waiting for us on the other end. It was a small child – maybe three years old. When he spoke, his mouth didn't move, but we heard his thoughts like an announcement in our heads. His voice was an adult's: calm, strong, and full of authority.

"Hello, Boone."

"Hey Pfister," Boone said. "This is my son, Seth. Seth, this is my good friend, Pfister. He is a Sarrow from the planet Treen. They look like our small children, but Pfister is what now... ninety-six?"

Pfister nodded and smiled. "It is a pleasure to meet you, Seth. Welcome to the CBC."

It was like an oversized ventriloquist's doll was talking to me and walking around by itself. Pfister laughed the moment I thought it, which creeped me out. I certainly wasn't ready for what came next. He turned around and smiled at me, and I heard his voice in my head say, "I can hear your thoughts, you know. You may want to be careful around us. We are very sensitive...like children."

"Sorry," I thought back. "I didn't mean to offend you."

"Could you stop having a conversation without me?" Boone interrupted our silent communication with a small added chuckle. "I'd like to know what's going on, too."

"Seth thinks I look like a ventriloquist's dummy," the adult voice broadcast, as the little boy cocked his head to the side.

"Don't worry, Seth, you'll get used to it," Boone nodded. "Comes in handy sometimes. You'll see. And if you were wondering how he knows what a ventriloquist's dummy is, he can see all your thoughts and feel the way you feel about them. Pfister is our main interpreter. He can read the thoughts of everyone on base and is able to get his point across in our heads."

"Is it telepathy?" I asked.

"A bit of mind reading and thought transference common to the Sarrows on my planet," Pfister thought.

"Telepathic thought transference is the muse behind our Brain designs," Boone said, shaking the black rectangle at me, "You know, just push a button and think what you want, and it happens."

"Cool," I said. It was only then I realized any girl from Treen would probably be a three-year-old-looking ninety-year-old, which took all the fun out of my dreams of hooking up with an alien girlfriend with telepathic powers. Pfister laughed again.

"Will you please knock it off?" Boone asked.

"I can't help it," Pfister smiled, "Seth has such comical thoughts… ingenious, really."

Unfortunately, Pfister decided to join us on the tour, and he led the way. I had to work double time to guard my thoughts. Rosco followed, and Boone and I took up the rear. As we continued the tour it dawned on me that Pfister was my first real alien encounter. He was a child sized BAH (Bipedal Alien Humaniod).

"You're the alien, Seth," his voice corrected in my head, "But I'm happy to be your first real encounter."

I was disappointed, but tried to hide any thought of it. I had imagined my first time to be different. I had not expected "Rosco the gurgling Boska Beast" and "Pfister the Childlike Telepathic geezer." I expected little green men and bug-eyed monsters and a few SHACs in skintight uniforms. My expectations were just as cliché as the commentators at the end of Connie's article had been. I tried not to think anything about how weird I thought they were, which left me feeling angry about not being able to have more of an open mind. I swear I could hear Pfister laughing quietly in my head about that as well.

In each room we visited, I found peaceful intergalactic engineers, dressed in white spandex, quietly working on their projects in perfect harmony with the galaxy.

"How do you know how to select people for the CBC?" I asked, wondering how a kid like me ended up in a place like this. I was already beginning to miss food smells, arguments, opposing fashion styles, and gum on the sidewalk.

"We listen," Boone said. "On Earth, it is through radio waves because they travel great distances at great speeds when amplified through our equipment. I tuned into you when you were living in England and went to your first SWGG campout at Stonehenge."

We'd been stationed at Mildenhall RAF, England when I was ten, and I'd run away from home and hitchhiked to Stonehenge so I could camp out with a chapter of the SWGG (Star World Gazers Guild) to commemorate the twentieth anniversary of their chapter leader's alien abduction from that exact spot. About the only thing that happened was that I heard some outrageous abduction stories from a bunch of drunken hippies who didn't know what they were talking about.

It had gotten me grounded for six months solid, and at the time, I had been frustrated that it hadn't led to abduction. How could I have known that it would have been the event that started it all?

"That guy had his stupid radio playing all night long!" I realized.

"Right," Boone continued. "You asked those guys some great questions, and so I began to follow your ideas and progress every chance I got. Germany was when I really began to lock onto your signal…"

"In the forest…"

"And then once you asked to be adopted, instead of abducted, I knew that you were serious. How did you catch onto us, by the way?"

I froze, wondering if it was secure to talk about Connie Jenkins. She had asked me to come back for her if it was safe, but I had no idea if it really was. Everything seemed nice enough, but one could never be too sure, especially after the unsettling dream I had that morning. I decided to proceed carefully and back-peddle if any tension began to emerge in the conversation.

"I looked up wind chimes and alien abduction on the internet one night and got a link to a woman who had written an article about you. Uh, nothing too descriptive… just that she had heard the wind chimes right before she had been taken, and she called it adoption, not abduction."

"Really?" Boone wondered. "She actually used the word adopted?"

By this time, Pfister had stopped walking and turned around to listen to our exchange.

"The woman had amnesia, so she didn't remember much, but her apartment was white and full of plants, just like your decor here. I'm guessing she was once a part of the CBC, but then I think something happened to her."

"It's unusual for one of us to ever leave," Boone said. "What did she say her name was?"

I panicked, not sure of what to say. I didn't want to give her away, but the expectant look on Boone's face made it hard to think of a pseudonym. I folded, "Uh… Connie… Jenkins."

"You don't think that it could be Constance, do you?" Pfister wondered in our minds.

"Topher's wife?" Boone asked.

"Yes. She went missing a while back. He still hasn't found her. He thought…" Pfister paused and then his thought whispered, "…the… Kashmaari… took her."

"There is no way the Kashmaari would dare take one of

us. They have never tried to make a move on the CBC...we still trade with them." Boone countered. He was unnerved the moment Pfister had whispered the word Kashmaari. Up to that point, Boone had been smooth and sure, but now he was floundering like a fish washed up on shore.

"Well," Pfister shrugged, "I only know what he said. Perhaps we should consult him."

"Did Topher go to Constantine?"

"I don't know."

By that time, I was pretty much done with being on the fringes of the conversation. "Uh, guys...Kashmaari what?"

"Oh, yeah, sorry, Seth," Boone said. "Not much to catch you up on. I doubt it was the Kashmaari." His voice was calm, but he was sweating, just like Dad did when he didn't want to talk about something.

"What are they?" I pressed.

"They are demons of light that have the ability to take over a person's body and control it." Pfister explained in my thoughts. "They don't have their own bodies, so they use other people's bodies in order to... experience things... physically... for themselves."

"They're disembodied aliens?" I asked, thinking of my dream and the accident.

Pfister nodded and his explanation continued, "Basically, Seth, Kashmaari wear people – they even call them "skins." They go on drug binges, orgies, and even killing sprees with the bodies they take control of. After they have used them up, they dump them and go on to find their next victim. They like to feel things... corporeally... for themselves."

"Whereas it seems like the CBC likes to avoid real experience as much as possible," I couldn't help from saying out loud, thinking of my breakfast and all the white uniforms and surroundings. It was suddenly silent enough that one could hear space crickets chirping. I back peddled quickly to the Kashmaari again. "Well, what those creatures do sounds like it could have happened to Connie. She even said she felt as though she had been used up and spat out again."

"Perhaps we should go see Topher," Pfister urged. "Especially if Constance was abandoned on Earth. He might have time to locate her before we move out. I didn't know her well and can't seem to figure out if she is the same woman that Seth sees in his mind."

I could tell the wheels in Boone's head were spinning. He looked like Dad did the morning I told him about the radio static in the forest. His answer was slow and deliberate, "I hate to upset him if we don't have all the facts. What if it isn't Constance? You know how hard it was for him when she left. Let's see if Seth can identify her first. We'll get hooked into the mainframe after orientation and review some of her images."

"As you wish," Pfister agreed. "I will leave you now. Seth, it was a pleasure."

"For me too," I said, taking the child-sized hand as it clasped at mine.

Then, the tiny Sarrow from Treen turned and walked quickly away while Boone ushered me into a room the size of a giant hangar, full of younger-looking CBC engineers. They were playing what seemed to be multi-dimensional video games. Each engineer was in an isolated section of the room that created its own realistic battleground full of sights, sounds, smells, and touches as they virtually fought and triumphed over tangible holograms. They weren't controlling avatars on the screen, or playing a two-dimensional opponent; they were in the middle of seemingly real-life adventures inside of the game – actually forging a path to victory.

"This is where the younger engineers spend most of their down time," Boone announced.

"Playing video games?" I observed, barely able to take my eyes off the realistic simulations being played all around us. There was a starship dogfight involving CBC fighter planes that caught my eye. I could tell that the engineer playing the simulation was a woman, but the helmet she wore obscured her facial features. Her ship was surrounded on all sides by enemy war ships, but she was able to cut right through their defenses. It was amazing to watch the skill involved, even though it wasn't real. The engineer piloting the game finished the fight by barrel rolling through four ships shooting each one down with perfect accuracy. She pulled off her mask and revealed herself.

Her facial features were similar to Boone's, only she was much prettier. Long black braids trailed down her back, fastened by delicate, clear, cracked-glass beads, which spiced up her standard-issue CBC attire.

"Seth, This is your new sister, Nellie," Boone announced.

Chapter 13

NELLIE

"Hi, Seth," Nellie said, shaking my hand firmly. "Welcome."

"Uh, hi." I said, feeling pissed that nobody mentioned a sister when I signed on. I had gotten past that part in my life where I did nothing but desperately wish for siblings. I liked being spoiled and having everything all to myself.

Boone continued the introduction. "She's ... how old are you now, Nellie?"

"I should be forty-one in Earth years, but my spacebody age is about sixteen."

"Nellie joined up with the CBC when she was, what... ten?" Boone stated.

"That's right."

I just shook my head. "I have no idea what that means."

"It takes us a lot longer to age in Space," she answered in a tone that suggested it was common knowledge and I was the village idiot.

"Interesting," I said, glancing at the young engineers playing video games around me. They had probably all lived a lot longer than me, but they were still in their teens – like Peter Pan – unable to grow up. "You're really good," I said to Nellie, gesturing at the game helmet she carried.

"Thanks," she nodded. "You wanna try this? You probably should, just so you won't ask me what we do for fun around here."

I could only nod as she hooked me up and placed the helmet on my head. After a few moments of instruction I found myself lost in the simulation's space battle. My first life ended in two seconds. Luckily, Nellie allowed me to play for what felt like an hour, and by the end of my time I had gotten good enough to last about ten minutes.

"You're a better scientist than a soldier," Boone observed when I took my helmet off. It sounded like he wanted me to stay home and play dominos every weekend for the rest of my life. I didn't like the thought of my new virtual existence.

"Just need a little practice and I might change your mind," I said realizing it was just as tempting for me to want to contradict my adopted father as my real one.

"You ready to go to orientation?" He shifted gears completely.

Actually, I wanted to keep playing and prove what a good space soldier I could be, but agreed to finish the tour because I could sense that I was starting to tick him off.

We left Nellie and the hangar full of videogame-playing quasi-teenagers and Boone led me into a gigantic stadium larger than any IMAX I'd seen. Of course, it was white, instead of the usual movie theatre black drab, and of course, there were potted and hanging plants everywhere. I surmised that the plants were there to help with the oxygen flow...some sort of bio dome idea. At least the oxygen was real.

I took a seat in the center of the middle section, and felt the massage and contour begin. Boone joined me, but Rosco stayed on the lower level, sniffing the ground for who knows what.

"Would you prefer a zero-gravity setting for this?" Boone asked.

"Is that an option?" I asked, sheer joy welling up inside of me.

"Oh, yeah," he said, pushing a button on his Brain. "We've found that it helps concentration."

Suddenly I became weightless and floated out of my chair and up toward the ceiling. The stadium grew dark and an automated movie greeting filled the four walls around us. We began panning through stars, planets, and solar systems as a voice spoke. "Greetings, Seth, and welcome to the Cillian Base Community, or the CBC. We're glad you have joined our ranks..."

I relaxed into the air, occasionally flipping cartwheels, but mostly just enjoying the weightlessness. The voice narrated a slideshow of different sites across the galaxy. In a nutshell, the CBC was the Ford Motor Company of the Milky Way. I had two major responsibilities to them: design and invent things and to be loyal. I probably missed a lot of the presentation because I was too consumed with backstroking around the room. As far as I was concerned, the antigravity feature blew my concentration completely.

When it ended, the effect switched off and I floated back down to the ground next to Rosco.

Boone joined us with an expectant look on his face. "Well?"

"Great," I said. "It was awesome."

"I'm glad you liked it." He smiled and clasped me on the shoulder. "This will be your instruction room. You'll learn most of your engineering, history, languages, and mathematics here. It also serves as a place of recreation. The system can call up any music or media you wish to watch, and we also host large multiplayer games in here. If you hadn't been scheduled for an orientation I'm sure Nellie would have been in here with some buddies doing some sort of large-scale battle assault on something."

I couldn't help thinking that the orientation room would have been an excellent venue for a dance. I hoped there were other teens like me on base, because if there weren't, I was going to be stuck with a bunch of forty-year-old engineers like Nellie, trapped indefinitely in puberty.

"Hey! Did you want to look at some images of Topher's missing wife?" I remembered. "See if I can match her to Connie Jenkins?"

Boone thought for a moment then shook his head. "Later."

"We're right here," I said.

"Nope.   Right now I think I'll take you on a little field trip," Boone announced and directed me out of the stadium. We walked back down a familiar corridor, Boone practically skipping along in front of me.

"We're gonna take you on a deep-space excursion – show you a little bit of the galaxy before you get bogged down with a heap of catch-up studies," Boone announced over his shoulder. "I'm in a negotiation with the Varlocks a highly advanced species who need to join the CBC. We don't speak their language, but have been able to infer that they want to share technology with us and commit to peace."

"Okay," I said.

"What would you say if we took off right now?"

"Uh… sure…" I said, desperately fighting the urge to ask if I could fly the ship, half-wondering if there was an age requirement.

We entered our quarters and found Nellie at the breakfast nook, playing with a smaller, pink version of a Brain. She stood up and asked, "You ready, boys?"

"We're ready to go," Boone said to her. "We thought with your language skills, Seth, you could come along… help us out…tell us what you think they're saying. With all those countries you've been to, you've learned how to get your point across without knowing the language."

To say that I was shocked would have been an understatement. I wasn't a translator, and I was pretty sure that I'd have less of a chance of success than he would.

"That's because we were all… you know… HUMAN," I objected quickly. "I don't know if I can translate for alien creatures yet."

"You were able to understand Meike well enough."

"Again," I said, "She was a human… not a Varlock."

"German female," Boone corrected. "Close enough."

I was embarrassed that he had listened to my last night with Meike – he knew about our relationship and how clumsily we communicated. It felt like I was talking girlfriends with Dad again. A pain ran through my heart when I thought about them – Meike and Dad – and then everyone else back at home. For some reason, I was having a harder time adjusting than I had anticipated.

"What's wrong, Seth?" Boone was staring into my face empathetically.

"I didn't say goodbye to anyone," I said, ignoring Nellie's strained look.

"You want to send them an e-mail?" Boone asked.

"May I?"

"Oh, come on!" Nellie gave an exasperated sigh. "I told you he wasn't old enough! Look at him, Dad, he's already homesick!"

"Go get Sistah ready," Boone instructed Nellie, ignoring her rude outburst.

"Fine," Nellie said and left the room.

Boone passed me his Brain, "Here. Push this button and speak what you want to say, and the name of the person you want to send your message to, and let the Brain do the rest. Only, please say that you are running away from home. We like to keep a low profile, and if you give too much away to the wrong people, your Brain will reboot, and you'll lose all knowledge about the CBC."

"That green juice?"

"Yup."

"Okay… I ran away from home because of the divorce," I said to myself.

"I'll let you send three emails. Then, communication with your friends and family must end, so choose wisely."

"Can they write back?" I asked.

"Yes, if they reply to sender," he smiled. "And if they do, I'll give you the messages."

"Thanks," I said. "I just didn't know I would miss them."

"You're gonna miss a lot, Seth," Boone said. "But it'll pass."

"Can I reply to their replies?"

Boone raised an eyebrow. "How 'bout we cross that bridge when we come to it?"

I said Dad's full name and then began to speak into the Brain, *"Dad, I want you to know that I'm fine. I ran away from home because Mom left. It's better this way. —Seth"*

The Brain beeped and the screen flashed the word *SENT*.

"Good," Boone said. "Anyone else?"

I wasn't sure what I would write to Rosa, so I decided to skip her and move on to maybe Miguel, not Nelson. I could only imagine the lengthy, newsy response he would send back to me.

I decided to send something to Meike, since she was my longest-running friend.

"Will it translate the message into German?"

"Sure. We've got her language in our Data Files."

I said Meike's name and then asked it to send my message in German. *"Meike, I know that I didn't get a chance to say goodbye. I hope that you are doing well. I really like Las Vegas. You should come and see it one day. I miss you and our forest. Germany is such a great country. Bye! Seth."*

"Your Mom?" Boon asked.

"I don't really have anything to say to her anymore."

She had left me without looking back, and I was going to do my best to do the same in return.

"Okay, well, is that it?"

"One more," I said. "For Rosa Gomez: *Rosa, I'm sorry that I will be unable to take you to Prom. Guess you'll have to stay home that night. Hope you can forgive me one day. — Seth."*

I waited for my memory to flush itself, scared that I had given too much away, but nothing happened. Instead, the screen beeped again and the word *SENT* flashed across it.

I passed the Brain back to Boone who put it in his pocket.

"Thanks," I said.

"Feel better?" he asked.

"A little." I tried to smile.

I must have looked worn out or something because Boone led me back to my room, instructing me to rest while he got a few things ready for the trip.

I lay down on my bed. It immediately wrapped itself around my torso and began a massage and heating pad. I sighed heavily and tried hard not to feel sad or homesick. I was in Space. It was what I had wanted all my life, and I knew for a fact that it was going to be a lot better than living through Mom and Dad's divorce.

Nellie and Rosco appeared in my doorway. I sat up quietly and waited for her to say something. Rosco waddled over to me and tried jumping up on my bed, but he was too short, so after a few failed jumping attempts, he lay down by the side.

After a moment of awkward silence, Nellie looked me straight in the eyes, cleared her throat, and spoke, "Okay, listen, you little loser! I don't want you here on base, so you better prepare to go home soon."

I sat up. "Um, I'm sorry. What?"

"You don't belong here and you're too young to make a decision like this!"

"You did, when you were ten," I interrupted.

"Boone's my real dad, idiot."

"Oh."

"And you're just some kid who threw away perfectly good parents to play in Space for a while. Boone thinks this is a great idea, but I know otherwise. He thinks you're a genius who's gonna invent a whole bunch of cool stuff for the CBC, but I know you're just some mediocre kid who has seen too many movies and has no idea what he's doing."

"Get out of my room," I said. I wished I could slap her in the face, but I was too shocked by her open hostility to move. Not to mention, she was a girl, and my newly-adopted sister, and I really wanted to play her video game again if possible. My only option was to listen to her tirade as calmly as I could.

She stretched, tossing her head gently from side to side as if she were preparing for a boxing match.

"You have no idea what you've done, but I'm going to do everything in my power to get you back home, where you belong," she continued. "Eventually you're going to be a disappointment to Boone. You know that, don't you?"

She called Rosco over to her, and he complied happily, completely unaware of her threats. As she reached down to scratch his back, she smiled coldly. "You could never replace the son Boone left behind on Earth."

"He had a son?

"Yes," she said, standing up again. "He didn't want this life, and neither will you when I get through with you."

I decided if I remained silent, maybe she would run out of steam and just leave. I waited, blinking at her. She turned around and began to walk out the door, but then changed her mind and walked right up to me. I grew nervous as she approached the end of my bed.

"Oh, and by the way, Seth," she said in a softer tone, "if you say anything about any of this to Boone, I will kill you."

With that, she turned and marched out of the room.

Chapter 14

FLIGHT

I don't know how long I waited for Boone to return for me. It felt as if I had fallen asleep again. Every part of me was numb when he gently shook my shoulder.

"Let's go have an adventure, shall we?" Boone announced. "Isn't this what you've been waiting for your whole life?"

"Yes it is," I said, shaking off Nellie's threats and nodding wholeheartedly in agreement. I jumped out of bed, grabbed my backpack, and followed him out of our family quarters. I could hear Rosco's gurgle-whinny call out to us pathetically halfway down the hallway. I was grateful he was being left behind. I didn't want him sitting on my lap or licking me during my first deep-space journey.

On the way to Hangar B, Boone pointed out some more sections of the base, but I wasn't really paying attention to the layout. What really captured my attention was the sound of wind chimes tinkling in the air around us as we walked through an all-transparent commons area.

"What is that?" I asked.

"The sound?" he asked.

"Yeah," I said. "I heard it through the radio. I thought they were wind chimes."

"That is the sound the light speed flux makes. Pretty, huh?"

"Yeah," I agreed, mesmerized by the soft tinkling. "Uh, what's light speed flux, again?"

"In very basic terms, it's Einstein's theory of relativity," Boone explained. "When you approach the speed of light, time slows down. When you are traveling at the speed of light, time stops. We set our base in a speed-of-light flux to camouflage us. What everyone sees off base is the way things looked before we set up camp. Time moves on around us, but inside this dome, time is frozen. It is an optical illusion. When we travel off base we adjust our travel so we catch up with time."

I nodded. "Okay," I said, trying desperately to track.

"Did you even follow that, Seth?" a voice called out from behind us. We stopped and turned. Nellie stood with her hands on her hips. I jumped a little as I faced her, not really sure how to act around her after her death threat. I couldn't help wondering if I'd end up like Connie when Nellie got through with me – spat out and abandoned without any memories.

"Oh I'm tracking, Nellie," I shot back, "but why do we even need to go into a speed-of-light flux?"

Boone said, smiling warmly at me. "It provides some anonymity for us not to be on the same time continuum as everyone, and it's also nice to add a few years without the aging process."

"We are frozen in time so that others won't be able to locate us too easily," Nellie interrupted.

"Other things are looking for you...I mean...us?"

"Not necessarily, but you can never be too sure," Boone said, calmly. "There are a lot of crazy things out here. We prefer to go unnoticed. Keep our distance. Just think of us as a neutral entity... like Switzerland. We are conscientious objectors to the fights and wars of the other species in the Galaxy."

"Why do we want to keep out of the wars?" I asked.

"Why should we get involved?" Nellie asked.

"I don't know... to help people out?" I asked as sarcastically as possible. I didn't know why, but my gut told me that the whole thing with Connie and maybe even the problems in Vegas were connected somehow possibly to those Kashmaari things, and that Earth needed a little help.

Boone shook his head, "You'll soon learn that it's best to keep a low profile and keep out of conflicts, Seth. They just waste resources and energy."

"Uh... information that would have been helpful before I signed on," I said, staring at the sterile white walls around us. There were no imperfections anywhere to be seen.

"You want to go to war?" Boone asked, almost as if he were shocked.

"I don't know," I answered. "I've grown up in the U.S. Air Force all my life, so I'm not exactly a pacifist. There is a point to having a good defense against all enemies foreign and domestic."

Neither of them looked like they understood, so I added, "You know... the pursuit of life, liberty, and all who threaten it..." I had always liked the Navy's motto.

Nellie rolled her eyes and sighed, then said, "We are engineers, not soldiers, Seth. We design and create space craft and travel systems, mainly, and then work with other technological advancements. We are a team of engineers and scientists who have been carefully selected to improve the Universe."

Blah, blah, blah, I wanted to say. What about her games... she had developed some real combat expertise in those simulations.

I glanced around, trying to see the improvement Nellie boasted of. Sure, there were advancements, but the only thing that was beautiful was the stars, and you could see those on Earth. Suddenly, Julia Gomez's food, and the different architecture of the places I'd lived, began calling to me. I was even missing the stupid separate hot and cold water faucets in England.

I wasn't sure why, but the whole "we don't want to help anyone – we're pacifists" idealology made me instantly want to start an argument, so I asked, "If you stay in the freeze time flux thing, what prevents others living in real time from advancing before you catch up to them?"

A twinge of guilt seemed to cross both Boone and Nellie's faces. Boone's mouth twisted up to the side, and he said, "We calculate it enough. We keep current on what's going on, and our bodies stay young when we jump ahead in time for more… inspiration."

"Time travel?" I asked. "And you don't age if you jump ahead in time?"

"Working out a few kinks, but yes."

"That's cheating," I observed.

"We only peek at what the CBC will come up with later. It's not like we steal it from anyone other than ourselves." Nellie butted in. She was ready to argue back, and I was ready to dish it.

"Whatever," I said, calling her bluff.

"Let's get going," Boone said, completely dismissing the mounting tension.

Nellie and I followed in silence behind him. My sneakers squeaked on the floor a few times as I kept stride. After a few more corridors we entered a colossal space hangar full of obsidian-looking ships, just like Sistah, and I completely lost my anger. It was the most beautiful sight I had ever seen.

"Is this the space dock?" I asked in wonder.

"This is Hangar B." Boone smiled proudly.

The space ships shimmered cobalt and violet in the soft lighting. They went on and on in rows – every one as beautiful and unique as the next. I looked up at the stars twinkling in the sky around and beyond us.

The *wow* I mumbled didn't really cover it and the frustration I had felt in the corridor had disappeared entirely.

I saw Sistah straight ahead of us, looking more like a space ship than a car at that moment. I climbed in quickly and claimed the front seat I'd ridden in before, setting my backpack next to me.

Nellie didn't say a word. She tripped her way past my pack and settled herself in the seat behind mine. Then she began to paint her nails using a little pink rectangle. She had beamed on red, then blue, then orange while we waited for Boone. I swiveled my chair and faced the front of the space craft, ignoring her back. I pushed a few screens. Nothing happened. I couldn't remember what Boone had said to get her revving.

He finally climbed into the driver's seat and said, "Activate."

The lights switched on and the engine hummed.

"Hey Sistah—you ready?" Boone asked.

"Voice command affirmative," Sistah responded.

"Take us to the Embassy Base on Krad," Boone ordered.

"Sure thing, Sugar," Sistah said. "Estimated travel time eight hours and twenty minutes to Krad."

"Don't worry," Boone smiled, "I packed some games."

"How far away is Krad?"

"Won't make sense to explain the distance to you now," Boone said, "but let's just say that we'll be hitting real acceleration way beyond your concept of light speed."

"Do you ever drive Sistah manually?" I asked.

"Not anymore," Boone said. "But, do you want to try driving her?"

"Yes please."

"Sistah, looks like Seth is taking you out on a little ride."

"Switching to manual operator mode," Sistah said as a transparent star chart appeared on the windshield.

Boone switched seats with me and handed me the steering mechanism. The grips bent around the shape of my hands and the seat automatically adjusted to my height and build. I listened to the engine's humming as I waited for instructions.

"Now, this is a little CBC secret, just in case you ever need to take over someone's craft. The protocol is simple." Boone explained. "Just say 'Activate,' then 'Code 1162,' and you should be ready to go."

"Really?" I asked.

"You can commandeer any CBC ship," he said.

"It's that easy? You aren't all scared that someone will steal your space ships?"

"Nobody in the CBC will. We all have what we need. And if they did, we'd just get a new one," Boone smiled. "Just thought I'd let you in on one of our little secrets. It will work for all space craft, if there's a CBC emblem on it. We design and build ships for just about every advanced civilization in the Galaxy. That's mainly what we do – vehicles and deep space travel."

"Activate… Code 1162 ," I repeated.

"Affirmative," Sistah said. "Welcome guest operator."

"What next?" I asked.

"The coordinates are already programmed into Sistah, but if you needed to do it manually, you would just consult the star charts. They basically act like an intergalactic GPS. You'll love it. It will ask you your destination. Just tell it where you need to go, and it will tell you what to do and when to do it."

I spent the next few minutes trying to memorize every instruction given to me. Luckily, Sistah was just about as user-friendly as she could get.

"Alright," Boone said, "Let's take her out of dock. Just push the steering column away from your chest. The harder you push—the faster it goes. And watch out, it's very sensitive. Pull back to brake. Turn left and right as per usual for left and right."

"Okay," I breathed. "Just like a plane?"

"Pretty much," Nellie interjected, "but not really."

Shut up, stupid cow! I thought, grateful that she wasn't Pfister and couldn't hear what I was really thinking.

Boone smiled and patted me on the back. I shook off Nellie's sarcasm and inhaled deeply

"All right, Seth," Boone said. "let's roll."

"There's a wall there," I pointed out, not really ready to steer straight into it, but guessing that's just what I was supposed to do.

"Just do it, Seth—see what happens," Nellie said, passing each of us a bottle of cream soda. Her nails were pink, and her voice was kinder. "I'm so glad you scored some of these, Daddy."

I was getting sick of her mood swings. She was my friend, she wasn't my friend. She wanted to kill me, she was hooking me up with cream soda: it was gonna be a long flight.

"Cheers," Boone said, and clinked his bottle to mine. "Here's to Seth's first launch."

"Thanks," I said, taking a swig, wishing Nellie wasn't there to see me at a vulnerable learning moment. I just needed to relax and not let it get to me. "Do you have any music?" I ventured.

"What would you like?" Boone asked.

"A little rock and roll," I said thinking about the first time my dad took me out flying. We listened to his big-hair-butt-rock music as we tore up the sky.

"Sure thing, Sugar," Sistah said. Instantly something with rich power chords started playing. I took a swig of my pop, placed the bottle between my legs, and gently pushed forward on the steering column.

We shot through the space dock walls like a crack of lightning in the night sky. The wall let us pass through without rupturing—like a bullet shot through liquid mercury—then it coagulated back in place once we were through. The base vanished completely. In the place of it were moon rock formations and wisps of dust trails from take off. A small rear-view screen had appeared which gave me a visual of everything behind us. It was better than a rear-view mirror, although hard to get used to.

"The base is still there," Boone observed. "Just frozen in time. You can't see it because you have already moved ahead three seconds. We'll have been gone a few days, but for everyone on base it will have been moments. Some men in the CBC come home with full beards from their missions, when they were clean shaven right before they left."

"Whatever you say," I shrugged, wondering if I would ever catch up.

I pushed the steering column further forward and we sailed over the rugged terrain of the moon like a slick fish through smooth rocks. Driving Sistah was like riding a dune buggy on ice skates. We felt every bump and crater. Because of the difference in the moon's gravitational pull our leaps and bumps were several stories high. I pictured a giant ballerina leaping across the desert in slow motion as we shot up and crashed down.

"That's where we transfer our water from," Boone announced as we passed a formation. "I believe that one of NASA's shuttles finally picked up evidence of water here on the Moon, not too long ago, which is some progress, eh? There's another station there—you just can't see it…"

"Because it's frozen in time?" I interrupted.

"Exactly," Boone said.

As I got my bearings I realized we were coasting over the Sea of Tranquility, which was where Neil Armstrong took his first step… his giant leap for mankind. Although it had been decades, I couldn't help scanning the area for the American flag they had left or their footprints in the sand.

"This is the Sea of Tranquility. This is where they landed." I said, more to myself, but somehow saying it out loud made it real for me.

"Is it?" Nellie sounded bored. "You know we have done a lot more than collecting moon rocks and walking on the surface, so pardon me if I'm not really impressed."

"Get ready for transition," Boone interrupted.

"I'm sorry, but you just don't knock Neil Armstrong!" I couldn't let it go.

"He's practically a caveman, Seth." Nellie enjoyed how angry she was making me.

"Excuse my French, but the man had to have had balls of pure steel to do the things he did!"

"You're so dumb, Seth!"

"Wench!"

"Idiot!"

"Hey!" Boone interrupted. "It ends right here, right now."

Upon reflection, I realized I was probably experiencing sibling rivalry for the first time in my life, and I was elated. I had just found my major purpose in Space—to outshine my adopted sister and make her life a living hell until such time as she managed to kill me or send me home without any memories.

I glanced back at Nellie and found that her hairdo was different from before. Instead of braids, she was sporting dreads. Her make-up was different as well.

"I'm having a hard time seeing how an exploration into the realm of cosmetology is a giant leap for anyone," I mumbled.

"Beg your pardon?" Nellie asked, but I knew she heard me.

"We're coming up on a right turn if you want to hit the proper trajectory for Krad," Boone interrupted, "You need to slow down, Seth."

I pulled the steering column into my chest and we decelerated too quickly. Sistah bounced around like a pinball, but Boone only laughed. I shook myself into focus tried to slow her down. Who knew how fast we were going? Everything was flashing past us like a blue-ray disc on fast forward and I was about to be sick.

"Approaching right turn, Sugar," Sistah said, "in ten seconds, nine, eight, seven, six, five, four, three, turn right now."

Instead of a dinky ding noise there was a grand gong reverberation. I turned the column to the right as slightly as I dared, but about fell out of my seat anyway. Boone laughed even harder. I overcorrected and Sistah barrel-rolled three times. Pushing hard on the column, I propelled us out of the spin and back on course.

"Good instinct on that one," Boone smiled proudly. "You're really getting the hang of it."

"Thanks," I said, "But I think I need to throw up, now."

Boone tapped a button on his rectangle and a light transported the queasiness from my stomach, along with whatever else was about to come out with it. I immediately felt better.

"I didn't expect that kind of reaction to the turn," I managed.

"I think Sistah was just trying to have a little fun with you," Boone confided. "It shouldn't have been that bad, especially with such weak gravity."

"Dad," Nellie interrupted excitedly, "I think I worked out the bugs, look!" Her hair was a short pixie cut twisted up with crystal butterfly and flower clips.

"Very nice, Nel," Boone said. "She's working on a beauty beam line, Seth. You can play around with your hair, nails, and makeup—just transfer the styles and colors on and off. Not really useful for our group at the CBC because we tend to be a little more practical, but it could be marketed to a few of the more… how to say it…up-market and savvy star systems."

"You could say vain," Nellie suggested. Her hair was back to the braids she wore earlier, although she kept her new sparkly nails.

Boon shifted in his seat and asked, "So, Seth, you want to hold onto that column for the next 8 hours, or do you want to put Sistah on auto pilot and relax a bit?"

"Auto pilot would be great," I said, letting go of the column. The ship sped up and began to veer off course.

"Sistah, take over, would you?"

"Will do, Boone," Sistah cooed.

The ship straightened up and merged with a clear, tube-shaped current like the one we traveled in from Earth. Our speed increased dramatically. Soon we were moving so fast that it almost seemed like time was slowing down and we were in slow motion. I shook my head in wonder.

"Have a few questions, huh?" Boone asked.

"A few hundred." I nodded. "How does it work?"

"Well, I hope you won't mind, but I'm going to leave you in the dark for a while, Seth," Boone said. "I want to see what you will come up with on your own, before I start teaching you our science. It's part of the reason I wanted to take this trip. I haven't really introduced you to anyone on base, or put any biases in your head. Don't want to start limiting your possibilities with our theorems and equations until you have a little time to move around in my world and see what we're missing. I want to see how you react to this situation without any coaching. Does any of that make sense?"

"Uh…" I said. "I doubt I'll be much help, sir."

"What do you think we are traveling in?" Boone asked.

Nellie, reclined comfortably in her seat, was already asleep. Her snoring interrupted my thoughts. I almost wished I could do the same. There was no way I was really going to bring something new to the group. Perhaps Nellie was right, and I was just some punk kid who had watched too many movies and had his head in the clouds. It was like I had just shown up to a science fair for geniuses with an ant farm. Boone was way beyond Einstein, Heisenberg, or Tesla, and I was an outclassed infant.

He cleared his throat, obviously still waiting for me to answer his question.

"I figure we're traveling in some sort of naturally occurring tunnel because there is no civilization that could lay down a freeway system across the galaxy... it's a channel or current ... but seems to act like the Underground in London with several different tracks. It somehow accelerates travel speed... I don't know."

"You're on the right track," Boone said smiling at his own pun. "There are pathways like this all over the galaxy. They are channels of energy, made out of a naturally-occurring substance called cillian."

"Which is why you're called the Cillian Base Community."

"Right. And our ships have been constructed to accelerate to the speeds possible in these channels. We've mapped out pathways to every civilized place in our galaxy and have begun to map out pathways to a few galaxies beyond."

I shook my head in disbelief. "I'm sorry, but I'm having a hard time with that, sir. Even if we traveled one hundred and eighty-six thousand miles a second for a whole year it would take us something like five hundred years at that rate to make it from the Earth to Polaris. Even Alpha Centauri is over four light years away.

"Now, Seth, repeat after me," Boone said, "Light speed is a variable, not a constant. Time is a variable, not a constant. What if I were to tell you that we had a team cross the Milky Way in just under a week channeling these currents. There's a way, Seth."

"Okay." I nodded.

"We're mostly powered by the Day Star," Boone continued.

"You mean, like, the Sun?" I asked.

"Yeah—solar power is what it's called on Earth, now," Boone said.

I nodded again. Solar power is free, clean, always available, but not developed to its full potential.

"Bet you're wondering why you don't have this kind of power back home," Boone observed. "Mad there isn't more progress?"

"Yeah..." I stammered.

"There are conspiring and greedy people in power on Earth who always seem to stop progression so they can have money and control. Until there is no more greed, there will always be corruption and damnation down there and I don't care which side you are talking about."

"Damnation?" I blurted out.

"It's a little harsh, I know, but it means that progression stops, and that is what happened with the Earth. Consider yourself saved, Seth. Enlightened."

"Is that why you left?" I asked.

"I was an engineer who couldn't get a break because I was black. Kept getting passed up for promotion. Didn't really want to have to get the law involved – didn't see why I should make people appreciate me. The CBC approached me and asked if I wanted to join them, so I left and got to go a little beyond my limitations. Things have changed a bit since I lived down there, though. You can dare to dream more...when you're... well, like us, I guess."

I nodded and thought of the top three jobs list I had made on my first day at Central. Whatever was in store for me in Space had to be more exciting than a professional basketball player, civil engineer, or Air Force fighter pilot. At least, I hoped it would be since I was pretty much stuck forever with the CBC.

I asked, "Have you ever regretted leaving?"

"Yes, but I think all paths of life have regrets," he observed, leaning back in his chair. "You can't have one hundred percent perfection with any choice you make. There's always a tradeoff, son. Up here, I got to be something, somebody, which means more to me than anything I left behind. But I do miss a cold cream soda now and then."

I waited for him to talk about the son he'd left behind, but he never did, and he never asked me if I regretted my decision to leave.

Chapter 15

KRAD

The rest of the flight to Krad was spent napping and having food and waste transported in and out of my body while I checked out Sistah's entertainment options. I was delighted when I found I could call up almost anything including the game I played back on base. If I named it, Sistah could get it—movies, music, video games—even the stuff I'd learned to love in other countries where Dad had been stationed. Boone played a few games with me and then took a five-hour nap while I called up all my favorite music and had Sistah create a gigantic playlist for me.

After a while, I turned to a tour of the ship's specs on the mainframe. There was a weapons system on board. I was just working through a battle simulation, when Nellie woke up, so I decided to try sleeping. There was no way I was going to engage in another brother-sister heart to heart. But my rest wasn't all that great because I was subconsciously worried about what she might do to me if I got too deep in a REM cycle. I must have pretended to sleep more than I actually did.

"Seth," Boone shook my shoulder as he spoke, "you wanna take the last little stretch to Krad?"

"Oh, like drive, you mean?" I asked.

"Fly, but yeah," he answered.

"Uh, no," I said. "I don't want to tear up the Varlock's landing field–wouldn't be good for diplomacy."

"Have it your way," Boone said and chuckled.

"Arrival in five minutes," Sistah interrupted. "Prepare for a cold climate."

Boone whipped out his rectangle and suddenly, extra layers of white spandex appeared on their bodies along with matching white boots and coats for all of us. I was grateful he didn't ask me to change out of my jeans yet.

Sistah gradually filled the cabin with cold air to acclimatize us. Nellie shivered and rolled her eyes. She ended up beaming on two extra layers of clothing, adding additional socks and gloves as well.

A small, speckled, brown and aquamarine planet appeared ahead of us, right about the time we began to slow down. From what I could make out, our landing site seemed to be in the middle of an Autumn jungle instead of a city. I sighed deeply, trying to remind myself to breathe. We touched down on the planet's surface with a smoothness that was just like a feather landing on the water. Boone tossed me a head covering, and then passed one to Nellie.

"Do not remove this oxygen mask," he ordered. "It's awkward and will inhibit your ability to communicate as well as you would like, but at least you'll be able to breathe. The air here is extra heavy on the chlorine and will be poison to your lungs."

The mask covered my whole face and the oxygen felt like flour as I breathed it in and coughed it out. I reached for my backpack and listened to Nellie sigh in complete exasperation when I slung it over my shoulder. She muttered something about how I was carrying around a security blanket. Sistah's doors hissed open and we piled out.

"Sleep and draw Day Star Power," Boone instructed Sistah, and she powered off.

My depth perception was so off that I tripped over my left foot and fell onto the frosty ground, which felt like a frozen sponge. I was annoyed to find that Boone and Nellie were getting around effortlessly in their masks. Boone scooped me up by my left arm and pointed me in the direction of the delegation ahead.

Three tall figures approached us. They were BAHs –

bipedal alien humanoids – but moved like fast and tense predatory cats. Their skin was a dull, light gray, and ivory hair shot out every which way, like the troll dolls Meike collected back in Germany. Not only could I not distinguish gender, but they all looked exactly the same to me. Their eyes were each violet and they spoke in quick, deep, whimsical tones... nothing I could pinpoint. They wore what seemed to be their equivalent of leather looking animal skins, but with a slight CBC influence since the skins were more white and buff.

As they grabbed our arms around the elbows, I realized we were being greeted. We shook elbows back and although we smiled, nothing in their responses indicated they were smiling at us.

The tallest one spoke and nodded toward a dullish copper-looking, Frisbee-shaped structure ahead that melted into the surrounding fall-colors landscape perfectly. The trees nearby it were shades of browns and orange like the desert, although the air was frigid.

We followed them as they walked in the direction of the structure, the ground crunching beneath our feet as we went. Everything was dusted in frost, and the part of Nellie's braids that hung past her mask had turned white, frozen solid. I wanted to reach out and break one off like an icicle, but stopped myself for the sake of the mission.

We entered the structure and marched to a diamond-shaped room full of soft orange benches. The three Varlocks sat down and pointed out seats for us across from them. We sat down, and I coughed out another breath of heavy oxygen, wondering why someone hadn't fixed the flour-air problem years ago.

The largest Varlock spoke directly to Boone, then nodded and waited. When Boone turned to me and smiled, I realized he was really serious about having me translate. I had no idea what the Varlock was saying, so I shrugged, hoping it would be enough to get everyone off my back. Nellie nodded for me to look at the beasts again, but it was practically impossible to focus or pick up on anything because the mask was so useless. I looked down at my backpack on my lap and realized that my fists were clenched tightly around the midsection. I looked back over at Boone, then to Nellie and shrugged. Then, the three of us stared back at the creatures.

A different Varlock spoke a few sentences and then stood up. Boone and Nellie looked over at me. I decided to stand up too, but everyone else remained seated. The standing Varlock howled once and sat back down again. I didn't howl, but I sat down as well. Then it was silent. Boone looked at me again, and I shrugged again.

"If you're looking for a translation, you've got the wrong guy," I said, my voice tried to push its way through my mask. "I have no idea what they want… you should have brought Pfister."

Boone made a sound like he was trying to stifle a laugh. Another snort escaped the tallest Varlock, which got everyone in the circle laughing along with them. I felt disoriented. Had I missed a comical moment?

Nellie suddenly removed her oxygen mask and said, "These things are terrible."

I reached over to stop her, "No!" I cried. "You'll die!"

Everyone laughed harder, Nellie joining in with them. Boone removed his mask and breathed in a huge gust of air.

"So, this is the newest adoptee," the largest Varlock said. "Welcome to Krad, Seth."

It still took me another second to register they had all been playing a joke on me, and then I removed my mask, completely humiliated. By the time I got it all the way off, everyone was in complete hysterics. Boone slapped his knee as he wheezed out air between the shockwaves of his laughter. I relented and smiled, shaking my head in submission.

"Well, I can tell you one thing," I announced, "these masks do suck. Do you ever really have to use them?"

"We try not to associate with those beings who don't breathe the same air as we do," the Largest Varlock stated in a strong voice, sounding as if he were completely serious. It surprised me how good his English sounded. It wasn't

British English either. He was speaking American English, and his dialect was spot on.

"Nobody wants to use those," the gentle looking Varlock on his right added, only he had a bit of a strange accent I couldn't place.

"It's like breathing mud," I said.

"Exactly," said Boone. "We set this up to see if you could do anything about it."

"Me, sir?" I asked in disbelief. I was clutching my backpack again and tried to ease up on my grip.

"Jim-bo has a lab. He can build any idea you come up with," Nellie said. "He's going to help me streamline my new beauty Brain devices as well."

"Uh… Jim-bo?"

The largest Varlock saluted, indicating that he was *Jim-bo.*

"Sorry, Seth," Boone apologized, "We just wanted to give you a real experience with our communication problem before I asked you to fix it. The CBC is light years ahead in transportation and deep space travel, but not so hot in other areas."

"Maybe you should adopt a few linguists as well as engineers."

The group all nodded and mumbled in agreement. I decided to shake off the feelings of embarrassment and anger from their practical joke on the new guy and began to focus on the problem. "So, it's uncomfortable," I began, "too uncomfortable for me to even care if I can understand anyone while I'm wearing it."

"Right," Boone said.

"A bio-dome?" I offered, then cringed at how stupid my suggestion sounded. The CBC was already doing a version of it with all the plants they had everywhere. Surely they would have come up with a similar idea by now.

"What is that?" Jim-bo demanded.

I quickly explained that a bio dome was a self-contained eco system in a glass jar, and that the plants created the oxygen while an organism, like a frog, created the carbon dioxide. I gestured to the palm tree looking thing potted next to me. They didn't get the connection. As I summed up the process, and idea came to me for a bio-suit lined with blue-green algae and covered with the same matter the walls of the moon base were made of. I thought it might be thin enough to create an illusion of being mask-free, and would allow for a more intimate relationship with foreign species that breathe different air.

"Or we could beam in oxygen to a mask instead of having it filter on site," I suggested as a second idea.

"I like the first thought," Jim-bo said, "We should work on that one. Transferring is sometimes hard to do as a consistent, life-support measure. We would have distance to take into account as well. I like the idea of creating re-usable atmosphere in a cillian shell."

We discussed our options, but the thought that other life forms in the Galaxy didn't all breathe our own type of atmosphere kept distracting me. There weren't just alien species language barriers to contend with, but atmospheric ones as well.

The Varlocks walked us over to the lab, which was an intergalactic tool shed, complete with green plants and white plastic. Big, shiny, metal, tool-type objects hung on the walls. Jim-bo directed me to a corner of the lab and sat me in a white chair next to a giant fern. My seat wrapped itself around my body and began to massage and heat my buns.

"Yeah, so the CBC built this little lab for us—can you tell?" he asked with a sarcastic grin.

"Sure, white walls, plants…"

"Bio dome plants." He smiled and plopped down in an identical seat across from me.

I sighed.

"You sick of it yet?" he asked quietly so that nobody else could hear.

"What's that?"

"Sterile living."

"I miss colors," I said.

"And food?" he asked.

"Yes!" I said. "How do you get to keep your base the way it is?"

Jim-bo nodded and whipped out a Brain of his own, and started pushing buttons. "We are not a part of the CBC," he answered finally. "We work with them but haven't adopted all of their practices. I can take leaks whenever and wherever I want."

"Where did you learn your English?" I asked.

He glance up and actually looked embarrassed. After a mighty sigh, he said, "American TV shows and movies."

I was shocked.

He continued, "I can't get enough of them, really. That's why I like to work with Boone and Nellie. I'm fascinated with Earth... so messy and angry and chaotic and wonderful."

I smiled, trying to take in the conversation I was having. So many of the people I had met in the countries we'd been stationed in gave me the same exact answer. Everyone learns English from American movies... even BAHs.

"What are you smiling about?" Jim-bo asked.

"You are my first BAH," I said, deciding that Pfister didn't count because he was a BACH (Bipedal Alien Childlike Humanoid) and I definitely wanted someone like Jim-bo to be my first official BAH contact.

"What's a BAH?" he asked.

"Bipedal Alien Humanoid – like almost every alien on Star Trek."

He smiled and shook his head. "You are my first BAV, then... Bipedal Alien Varlockoid."

"You sound like a nerd," I said.

"I'm just following your lead, Seth," he nodded, "But I know what you mean about Star Trek. All their BEMs can walk on two legs. That being said, I still enjoy the show. You have such great entertainments on Earth... you and Tralis Four produce the best stories. But Tralisasians must have larger bladders because their entertainments last for hours on end, and yours usually last up to two at the most. Don't worry, Seth, I'll take you to see some real BEMs."

I smiled, happy that he was a big enough nerd to know the bug eyed monster reference, just like Rosa.

"Is your name really Jim-bo?" I couldn't help asking, staring into his blazing purple eyes. They were so cool. There was a brown ring in the center around a darker sphere that must have worked like a pupil.

"Jim-bo's the nickname they gave me," he said, fiddling with his Brain. It was larger than Boone's to accommodate his large hands. He also had multi-colored, intricate designs etched into the cover surface.

"What's your real name?"

He answered in a deep, resonant and very long string of consonants and glottal stops that I wasn't even going to try to pronounce.

"You can stick with Jim-bo, Seth," he said after a moment, and laughed with a broad smile. "I don't expect you to be as advanced as I am."

"Sarcasm?"

"Truth," he shrugged.

"I'm surprised you would condescend to watch our shows or learn our language," I shot back.

"Whatever," he smiled. "I learned your language in a week. Just added it to my vast collection of intergalactic wisdom."

I wanted to say something pithy in response, but nothing came to mind: Jim-bo was better than any alien I could have possibly imagined and I was taken completely off guard. Luckily, he was concentrating on his Brain too much to notice that I was at a loss for words. After a few silent moments he adjusted the position of my head and said, "Think."

"I'm sorry?" I said, unsure of his command.

"I want you to think about that bio dome thing and your design ideas right now."

As I thought, my ideas began to appear on the screen of his Brain.

"It's picking up my thoughts?" I asked.

"Just relax and think," he instructed, like a doctor giving an examination. I thought through my ideas as succinctly as possible and found them all appearing on the screen. As we discussed a few possible variables and alternatives to my brainstormed invention, the plans on the screen changed or were added to, almost like we were sketching and erasing. Through the thought processes of the conversation, a whole plan for a prototype was drawn up. It looked exactly the way I had envisioned it. As each idea appeared on the screen, Jimbo would think his own notes and make counter-changes.

To my great satisfaction, he seemed only interested in my projects, and completely ignored Nellie, who just hung around the lab like a bored girlfriend at band practice. And after a few hours, one of the other Varlocks brought us food. Not beam-me-up-Scotty food, but plates of seasoned meats and roots on some strange-looking grain. Flasks of actual water accompanied the meal.

"Thought you might appreciate this," Jim-bo said softly as we ate.

I stuffed myself almost out of rebellion for the perfect-serving-sized rations which had been forced down me since I left Earth, and I drank down three flasks of water, although I wasn't really that thirsty.

Boone just kept shaking his head and laughing at me from across the room. He had been working with the shortest Varlock on one of his projects.

"Hey man, I don't care what you think," I called over to him. "There's no telling when my next real meal is going to be, and I didn't realize how much I'd miss eating—spilling food on my shirt... burping—little things like that... not to mention how unhealthy it must be to bypass this most basic of processes!"

"You'll get used to it," Nellie told me from her side of the room. Although she was twenty feet away, she still felt like she had to be a part of the conversation.

I rolled my eyes and glanced back over to Boone, who was back to studying his Brain. He looked up and smiled widely, "Just checking my messages. Looks like Meike wrote you back."

"What did she say?"

"It's in German."

"Oh."

"But the translation says she's glad you're happy and that she has a new boyfriend now, so please don't write anymore."

"Oh."

Boon went back to his messages while we finished eating. Once our plates were empty, we resumed our project. My stomach felt like it was going to burst, and I actually felt a little sick, but it was worth it, if only to feel something real.

Jim-bo named our prototype "Bio Suit" and cleared his screen for more of my ideas. Another one appeared on screen – one that I didn't realize that I had been working on. I guess it had been in the back of my head ever since Boone and Nellie told me that the CBC were pacifists.

"What's this?" Jim-bo asked.

A picture of me in an impenetrable suit, similar to the one we had just created, appeared on the screen. The green alien, like the one I had seen on the day of the accident, sparked and crackled on the screen. It ran full force into me, but couldn't enter my body because of the suit. Then the Seth on the screen took out a gun that sucked the DH (Demonic Humanoid) into it.

"You got a Kashmaari problem?" Jim-bo asked slowly in a hushed whisper. His eyes were glued to the image of the green DH on his Brain. He used the word that Pfister and Boone had used that morning.

"I don't know," I whispered back, inadvertently looking around the room. "Is that what a Kashmaar looks like?"

"Yeah."

Nobody was paying attention so I told him everything I knew about the accident, which had been real, and Connie, and Boone and Pfister's conversation about Topher's wife, then asked him what he thought.

Jim-bo nodded. "Sounds like you probably have a Kashmaari infestation back on Earth."

"Oh, like the weird stuff going on in Vegas?"

"Yeah, and your Dad flashed what badge at it to make it go away?"

"His Air Force personnel badge."

"Wow, and it worked?"

"I guess. It just disappeared."

"Interesting."

It was, but I didn't want to think about Dad's association with those things, so I changed the subject. "Why doesn't Boone want to talk about it?"

"Doesn't want to get involved," Jim-bo observed in a cautious tone.

"Do they really possess people and make them do terrible things?" I asked, thinking about my dream that morning.

"As far as I know, most of them do," he said.

"Why?"

"I'm not sure," he stated. "They don't have bodies. Maybe the only way they can feel things is by taking over somebody else. We've only just begun to realize what they're up to. They seem to pick on the less advanced worlds for their skins so that no one will be able to stop them."

"Can anything stop them?"

"I don't know," he said, "Maybe Constantine has something."

"Whose Constantine?"

"He's like the Van Helsing of the Kashmaari world." Pfister and Boone had mentioned him that morning as well.

"Why doesn't the CBC do something?"

"We aren't really prepared to go up against them. They really just scare the pants off of everyone."

I couldn't help smiling.

"What?"

"Scare the pants off of everyone is a little outdated."

"Oh... well, they are freaky beyond freak."

"Got it."

"They're bad news."

"And you don't have weapons to protect against them?"

"Nothing like you have dreamed up in your head," he pointed to the gun. "Only, a gun is so passé, don't you think? Maybe a lasso?"

The picture morphed from a gun to a lasso, and then as

I said it out loud it changed into a whip.

"A plasma whip."

"A whip would work to defend against corporeal beings as well as Kashmaari," Jim-bo agreed. "Now, that would be cool."

"Oh, you mean have two functions, one against the DHs, and one for enemies with bodies."

"Yeah," he nodded, pushing a few buttons, "you gotta be able to whip a target, but also whip through it to draw out the Kashmaar, or DH, as you call it."

Demonic Humanoid appeared in small lettering next to the Kashmaar on the screen. Then the words *Kashmaari Armor* appeared over the prototype of the suit.

"And then have some sort of way to draw it into a containment chamber housed in the handle," I said. "to keep it prisoner."

Jimbo's Brain sketched the energy containment chamber I'd been working on to fuel my rockets as I thought. I tried to be as thorough as possible while I reviewed every detail of my invention. Jim-bo added his own engineering thoughts as I went. It was a meeting of the minds – the one I had always wished for.

"This chamber could be hard to pull off," Jim-bo muttered. "As far as I know, nobody has tried to imprison a Kashmaar. If it didn't work the first time, they'd possess you and have you end your life in seconds. You couldn't mess this up. There's no test run for something like this, Seth."

"That's what the suit is for," I said, pointing to the armor on the Brain. "The Kashmaar shouldn't be able to get through to him."

Jim-bo nodded. "A fire-fiend fire-wall."

"Yes! Could you build something like that?" I ventured.

"The CBC wouldn't like it," he said, frowning down at the screen.

"What is up with the CBC?"

He shushed me and I sighed, trying to clear my head of the frustration and total hopelessness that was surfacing. I glanced over at Nellie and Boone who were still quietly working on projects, oblivious to our contraband conversation. Jim-bo nodded to the door.

"Hey, Boone, I'm taking Seth out for a while," he announced.

"Sounds good," Boone said, not glancing up from his work.

"Yeah... let's get some air," Jim-bo said, heading for the door.

Chapter 16

JIM-BO

We hurried out of the lab and into a darkened corridor. I ran, the way Nelson used to work it double time, to keep up with Jim-bo's large strides. He probably had about a foot on me, and I wasn't short. Occasionally we passed a random Varlock as we shuffled down the passageways, and each time Jim-bo said something to them in his native tongue. There was no way I was ever going to learn something like what the Varlocks spoke. One thing was certain: Jim-bo wasn't an introvert.

We entered a hangar full of obsidian CBC space craft and a few other vehicles. Jim-bo stopped in front of two stealth-looking hovercraft motorcycles glistening cobalt and violet under the lights.

"You wanna try this?"

"Yup," I nodded.

"You can bring your back pack," he pointed to it.

"It's all I have left of home," I admitted.

He shook his head and said, "I'd freak if they made me make that deal."

"What deal?"

"The never go home deal," he said with disgust. "What do you have in there, anyway? You have a picture of that girlfriend who doesn't want you to write back?"

"Meike?" I asked, "Yeah."

I grabbed the photo book and found Meike's picture. She was leaning next to a tree in our forest.

"She's beautiful," he said. "I sure like your Earth ladies."

"Here," I said taking it out of the book. "You can have it I guess."

"Because she dumped you?"

"Yup."

It was weird for about two seconds until Jim-bo thanked me and put Meike's picture in an upper pocket of his white leather shirt.

"What's this?" he said, taking the walkie talkies out of my pack. I had a quick Nelson-on-the-first-day-of-school moment.

I showed him how they worked, and he beamed brightly.

"Let's use these on our ride," he said as he presented me to my Harley. It wasn't a real Harley, but it sure seemed close.

He spent the next few moments instructing me on the way to use my CBC hovercraft motorcycle. As soon as I sounded like I knew what I was doing, we took off through the hangar door. I shuddered when I inhaled the outside air for the first time. I knew I didn't need my oxygen mask, but was still expecting to keel over and croak. A glance at maskless Jim-bo reassured me that I'd live, and I reminded myself it had all been a hoax and that the air was fine.

Although fine, the air was glacial as it beat against my face, but I didn't care. It was good to be outside. We rode about ten feet above the ground. Our speed was good enough that I felt free, but could still stay in control of the craft.

"BAV 1, this is BAH 1, do you copy?" Jim-bo's voice crackled in my walkie-talkie.

"I read you BAH 1," I answered, trying to keep control of my hovercraft at the same time. "But I need to concentrate."

"I'll talk, you listen," Jim-bo announced and then launched into a tour guide's explanation of the terrain. There wasn't much to say, since we were in the middle of nowhere, but I could tell he was trying the best he could. Krad, with all its muted earthy colors, reflected warm light tones which were soothing as we rode. The air was crisp and fresh, like the forest in Germany had been, seemingly untouched by civilization. I could breathe again, and my heart felt lighter than it had in days.

Slight, dune-like formations, called the Dry Sea Bed, blurred beneath us as we rode toward the brilliant pink and golden yellow light of the setting sun. The cold clouds pushed contrasting blacks and blues against the brilliant orb in the distance. A few sunbursts escaped through them, becoming golden and silver streaks against the sky.

Jim-bo slowed down and parked his hovercraft next to a forested cliff overlooking a valley. There were small, copper-like domiciles in the valley which seemed to be part of a small Varlock village. I got off my motorcycle and joined him on the ground. He cracked a large canister in half and a blue fire appeared on the dirt between us. I felt its immediate warmth. The glittery, silver and green flashes popping in the flames competed for my attention with the sunset and valley. We watched the fading light and tiny village for a long time in perfect silence. The sun was larger than ours, but not as hot, I supposed, given the fact that the planet was freezing cold.

After a while, I stared at Jim-bo. His features, although strange and still alien, were beginning to grow on me, and I decided that he was what would probably be considered good-looking for any Varlock girl's standards. I didn't know if I'd ever find a Varlock girl attractive, even if Boone had compared Meike to one, but perhaps I could date one.

"It's rude to stare," Jim-bo observed, eyes still fixed on the settting sun.

"Sorry, just trying to figure you out," I said. He reminded me of the boys in school who shaved daily – the mountain men types who were lucky enough to get their manliness early and never had to go through the voice-cracking, awkward stage that Nelson seemed indefinitely stuck in. "How old are you?"

"I'm your age," he answered. "I'd be considered a teen on Earth, but we get out on our own much sooner than you. I've been working since my eighth year. You'll probably be stuck in your mom's basement 'till you're thirty-five.

"Don't you be talkin' 'bout my mamma," I joked, but couldn't help feeling sad. I wouldn't live with my mom ever again.

She left me.

The blue fire crackled and sparked suddenly and I heard the distant noise of the evening insects singing their songs. They didn't sound like crickets, and I couldn't compare their sound to anything back home, but it was soothing anyway, and when I closed my eyes, it almost felt like I was camping.

"So, what are Earth girls really like? Not like Nellie, I hope," Jim-bo asked.

"They're good, I guess, I don't know."

"Some of them on your entertainments are very beautiful... but why must they always be the objects of desire? Don't they serve any other purposes?"

"They have several purposes," I said, not really interested in talking about Earth girls. "What are Varlock girls like?" I decided not to ask him what purpose they served.

"Ahh....," Jim-bo hesitated for a moment, then said, "My kind isn't as advanced as the few of us are back on base."

"What do you mean?" I asked.

"They don't believe in aliens."

"What?"

"My work is very top secret. Most Varlocks live simply, without any knowledge of the wider Universe. That's why our base is in the middle of nowhere. You and I don't even exist. My parents think I moved to another region to study war, but I really got a secret job offer from the CBC because of my superior engineering capabilities. I get to visit my folks now and then, but our visits are getting stranger and stranger. I'm too advanced now that I have become so educated. I've almost been with the CBC longer than I was with my parents."

"Why don't Varlocks know about other aliens?" I asked.

"Varlocks are no good."

"What do you mean?"

"Just picture a bunch of Vikings on steroids, killing things and drinking and pillaging... fighting to dominate other regions...and you might be able to comprehend my upbringing. It's kind of hard to spend your whole life outside of your world learning about other worlds and then fit in around here."

"You ever gonna get a woman and settle down?"

"With whom? What Varlock in her right mind is gonna ever settle down and watch as much of Earth's pop culture as I have? I know I probably have a soul mate on Earth, but until she materializes..."

"Anyone in the CBC?"

"I'm scared of Nellie. She's cute, but she'll kill you."

"I know."

"Besides, she's old, like forty."

"You seem more mature than her."

"I'm wise, indeed," he smiled. I couldn't tell if he were joking or serious. He continued, "My real hope is to get with a Naylaa who has been on embassy assignment on Earth or Tralis Four."

"What's a Naylaa?"

"They are the most beautiful species in the CBC coalition. I've only met two in my time, but they are amazing."

"Super hot alien chicks?"

"Yup, only it's normal to be "super hot," as you say, where they come from, so they aren't all that and a bag of potato chips."

I shook my head and smiled.

"They're actually pretty down to Earth, as you'd say," he continued, "Not prideful at all. Looking like a goddess is an everyday thing for each of them so there's not a lot of competition."

"Man, I could use a SHAC myself," I said, trying to envision an entire planet of beautiful, humble aliens, but the more I tried to get excited by the prospect, the more I found myself missing Rosa. I tried to push back thoughts of her eyelashes and said, "Can you take me to their leader?"

"Seth, I doubt very much that Boone is gonna let you out of his sight. He's been waiting for years for you to be old enough to join him. You've been his goal ever since he found out he had a grandson."

"Grandson?"

There was an awkward pause and the alien almost-cricket chirping noise grew louder. Jim-bo chose his words carefully, "Do you not know why Boone picked you?"

"He said he thought I'd be a great asset to the CBC... that's all... never mentioned..."

"Oh, crap...sorry.... my bad..."

"I'm his grandson?"

"Yeah..."

"That means Nellie's my aunt..."

"Yeah... I'm really sorry about that."

"Dad is the son Boone left behind on Earth," I realized.

Jim-bo blew out a deep breath and said, "Seth, it sucks that I'm the one to break it to you."

"No, this is good... it's good to know," I said, punching the anger back down into my stomach. "I'm sick of not knowing what's going on. And now it kinda makes sense why I'm so important to Boone."

The sun was slipping down behind the dunes and the sky was growing darker. I watched it slowly slip the last of its way down into the horizon as my mind raced for an anchor to reality. Dad wasn't talking. Boone wasn't talking. Nellie just wanted to get rid of me... I wasn't special...I was just related.

The sky grew darker.

Mom probably didn't know about anything, I decided, she was just sick of being left in the dark, too, or she was in a depression.

The sun completely disappeared, leaving a small pink glow in its wake. Jim-bo stood up and walked over to his hovercraft. I shivered as the last of the blue fire smoldered its way into nothing as well. Without saying another word I joined him.

A sudden scream rang in my ears. Only after the third

outburst did I realize what was happening: another Varlock had approached us and been startled by my presence. It pointed at me and screamed a few more times, then ran back as fast as its feet could go into the bramble of the jungle.

"Aren't you going to do something?" I asked Jim-bo, watching the poor thing run. "Stop him from running away?"

"She can tell anyone she wants that she saw an alien here," he shrugged. "Nobody will believe her. It's dark, anyway."

"Oh." I said. "That was a female Varlock?"

"Let's get back to base," Jim-bo smiled.

I was definitely not interested in hooking up with one. The females seemed more masculine than the males – bigger and huskier, if that was even possible.

My head started spinning. Nothing seemed right. I wanted to get back to base because I didn't want a whole bunch of Varlock villagers showing up with their equivalent of pitchforks, but I wasn't ready to face Boone yet. I was floundering – not sure what to do or how to proceed. Jim-bo studied me for a moment, then gave a huge sigh.

"Look, Seth," he began, "I have no idea what you must be feeling right now. I thought you knew. For whatever reason, you left your home on Earth to go with a man that you didn't even know was your grandfather… which means that something's not quite right back home for you. And now, something's not quite right here in space…"

I shrugged. "I just have always wanted to visit outer space."

"That's it?"

"And my parents are getting a divorce."

"You signed the CBC never go home clause because you're a stargazer and your parents are splitting up?"

"Uh… yeah," I said.

"Are you mental?" He was serious.

I didn't answer. I didn't know. I had just really wanted to go to OS my whole life. Why couldn't anyone understand that? I searched myself for an answer. Maybe

I was like Boone. I had left everything to go to Space and become something, no matter who I hurt or left behind. In thirty years would cream soda be all I missed back home?

"What are you gonna do now?" he asked. I could barely see his face in the darkness.

"I'm gonna find a way to kick some Kashmaari butt the heck out of Vegas, that's what I'm gonna do," I realized. It was destiny. I went up to Space to find a way to save Earth, although I didn't know it at the time. I went to Space to find an answer to my problems back home.

Jim-bo nodded and leaned against his hovercraft, facing me head on. His violet eyes were electric as he spoke, "I don't have a great love for the Kashmaari. They are nasty aliens, and I don't think the CBC should be trading with them. But you have joined the wrong group if you think you need to do something about them."

"I didn't know the CBC was full of a bunch of pussies," I challenged.

"Hey now."

"You guys are so lame!"

"We are... we really are," Jim-bo nodded and sighed. "I'll create some prototypes for you when we get back."

"What?" I couldn't believe what I was hearing.

He smiled and shook his head like he couldn't believe what he was saying, but he continued, "I don't relish the idea of Earth being taken over by the Kashmaari. I'd give up my Tralis Four entertainments before I'd give up Earth's. I'll make your weapons and help you get rid of them."

I looked deeply into his bright violet eyes. "I don't think you'll blend in on Earth, but thanks."

He smiled. "I'll be wearing the suit you designed, hello!"

"Right, and then you'll blend in just fine," I smiled back.

"Maybe we can try it out on Halloweens?" he suggested.

"Halloween," I corrected.

The ride back to base was glacial and I was frozen to the core when we got back. Jim-bo had me warm up next to another blue fire in the hangar, and then we returned to the CBC work room. Boone and Nellie were still in there and both nodded when we entered. I couldn't help staring at Boone, completely in shock at the resemblance he had to Dad. He still looked to be Dad's age, maybe a little older, but I would never have thought him to be my Grandfather, or Nellie to be my aunt.

I decided that if I was going to save the Earth it was better to not mention anything about being related. Business as usual until I made a break for it. Besides, they obviously had a reason for not telling me, and I was interested in finding out how long it would take for their big reveal.

Jim-bo and Nellie looked over her rectangle invention together. *How original,* I thought spitefully, *another rectangle—or Brain—whatever.* Although, I had to admit the invention was a cool piggy-back onto an already existing idea. Both Roxy and Mom would have flipped for something like that.

I lay down on the old orange couch in the back corner of the room and decided to take a nap.

Chapter 17
SPACE FLU

When Boone woke me I had no idea how long I had slept. I was starving and cranky. By the way my knees ached from curling up on the couch, I guessed it must have been hours.

"Hey, I just got a message from Base," Boone shook my shoulder again, "Seems they adopted a friend of yours, Seth, and she's pretty sick with space flu."

"Space flu," Nellie gagged in my other ear. "Ew."

"Nobody will go near her," he continued. "She's stable, but very ill. She's been calling for you, Seth."

"For me?" I struggled to wake myself and sit up.

"Oh man! We just got here," Nellie whined.

My mind raced. A friend... a girl...*she* had followed me? Who? Was it Rosa? She was the only one who knew where I had really gone. Did she follow the chimes and static to get picked up too? I thought of the family she left at home. Miguel would never forgive me, but I couldn't help the smile forming on my face when I thought about those eyelashes. Had she really followed me?

"Jim-bo," Boone said, "I think we'll need to head back. Do you have enough information?"

"Yeah," Jim-bo said, scratching his chin, "this should be good for now. Although, Seth and I are working on a few projects. You are going to need to lend him to me soon."

Boone's smile faded. "Why?"

"He's got some great ideas. We work together well," Jim-bo explained. "I'm gonna need to put in a request to have him stationed here for a few months."

"Well, I knew you'd get along, but I didn't think I'd need to share him so soon," he forced a smile. "I just got him. Don't put a request in just yet. I'll figure out some time for him to come back in a week or so."

"Fine," Jim-bo said. "But I'm serious, Boone. I'm gonna need him for a while."

"Sure thing," Boone agreed, suddenly snapping back into his happy-go-lucky self.

Jim-bo handed me my backpack. "I made a few upgrades to your stuff, hope you don't mind."

"What kind of upgrades?" I muttered, still trying to wake myself up.

"Let's just say that BAH 1 can talk to BAV 1 across the intergalactic radio waves any time."

"Oh, yeah?"

"Also, I made a few adjustments to your Knife so that I can keep track of your position – stuff like that," he said, helping me to my feet. "And I stamped your passport for you... I'm assuming that's why you brought it."

I opened to the place he had marked and a multi-colored design, similar to the one he had on his Brain, spread across both pages where the staples showed.

"Thanks," I said.

"And here's your bio suit, too," he said and held it up. "Good luck with the test run. Let me know via Walkie Talkie how it goes."

I nodded. "You've been busy. How long was I out?"

"About twelve hours," he answered as if it were perfectly normal. "Oh, and I looked through your design book. We definitely need to empty all those ideas in your head onto my Brain when we get the time." He stated that loudly, more for Boone's benefit than for mine.

I shook my head, not really wanting to leave Jim-bo behind. I wished I could tell him that he made everything I'd gone through so far worth it. Instead, I simply said, "Later."

He nodded.

"Let's move," Boone instructed.

He was still consulting his rectangle as the three of us walked out to Sistah. He looked up at me and laughed. "Seth, your dad wrote back. He says to get your butt home immediately or he'll send someone to get you. Well, we'll see about that, now, won't we?"

I cringed at the thought of my father, all alone on Earth , worried sick about me. It was the first moment I felt guilty for abandoning him – made worse by the fact that I was with the Father who had abandoned him. He'd never know where either of us had gone.

The ride home was uneventful, until we approached the Moon. Earth loomed up large and blue outside my window. I thought it was strange to see it there, a landmark signaling me that we'd soon be home – like the Esso station on the corner of our street in Germany. From a distance it looked insignificant, but it was my whole world, literally, and I missed it. I looked away to the dim stars out the other window in an attempt to put it from my mind and to reconnect with my childhood dreams of being abducted.

A few minutes later, the Moon rose into view. Sistah soared over its surface, slowing down as we approached the Daedelus crater, and then suddenly we tore right through the base's barrier wall. The rupture our ship had caused grew back together immediately.

"Hangar B – Earth Moon Base – we have arrived," Sistah announced.

"Thanks, Sistah," Boone said. He climbed out of the ship, ordering, "Draw Day Star Power and sleep."

Nellie and I followed. She hit my shoulder as we left the hangar. "Well, I'm gonna go check on Rosco. Good luck with all that space flu and girlfriend drama. Yikes."

I don't know why she was pretending to be supportive but I didn't believe a single word. She was probably plotting a way to ship us both back home immediately, and I was glad when she disappeared out the doorway. Boone led me down a new corridor with transparent walls displaying the beauty of the stars beyond. I looked up to the ceiling at the green ferns that hung between silver lanterns in a symmetrical pattern and felt a little calmer.

Pfister was waiting for us on the other end of the corridor.

"Hello, Boone, glad you got here when you did," he thought. He seemed shorter than I remembered. Probably because the Varlocks were so tall.

"Hey Pfister." Boone nodded.

Pfister looked at me and smiled. "Your friend is very ill, Seth. I advise you to be extremely careful around her. No one on base will see her. Space Flu can be deadly and is very contagious."

"Who adopted her?" Boone asked. I could tell he was upset.

"It was Topher," Pfister explained. "He said he had been in communication with her for a long time and decided to move unilaterally because he was worried the council would turn his request down."

"Topher? That's the biggest cock-and-bull..." Boone began, then looked over at me. "I wonder what his real motive is."

"He's in the other wing of the Medical Center. He shows no signs of the disease, yet, but he's been quarantined."

We turned down a dim corridor. Because the walls were transparent, I almost felt as though I were walking outside on the Moon itself.

"How's she doing?" Boone asked.

"She's on life support—they're doing everything they can to keep her alive."

We stopped and Boone put a hand on my shoulder. "Seth, getting sick in space is worse than anything you could ever imagine. Space Flu is basically like having leprosy of the intestines. If it doesn't pass, everything eventually falls apart inside the victim and is vomited out of the body. I'm so sorry this happened to your friend."

"Can I see her?" I asked, wondering for the first time if people actually died in Space. I don't know why I thought we'd be exempt.

"Yeah, here," Boone said, touching the Bio Suit

prototype Jim-bo had given me. "Wear this. You'll be able to breathe your own oxygen, and still get up close and personal. Not too personal though; we don't know how well this thing works."

The look on Pfister's face told me everything. Boone was crazy to let me go near her, with or without the bio suit, I thought. Pfister laughed and nodded. We exchanged a look.

I knew it would work, though. The design we had come up with was good, and although it barely felt like I was wearing anything over my face and body, I was positive it would protect me. The only drawback to using algae was that the air I breathed smelled like rotten seaweed. Still, breathing rotten seaweed was better than breathing flour.

When we reached the door leading to the sick room, Boone clasped a hand on my shoulder and smiled.

"Good luck, son," he said. "They'll be monitoring you. Do you know the way back home when you are finished?"

"Pretty sure I do," I said.

"Okay, well, see you soon." He turned to walk away from me. I could tell he was upset, but was doing his best to keep in control as usual.

I nodded and walked through the doors of the infirmary. There was nothing that could have prepared me for what happened next. Meike was lying on the bed in the center of the room instead of the Rosa I'd been hoping for.

"Meike?" I stammered.

"Hey, Seth." she smiled at me, shivering so violently that she could barely get the words out. I knew something was wrong the second she said my name. She pronounced the "th" effortlessly.

"I'm sick," she said and held out her hand for me. Her face was lime-green, and her once-perfect hair was drenched in sweat. As I took her hand in mine; it was ice cold. I began to rub her hands and arms to warm them and she smiled weakly at my attempt to help.

"A blanket maybe?" she asked.

"I can't believe you're here," I stammered.

"I can't believe that you are here!" Meike said. Her

voice was upset and unnatural. "Do you have any idea what I have gone through to follow you to this stupid place?"

I didn't. She grimaced and closed her eyes. I could tell that a load of vomit was beamed out of her at that moment.

"Can I get a blanket in here?" I called out, hoping that the person Boone said would be monitoring us would send one. A folded blanket appeared at the foot of her bed, then another. I wrapped both of them around her. She wasn't shaking as much, but she still looked terrible.

"Can you give me that shot?" she asked, indicating a needle on the stand next to her. "They wanted you to give it to me when you arrived."

"Where do I stick it?" I asked, picking up the needle and hitting it on the side to get the bubbles out.

"Why didn't they beam this into you?"

"Just find a vein in my arm!" She tried to lift her other arm.

I found one and stuck in the needle. I pushed down on the end and watched the orange liquid disappear into her pale, green-hued skin.

"Very good," she whispered and closed her eyes.

"What is it?" I asked.

"Medicine."

It was wrong—the whole situation was wrong, but I couldn't put my finger on what was happening. And why were we having a conversation in English?

"I'm glad you came to see me, Seth," she smiled, pronouncing the "th" perfectly again. I felt queasy.

"Of course," I said. "I can't believe you're here."

I thought that you said you had a boyfriend and not to contact you anymore! the thought yelled itself in my head. None of it was adding up correctly.

"Your Dad misses you so much—we all do," she said. "What were you thinking, Seth?"

I was about to ask Meike the same thing, when she closed her eyes and grimaced again. Then she grew calm and drifted off to sleep. I wondered if I had given her some sort of sleeping drug to put her out of her misery. Her face lost the green tint, and a creamy tone appeared on her cheeks.

I paced the floor trying to decide what to do next. I was definitely angry that Meike had been the one to follow me. If she died, it would be my fault, and if she lived, I would be stuck with her forever. We were stuck in the CBC for the rest of our lives with no way out. Whatever happened, I was responsible for her. If it was Meike. It didn't seem like her.

Suddenly, the room smelled like oranges, and she began to stir. I touched her hand and found it was warm, and her skin tone was no longer green. Her eyes opened and the pain that was previously in them had disappeared. A smile spread across her face as she looked up at me.

"Better?" I asked.

She sat up and stretched. As she tossed her hair, it fell to her shoulders in thick, black layers and I reached out to play with it between my fingers.

"I'm much better," she said, holding out her hand. I sat on the edge of her bed and held it. "I think it's because you're here with me."

I wanted to gag. There is no way her English should have been that good.

"Must have been the shot," I observed.

"Maybe." She leaned in, which scared me, because I didn't know what she wanted, and her hand pulled me closer. I half expected her to kiss me, but instead she began to whisper. "Seth, we need to get out of here now!"

"What?"

"You lead me to the ship that brought you here, and I'll do the rest. I've come to rescue you as a favor to your dad."

I was stunned, not knowing how Dad knew I was in space in the first place.

"I don't know where Boone landed his ship," I lied, trying my best to sound natural. "He dropped me off so I could come here directly."

"Do you think you could go find out where it is and then come back to get me?" Her voice sounded strange… metallic and edgy.

I nodded. She pulled me closer and kissed me on the

cheek. Her lips were warm, even through my bio suit. My heart pounded. There didn't seem to be enough time to think clearly, but my gut told me to get out of there and not to look back.

"I knew you'd want out of this place when you saw me," she whispered confidently.

"You don't want to stay here?" I asked.

"No," she said, "And don't worry about that stupid little pledge you made. You'll be fine; I promise. They won't dare come after you when I get through with them. You're safe, Seth. It's over now. You can go home."

She was so unlike Meike, so sure of herself. For a moment, I thought maybe she was being possessed by an adult special agent for the CIA or something. I nodded again and took a deep breath, but my heart refused to slow down. She wasn't giving me time to make a rational decision.

Her face contorted and looked pained again.

"I'm so sick," she said in her normal voice, complete with a German accent. "I don't feel good at all. Please help me."

As Meike writhed in pain, I squeezed her hand and stroked her face, but it obviously didn't do any good. The shivering ceased after a sudden, violent shudder.

"I'll be fine." The metallic CIA operative voice was back. "I'm just happy you're safe. We're going to be fine. We just need to get to a ship." Her smile was hollow and arrogant.

"I'll go find out where Boone parked his ship," I said, keeping my voice level as I backed slowly away from the Meike impostor.

She smiled and relaxed. "We're getting you out of here, Seth Carter."

"I'll be right back," I lied.

I kissed her forehead and took one last look. She looked fabulous in her white spandex CBC uniform. It was a pity she was insane.

Chapter 18

ESCAPE

On the way out of the Medical Center, whoever was manning the station, promptly confiscated (via beaming action) my clothing, along with what felt like the first layer of my endocrine system. A standard-issue CBC suit and boots were beamed on to replace my lost clothing. Once I got the green light from the disembodied voice giving out orders, I ran as fast as I could to Boone's quarters.

"How's your friend doing?" he asked, rising from his chair.

Nellie was there experimenting with her nails again. I hesitated. I didn't really want to dish her in, but could tell she wasn't going to leave any time soon.

"Meike's possessed," I answered. "She's crazy. She wants me to leave with her, and go back to Earth."

"I thought she had another boyfriend," Nellie said, sounding disinterested, although I was pretty sure that she was behind the whole thing.

"She says she's here for my Dad," I added.

"What makes you think she's possessed?" Boone asked.

"There's a strange metallic tone in her voice," I said, "It's not like her. It's also not like her to come up to the Moon to get me. She's the last person on Earth I'd expect to do a recon mission for Dad. And she can pronounce things in perfect English without her accent. Weird."

Several beads of sweat sprouted on Boone's forehead. Nellie stopped what she was doing immediately and rose from her seat.

"What?" I asked.

"A metallic quality?" Boone asked.

"Yeah," I said.

"Does she smell like oranges?" Nellie asked.

"Yeah," I said. "She had me give her some medicine, in a shot, and now she smells like the body lotion shop at the mall!"

"Okay…this is not good!" Boone said, grabbing his rectangle from the table and launching into a series of expletives.

He sounded like my dad when he was really upset, and I almost went into my usual routine of playing swearword bingo in my head, when suddenly both he and Nellie ran out of the room. I followed them, trying to keep up with their frantic pace, not sure why we were running.

"What is it?" I asked. "What's wrong?"

We turned down the passage that led toward the Hangar B launch sites.

"I've got to get you out of here," Boone said. "Get your butt home to your dad, Seth! Now! You ran away from home. That's your story. Say nothing about us to anyone. I'll contact you as soon as I can. This is bad."

"What's bad?"

"Your girlfriend's possessed by a Kashmaar."

"Wait, you mean, like, those things you told me about that wear people like skin? I thought you guys traded with them!"

"We do." Boone nodded. "But we don't exactly have a peace treaty, we just do it to keep them from hurting us. I had no idea your Dad was caught up with their kind. I knew he was a little misled, but I had no idea how much."

"Leave it to Samuel…" Nellie began, but Boone cut her off with a glance.

"Drop it."

"Okay," she backed down.

We turned down a corner into Hangar B. Sistah was straight ahead of us. Boone pushed a few more buttons on his Brain. The clothes I was wearing on the day he adopted me appeared in his hands.

"Here," he said, "you'll need to wear these when you get back home."

He shoved them into my hands along with my backpack and sneakers. One of them fell off onto the floor, and I picked it up and returned it to my awkward pile.

He cursed again, under his breath, avoiding my gaze.

"You have got to get out of here... we all do," he said. "Jim-Bo fixed your Walkie Talkies and we'll have him contact you when everything settles down."

"Why can't I stay with you guys?"

"Because it wants you!" Boone hissed. "And I can't let it have you. And, I don't know if there are more of them. When I feel it's safe to contact you, I'll reach you through Jim-Bo. Do not, *do not, do NOT,* let anyone know about this, and always keep your pocket knife with you. It will help us locate you, and it will protect you, in a way."

"Yes, sir," I said, not knowing how I'd be able to get it through the metal detectors at Central if I was really going home. It just didn't seem like the right time to bring it up.

Boone cursed again.

"The Kashmaari must have taken Constance," he realized.

"Topher must have made a deal with them to get her back," Nellie said, angrily. "He'd do anything to find her."

"With the Kashmaari, though?" Boone said. "They destroy his life and he helps them to get her back? It doesn't make sense."

"We didn't really help him when she went missing," Nellie muttered. "Maybe it's a kind of payback?"

"But how did he get her through our scanners?" Boone wondered.

"He waited to give the body assimilation shot so we thought Meike had the space flu...no one took a good look. "

"Assimilation shot?" I asked.

"The medicine you gave Meike helps the Kashmaari stay inside their victims. A body usually doesn't tolerate being possessed without massive doses of the stuff. It calms the victim and leaves them smelling like oranges.

What we mistook for space flu was really Meike fighting to get that thing out of her."

Boone interrupted, "We'll figure out how it infiltrated us later, Nel. Right now, we just need to get away from it." He turned back to me, "Especially you, Seth. You're why it's here. Your Dad sent it up here to get you."

"Are you sure Nellie didn't hire it to get rid of me?" I asked. The Meike Kashmaar had already informed me that she came as a favor for my Dad, and not for Nellie, but I wanted to be sure.

"I didn't send it, you idiot!" Nellie said, her arms folded across her chest. She was struggling to keep her composure, but had begun to cry. "Look, I know I said that I wanted to get rid of you, but there are better ways than using a Kashmaar."

"You didn't threaten Seth, did you?" I could tell Boone was disappointed.

"He shouldn't be here."

"Later," he decided. "We'll figure this out later. We don't have much time before it realizes Seth isn't coming back."

Boone led me away from Nellie's gaze and over to a space craft that was similar to Sistah, but had more rounded features, and was slightly smaller in its dimensions. Its violet and cobalt shine refracted the lights above our heads. Boone opened the door and pushed me into the driver's seat.

"Don't blame Nellie for this, Seth. She doesn't like that you are here, but she wouldn't get the Kashmaari to help her. Nobody in their right mind would make a deal with them. Now, listen, Son, you gotta trust me. Get back to Earth and hide this craft—you understand? Do not attempt to fly it again, or you will get yourself into big trouble. This is an emergency, so you will have to solo for now. Tell your dad you ran away and that is it. You have no dealings with the CBC and you have never been to outer space! I'll do my best to keep the Kashmaar from returning to Earth and blowing your cover. Do you understand?"

"What about Meike?" I asked.

Boone shook his head, "Nellie will try to get her back home to Germany. I promise."

Nellie nodded from behind us. Boone continued, "If we can lead the Kashmaar out of Meike, Nellie will retrieve her body and take her back home. Hopefully, she won't even remember what happened to her—or feel any of the after-effects."

Nellie's face was all scrunched up like a wilted cabbage. I couldn't tell if she was angry or worried. Tears streamed out of her eyes, but she kept brushing them away and smiling encouragingly at me. As much as I didn't want to admit it, I couldn't pin the Kashmaar on her. She was terrified.

"Okay, I'm on it!" she said. "I'll get her back home."

"Good," Boone said, "let's do this fast."

He tapped his Brain once and a large screen on the hangar wall called up an image of Meike waiting for me in the Medical Center. She was pacing the floor like a panther trying to figure out how to get to its prey.

Boone held his Brain to his lips and announced, "Please deliver this message quickly and quietly to all CBC personnel. Attention please. This is Boone. There has been a breach in the Medical Center. A Kashmaar has smuggled its way in with our last adoptee. We need to seize Topher for questioning and evacuate the Base immediately. Rendezvous at the usual spot. Out."

An alarm sounded and Boone cursed. "There goes our element of surprise."

Screams of panic rose up through the corridor just outside of the hangar. I glanced up at the image of Meike that was still on the screen. She obviously knew what had happened. Her body convulsed in some sort of seizure, then, the fluorescent lime creature burst out of it, and Meike fell to the ground, lifeless. The Kashmaar hissed and crackled as it glanced around the Medical lab, assessing its situation. Its eye slits were like two black holes. The familiar metallic voice hissed, "Give me, Seth Carter now, or I will kill all of you!"

There was no doubt in my mind that the Kashmaar

would be able to make good on its threat.

"Go and get Meike, Nellie," Boone ordered. "But take the least obvious route. I don't want you to become its next skin."

Nellie nodded and abandoned the hangar instantly. I wanted to yell and kick something. It was all going too fast for me to keep up. I watched the screen, mesmerized, as the fire-lime creature disappeared through the wall, leaving Meike all alone, still lying motionless on the floor.

"Seth, you gotta get out of here now," Boone said. "I promise I will get you later—just take Prudence here and go. And... uh, I love you, Son."

He gave me an awkward, but long overdue hug. I was about to tell him that I knew that he was my grandfather, but another alarm sounded next to us, and the hangar screen showed the Kashmaar in the hallway directly outside.

Boone yelled up at the screen, "It's almost here. Hold on, Seth. Stay put. Count to a hundred, then leave."

He closed the door of my craft and bolted in the direction of Sistah. The Kashmaar entered the hangar, glowing even more eerily than it had on screen. I thought Boone had made it to Sistah before it entered, but wasn't sure. I froze, unable to think or move as I watched the Kashmaar float in the middle of the doorway, its dark eyes searching.

"Wait," a voice sounded in my head. It was Pfister. I couldn't see him, but he continued to coach my thoughts as the Kashmaar stalked through the hangar aisles. "It's waiting for you to move. It tracked Boone's announcement to the hangar. Just stay still and let it follow Boone."

"Will Boone die?" I wondered. "Would it kill him?"

The Kashmaar slowly glided down the center aisle. It passed right through the space ships as it searched. It had nearly reached my craft when I heard an engine roar to life. The dark, oval eyes of the Kashmaar locked onto Sistah. It rushed toward Boone, but before the moment of impact, Boone veered left and Sistah vanished through the hangar wall. The Kashmaar followed, leaving a streak of light behind it as it went.

It didn't even need a spaceship or anything.

I pushed forward on the steering column to follow, but my ship didn't move.

"Activate," I yelled.

"Voice command incorrect," the space craft said. It was another woman's voice; this time she sounded English.

"I'm a guest driver. Activate code 1162!" I yelled.

"Voice command correct," the car said.

I grabbed the column and prepared to chase after Boone and the Kashmaar. There was no way I was going to go home without knowing what was going on, and I wasn't going to let Boone deal with it by himself, either.

"Go back to Earth, Seth," Pfister's voice instructed in my head. I looked out the window and saw the little child-man get out from the space craft he'd been hiding under, about thirty feet from me. The eyes of the tiny Sarrow locked with mine. "Do not let Boone's sacrifice be in vain. He's saving your life. Don't try to find him. Go home."

"But I don't want…"

"It doesn't matter what you think you want anymore," Pfister yelled in my head. "You don't understand anything! Get home and keep quiet. We'll come for you. You have my word."

"It's not about me!" I screamed at him in my thoughts. "It's about Boone."

"Don't worry about Boone. You just need to get out of here, now, before it comes back for you. It named you. It wants you."

His voice set my arm hair on edge. It wanted me. I needed to get away.

I grabbed the steering column and rammed it all the way forward. The ship tore through the base wall. Despite my orders, I raced out over the surface of the Moon, trying to get a glimpse of Sistah, but there was nothing but rocks and empty craters. The base had already disappeared, leaving me completely on my own. I pushed the column harder, trying to picking up enough speed to catch Boone, but there was no sign of him. No

Boone. No green Kashmaar. No CBC Moon Base.

My throat tightened as I realized that I was flying a solo mission. I was a small, insignificant speck in the vast black expanse around me. Nothing makes you feel smaller and weaker than being all alone in the middle of OS. It swallows you up just like you're a tiny grain of sand lying on the ocean's floor. I had just lost my only anchor in a void that was consuming me.

"Take me to Earth," I said in defeat.

"Copy that," the craft said, "Estimated arrival time to Earth is forty minutes. My name is Prudence, by the way."

We connected with a current and accelerated quickly. As I catapulted through space, I grabbed automatically for the seatbelt that wasn't there. Defeat and fear welled up in the back of my throat and I swallowed them back down angrily. I just wanted to blow something up, but there was nothing in my path to destroy. Finally, I gave up and sat back in my chair, letting the tears flow freely. I spent the rest of the journey wondering why I was weeping. Nelson was the kind of guy that would cry, not me, but I couldn't stop. I hated it. I absolutely hated it.

Chapter 19

ABANDONED

"Arrival to Earth in thirty seconds," the ship interrupted my grief. I had no idea what had happened to the forty minutes since we left the Moon. Everything was vague and distant—like I was stuck in the middle of a nightmare I couldn't control.

I opened my eyes and saw the Earth looming up into view. It had been farther from sight on the way back from Krad, but as we slowed to a stop before it, my breath actually caught in the back of my throat. I was astonished at the beauty of my home planet and sat for several moments in quiet, reverent observation of its vast magnificence. It was beyond words. I'd seen Earth on television screens but that didn't even compare, and I realized how lucky astronauts were, despite the toilet situations on their shuttles.

The ship cut its throttle, and we drifted along with the gravitational pull.

"Where to now?" Prudence asked.

"Take me to Las Vegas," I commanded. The ship lurched forward and we plummeted sideways through the atmosphere. As the sky grew dark I realized it was nighttime back home. I could see a million little lights shimmering up from the massive dark space beneath me and was barely able to make out the faint outline of North America from its coastal cities.

I heard one beep and then Prudence stated calmly, "Day Star power is low. Powering off to reserve fuel."

That's when the ship began to free-fall.

"Ahh... that's a negative!" I yelled, pissed that she hadn't mentioned something about low power earlier and grabbing onto the steering column for dear life. "Stay on course!"

Prudence didn't answer. Instead, the ship tore its way out of the current and plunged downward. I pulled back as hard as I could on the steering column, but it did nothing to slow us down. The fall was so fast that the only thing I could do was brace myself for impact; I closed my eyes and prepared to die. The only consoling thought was that we were falling so quickly, I knew I wouldn't feel anything once the ship collided with the sandy hills below and we shattered into a million particles. My last thought, oddly enough, was for Rosa in her prom dress.

The ship bounced upon impact, almost as if it had landed on a giant invisible air-bag which cushioned our fall. We were catapulted up into the sky and then bounced three more times before finally settling down on the ground.

You know that physics experiment where you put an egg in a safety design and try not to have it break when dropped from the top of a building? I was basically that egg, and apparently the CBC had mastered that experiment.

"Crash landing gear is operational," Prudence's voice turned back on.

"Could have mentioned that earlier, Prude," I muttered. It was a miracle I hadn't wet my pants.

"Powering off," Prudence said, and the doors hissed open.

"Prudence," I almost yelled in a panic.

"Yes, sir," she answered.

I sighed, happy to be able to give her a last command, "I want you to draw Day Star Power as soon as possible and try to remain in light-speed flux camouflage... that will make you invisible, right?"

"Affirmative."

The ship's lights went out.

I changed into my clothes and placed my Swiss Army Knife in my pocket so that Boone or Jim-bo could locate me once they decided to do so. I thought about calling Jim-bo on my Walkie Talkie, but he was so far away. I doubted that he could really help me, so it seemed stupid to bug him. I knew I was stranded somewhere on the outskirts of Vegas, and there wasn't much a Varlock could do about it. I checked to see if my cell phone had any power, but it looked like it had been dead for days.

I dumped my CBC issued attire on Prudence's seat and stumbled out of the ship. It disappeared behind me.

"Sleep," I said, hoping I had remembered to say the right things. "I'll be back as soon as possible."

Prudence didn't reply. I plopped down on the ground and sat for a while, staring out into the empty desert darkness. There would be no way for me to fully process what had just happened until I showered, ate, and slept. The thought of real food and water was about the only thing that made me happy about being back. But there was no use going back home if I didn't know what I was going to say when I got there. I tried to figure out something convincing. The best excuse I could come up with was that I ran away from home when Mom left because I was so angry. I didn't even know what day it was, so it was difficult to figure out what I had been doing. I didn't know America or Vegas well enough to lie about where I had gone, and since lying wasn't really my style, I decided to not say anything at all, ever.

I don't want to talk about it, I practiced saying in my head over and over.

I knew it would be important to find Prudence again later on, so I stood up to memorize my location. There were outlines of rocks and little dry bushes, but no major landmarks. I made a giant X with several large rocks on the ground in front of my invisible space ship then headed in the direction of the freeway. I could hear the sound of semi-trucks passing by in the distance. As soon as I crested the hill, I could see the beams of headlights a slight walk from me.

I counted two hundred forty-three steps to I-15. Luckily, I had come out near a mile marker, so I added that number to my growing list of stats to memorize, then I headed for the city.

I was certain that the glowing city of lights illuminating the night sky in front of me was Vegas. No other city glowed more brilliantly in the darkness. The light was so bright that it illuminated the dark, deserted hills surrounding the city, and I could definitely make out the Luxor's flood light shooting straight up into the sky like a conduit to heaven.

Cars breezed past me as I trudged forward. As I reviewed the number of total steps and the mile marker in my head, it occurred to me that I should have asked Prudence for the latitude and longitude of her location. And if I had thought to give her my address, she could have flown over to meet me after she got charged up. Perhaps I should have just waited with her till morning.

I was just about to turn back when a red sports car flew past me and then screeched to a halt. As I approached, the passenger door flew open. I peeked my head inside of the car and saw that the driver was Dad's assistant. She was even more beautiful up close. I blinked twice and tried to remember how to close my mouth.

"Hey, Seth, I thought I was you," she said. "Get in... I'll give you a ride home."

"Thanks," I said and hopped inside.

As soon as I shut, the door the pungent smell of oranges washed over me. It was almost as if I were back in the medical wing with Meike. My forehead broke into a sweat, and I felt nauseated. The woman smiled and hit the power locks. Tires screeched as we peeled off the side of the road and accelerated.

I waited for her to say something, but she just turned up the radio. Her system was too advanced to be from Earth, although it was a good knock off.

"My name is Altaar," she said, finally. "Your dad will be happy you're home. He's missed you so much."

Her voice was just as creepy and unnatural as Meike's had been. The echoing sound of metal reverberated off the car walls as she spoke. I recoiled at the strangeness, but found myself drawn to her overwhelming beauty. My stomach churned in response to the memory of my almost encounter with the Kashmaar that was after me.

Then it hit me that she might have been the one. Did Dad know what she was? My heart was pounding so loudly that I was sure Altaar could hear it. I glanced around and found the CBC logo right under what looked to be the heating system.

"Mind if I take a nap?" I asked, leaning my head against the window.

"Go right ahead, Seth," the woman said with strained politeness.

I shut my eyes and focused on my next move, but there weren't any. I was locked in a spaceship disguised as a sports car with a soul-sucking alien disguised as Miss Universe. What option did I have but to just go with it for a while?

Even with my eyes closed, I could perceive the lights from the city. When I peeked out the window, I saw a Vegas City Limits sign and I realized how fast we had gone. We took an exit, and pulled up next to a gas pump.

"Fuel mode set to unleaded gasoline, currency, Dollars," Altaar instructed her ship.

"That's affirmative, dude," the car responded. He sounded like a stoned surfer.

I squeezed my eyes tighter, even though there was no way the Kashmaar next to me could possibly believe I was asleep. An arm reached past me and retrieved something out of the glove compartment in front of my knees. Then I heard her exit the vehicle. The smell of oranges lingered in the air as the door shut behind her. I peeked out of one eye and watched her walk into the station, obviously to pre-pay.

The glove compartment was still open and I noticed a wad of dollar bills was inside. I pushed a button next to it, and the money was replaced by some foreign currency.

"Japanese—Yen," the car announced. I pushed the button several times in succession, and each time the money was replaced and the car announced a region of the world and named the currency; British Pounds, Russian Rubles, and Euros. My eyes then darted back to the CBC logo on the dash board and I realized I had one chance for escape.

"Activate Code 1162," I commanded. There was no response.

I looked up to see where Altaar was. She was at the counter, already putting something in her purse. The attendant smiled and she walked toward the doors.

"Activate guest driver," I yelled.

"Voice command correct, dude," the car spoke, but it sounded a little unhappy to comply.

"Go manual driver," I said sliding behind the steering wheel.

I glanced over at Altaar. She had turned back to speak with the man behind the counter again. It was the only chance I was going to get. I gunned the gas and tore out of the parking lot. I glanced back into the rearview mirror, but as far as I could tell, nobody was behind us. I hoped beyond hope that she didn't know which direction we went.

"Go manual flight," I commanded and pushed the steering wheel forward. The car lurched off of the pavement and up into the air. We glided over the Vegas lights.

"Should we go incognito?" the car suggested.

"Yes, activate that!"

I rose higher in the sky, hoping we really were invisible. I knew where I wanted to go and moments later, I brought the ship down on the abandoned field where Boone had picked me up.

"Stay hidden and draw Day Star Power when able," I instructed the ship.

"My name's Dirk and you should let me go find my real owner," a shaky voice offered. He actually sounded worried.

"Ah, that is a negatory, uh.. Dirk," I said, a little worried myself. "Draw Day Star Power, and stay hidden until I come for you. Do not attempt contact with anyone but me."

"Copy that, dude." The doors hissed opened and I hopped out.

"Sleep," I said.

So there I was. I had two CBC spaceships hidden and

charging, I had some weird aliens called Kashmaari chasing after me, and I had just returned home to Earth after who knows how long in space.

As I walked through the darkness of the cul-de-sac, I could make out a dark shape lying on the sidewalk ahead of me. It didn't look like a person, but the sight of it made me jump. When I got closer, I realized that the mound was in the shape of a bicycle, my bicycle in fact. No one had claimed it the whole time I'd been gone. I picked it up and headed for home.

The cool air on my face helped my focus as I cycled toward my house. I found Mom's car parked out on the street and the porch light was blazing a welcome. I tried opening the front door, but it was locked. When I ran around the house to try the back door, I found Dad sitting on the patio in his bathrobe, waiting for me.

"You're back," he said calmly.

Did he know I had just stolen his assistant's CBC issued sports car? Did he know his assistant was a Kashmaar? I waited for him to do something. He stood up, and instead of beating me for running away, he pulled me into a long, tight embrace.

"Are you all right?" he asked not letting go of me.

"Yeah."

"You had me so worried, Seth."

"Sorry."

Dad pushed me away from him, "Why would you run away? You've been gone since Sunday! Mom and I have been going out of our minds—no note, and then finally that stupid e-mail. What were you thinking?"

"I'm sorry."

Dad grabbed me again and we hugged for a long time. It was the first time in a very long time that I felt that Dad cared about me. It had been so hard to trust him. Nothing made sense and I was beyond confused. I wanted to figure it out without blowing my cover, for Boone's sake.

"Well, it's two in the morning," Dad finally said and turned toward the house. "Why don't you go in and get some shuteye."

"Yes, sir." I followed him into the house.

He was so calm. Maybe he didn't know. Maybe he did.

Mom had just awakened and was in the hallway, also in a bathrobe, when we entered the living room. She wailed and screamed and held me so tight I couldn't breathe. We held each other for a long time as she wept uncontrollably. Every time she shuddered against me, mid-sob, I grimaced, feeling as though my heart would break for having caused her so much pain.

"Don't you ever leave me again!" she screamed at me. "Do you understand?"

"Don't you ever leave me again," I whispered back.

Chapter 20
ROUTINE

When I awoke, the sun had already risen. I ran downstairs and found Mom in the kitchen. Dad stood next to her, helping her cook. I blinked twice. They had actually been laughing at something, together, when I entered the room.

"Good morning, Baby." Mom smiled and walked over to me. She wrapped her arm around my waist and led me over to the table. I sat down, and Dad walked over, seating himself next to me. Mom went back to whatever was on the stove.

"Weird," I said, shaking my head.

"What?" Mom asked. Her smile was bigger than I had ever seen it before.

"Uh, sorry, just not sure what day it is or what time it is or what planet I'm on," I said, trying to make a joke. I had expected the CBC or a Kashmaar to come and get me in my sleep. Instead, I woke up to an eerie Twilight Zone meets the Brady Bunch for breakfast. Were my folks actually getting along now? Was the divorce off?

"Well, you're on Earth, and it's Friday," Dad announced.

"And this is how we are going to try to do things from now on," Mom said, catching onto what I meant. "You're father and I are going to therapy. Eventually, when we have worked a few things out, we'd like you to come with us."

"Okay," I said, looking over at Dad who had a big grin

on his face and was looking at Mom.

The phone rang.

"That'll probably be your buddy, Nelson," Dad said and nodded to the receiver, "He's called for you six times already this morning. He wants to know if you're going to the prom tomorrow night."

"What... wait? It's only Friday? I didn't miss it?"

"Nope," Mom smiled.

The phone rang a third time, then a fourth. Dad grabbed it and tossed it to me.

"Hello," I said.

"Hello, Seth?" Nelson's voice still sounded high and overly concerned. "Seth, is that you?"

"Yeah, hi, Nelson."

"So, Seth, are you on for tomorrow?"

"Uhh... let me check," I said, and covered the receiver.

"No way," Dad said. "You are grounded."

It figured. I had been waiting for him to hand out my punishment.

"Oh, Sam, you've got to let him go, or that poor girl will get stood up! There's no sense in penalizing Rosa for Seth's stupidity," Mom intervened. "Let him go, just this once."

"Alright, Seth, you're grounded forever," Dad amended, "but be home by curfew."

I held the phone up to my ear and said, "They just said I could go."

Squeals of delight blasted through the ear piece. "I just knew you'd make it! Koa and I will pick you up around five-thirty. We'll already have our dates, and then we'll take you over to get Rosa."

"Okay," I said, wondering what Nelson knew about where I had been.

As if reading my thoughts, Nelson added, "Don't worry about explaining anything, Seth, your dad already let us know what happened."

"What did he tell you?"

"He said that your mom left him and you went with her, but that he begged you both to come back. I'm glad you're all in therapy. I think that everyone could use it.

Although, it kind of doesn't work if people only change because they were talked into changing. And it doesn't work if the people around you don't realize that you're okay and continually treat you badly ...oh, hey, do you need a ride to school this morning?"

"Yeah… okay," I said.

"Great, see you in… oh crap, like five minutes."

He hung up. I high tailed it up to my room to get dressed. In my rush, I neglected to ask why Dad told Nelson I'd been with Mom for the week. It bugged me that we were lying about it. I was grounded, but not grilled, and it seemed like nobody was gonna be talking about anything that had really happened.

Nelson and Roxy picked me up and a short ride later I was back at school as if I hadn't been to OS at all. It was like I'd gone on vacation and was back to reality. In fact, all my teachers seemed to know the same story Nelson did; my mom and I left my dad but we came back for another try.

At lunch, Nelson, Koa, and I talked about Prom plans while Miguel just smiled and shook his head. I wanted him to come to, but decided not to pull a Nelson and bug him about it.

"What are you doing tomorrow night?" I asked him, while Koa argued with Nelson about which movie to show our dates after the dance.

Miguel shrugged. "Whatever, you know."

I nodded.

Nelson suddenly escalated, "Look, Koa, we have got to watch a chick flick or the girls will be bored. I know a lot about girls, and we are more apt to get a little action if we pander to their romantic sides than if we watch some man film!"

"Nelson, you're lucky that you're even going on this date, dude," Koa said. I could tell it had slipped out, but it hurt. Nelson automatically placed his lunch back on his tray and assumed his position on the bench across the way.

"I'm not watching anything written by Jane Austen, Nelson," Koa called over to him. "Those movies are so boring. It's not even worth the possibility of kissing someone, man."

I didn't really care what we did as long as I was with Rosa, so I didn't say anything.

When I reached my drama class, I realized I hadn't seen her all day. My heart actually skipped a beat as she entered the classroom right as the bell rang. I was really happy to see her until I noticed that she was holding a basketball and my Sunday suit.

"You ready for your monologue?" Nelson asked.

"Huh?"

"You're performing today."

Before I could even say a thing, Rosa shoved me toward the class dressing room to change. I tried to think of an excuse to get out of having to perform, but everyone seemed pretty sure it was my turn to get on that stage and make a fool of myself. They had all done it and I was the only one left.

Rosa adjusted my tie when I resurfaced from the changing room.

"Tuck in your shirt," she instructed.

"I don't think I remember my lines," I said. I had flown a flying saucer and been to a different planet in the galaxy. There was no way that I was going to remember that stupid monologue. All I wanted to do was walk out the door and just keep on walking.

"Seth," Rosa began, brushing some lint from my jacket's sleeve, "you have been a mystery to me since day one."

"Really?"

"Just shut up and listen."

"Okay." She was so pretty.

"This is your pep talk. You ready?"

I nodded. I wanted to kiss her.

"I can tell you're nervous, so here goes. Seth, you have been a complete mystery to me since day one. You play basketball, you're a space nerd... you have smooth lines, you say the dumbest things... you are a good friend, a good soldier, a good son, a good everything, but really hard to pin down. So this is what I decided. You are a chameleon."

"I'm a chameleon."

"You become good at whatever it is you're doing. You

always rise to the occasion, whether it's your thing or not, so, now you are gonna be a good actor and get out there and break a leg."

"Okay...," I said, not really understanding what she was trying to say. She handed me my basketball and pushed me onto the stage.

I remembered my lines alright. I even found that I could relate to my character, Jamal, so much more since going beyond Earth and coming back to Central. It really was as if nobody understood me anymore. Handling the basketball even felt alien and awkward, probably because I still wasn't used to the heaviness of Earth's gravity. As I neared the end of my speech, I yelled the last part of my lines out of my own real frustration, "Don't you get it? I'm still one of you. I'm still a human being!"

I paused and let the quiet beats go by as I really looked out into the audience. Nobody got it. I searched the faces of my classmates. I couldn't tell if Nelson really was crying or not, but he certainly looked touched. Rosa was smirking.

"You know, whatever," I whispered and then dropped the ball, letting it bounce down to a standstill as I walked off stage.

When I finished, everyone clapped. I was pretty sure the clapping was because it was over, and not because I had done well. Even though I had felt something powerful in the moment, the whole experience was worse than I had imagined. So much for Rosa's chameleon theory: although, it was nice that she had spent so much time thinking about me.

She disappeared as soon as the bell rang, probably because she didn't want to talk about how bad it was, but Nelson kept telling me how boss I was as we gathered our backpacks. One thing was sure, it really was hard to come back to the 'hood, once you've lived on the Moon. Everyone was just trying to pick up where we had left off, but I swear that it felt like I was having an out-of-body experience. Something just wasn't adding up for me.

On the way out to the Dent, while Nelson rambled on about our plans for Prom, I saw one of his bullies approaching us. The bully didn't even have time to raise his hand toward Nelson's head before I slammed his own head into the locker next to me. Then I slammed his friends' faces into a couple of lockers as well, just for emphasis.

Nelson stole a few looks at the boys as we passed them.

"Thanks," he said. He shook his head once, gave a triumphant smile, and then dove right back into our conversation. "So, I think that we should go to my house after the dance and watch a movie, a chick-flick that is, pop some popcorn—get a little action if we can."

I didn't have the heart to tell him I preferred to get my action alone.

It did feel good to protect him, though. I had found that side of me in Space, the side of me that wanted to help people, the side that wanted to be a hero. Although, I was super tired when I got home and all I really wanted to do was catch up on my sleep. I passed out on my bed and didn't wake up till late Saturday Morning. Mom and Dad were out shopping, so I rode my bike over to The Good Life Living Center. The same young girl was still talking on the phone. She held the same finger up to me and kept me waiting while she continued her oh-so engrossing "I know… I know, right?" conversation.

After what seemed an eternity of "No way…. Nu-uh… NO WAY," she said, "Just a sec," and turned to face me.

"Connie Jenkins, please," I said.

She consulted the chart for several seconds and then said, "Oh, I guess she was checked out for good yesterday. Her son came and picked her up. But, are you Seth?"

"Excuse me?"

"Are you Seth Carter?" she read my name from the chart.

I froze. Was it some sort of trap—and the gum-smacking ditz in front of me was about to turn into a creepy space creature and stun me with a laser? I could hear the clock ticking on the wall as I deliberated whether or not to say yes. Suddenly, I heard the words escape my lips, "Uh… yeah, I'm Seth Carter."

"Cool." The girl smiled. "Connie left this for you."

She passed me an envelope with my name on it.

"Thanks," I said, and she went back to her telephone conversation.

I walked out of the building and sat on a wooden bench near the side doors. My hands were shaking as I tore open the letter and read:

Dear Seth,

Words cannot express how grateful I am to you. My husband, Topher, came for me. I'm struggling to remember him, but I feel safe. He told me that I was abducted by the Kashmaari and sold on their black market as a skin. I was worn as a bodyslave for several years. I think that's how I became an alcoholic and drug addict. The Kashmaar who used me and swept my memory and abandoned me in Vegas when it was finished.

Some things I remember. Some things I don't want to try to remember. I have very unhappy memories—sick and twisted gifts given to me from the demon that possessed me for so long.

The CBC would do nothing to help Topher when I went missing. They don't like to get involved in problems of any kind. They expect you to be loyal to them, but are never loyal in return. What Topher did to locate me was wrong, and it put you and your friends and family in danger. I hope that you were able to escape and that the girl they used (a friend of yours, I'm sorry to hear) is all right.

Please forgive us,
Constance
P.S. Don't trust anyone.

Chapter 21

PROM

I only had twenty minutes to get ready for the dance by the time I got home. As I dressed, I read over Connie's letter a few more times. I had no idea how to feel about her apology. Part of me was happy that she was reunited with Topher, but an even bigger part of me had to wonder if the CBC would ever contact me again. I figured I was pretty much a giant problem they would want to be avoiding.

What was worse, Dad's assistant, whose CBC vehicle I had stolen and stashed, was in fact a Kashmaar. I was positive. Dad and I still hadn't talked about it. I didn't even know how to bring it up. "Yeah, Dad... so you know how I was gone for a week and I wasn't really with Mom... yeah, so I went to Outer Space with your Dad, actually, and that Kashmaar you work with may have come to fetch me home in the form of Meike... or maybe it is a coincidence and you don't know anything about the Kashmaari?"

Something sinister was lurking in the shadows of my mind, but I wasn't focused enough to figure out what was going on, or how to get Dad to fess up about anything, or perhaps I really didn't want to know the truth. I kept waiting for his assistant to come to our house and demand Dirk back, or for Boone and Jim-bo to show up and take me back to Moon Base.

I focused my thoughts on the dance instead. Luckily, it was going to be a no-brainer. Mom had rented a tux for me when she was out shopping that morning and had also remembered to order Rosa a corsage. I hoped that was all I needed.

I ran out to the limousine and was happy to find that Koa and Nelson had also rented tuxes. I'd figured as much since we were renting a limo, but still hadn't been positive. Koa's bow tie and cummerbund matched Cami's peach dress. Nelson's date, Melissa, who had finally said yes, was wearing a billowy white dress, and Nelson was wearing a top hat and tails—which cracked me up, but kind of worked at the same time.

Only the moment after I rang Rosa's doorbell, I had the awful feeling that she might not even know I was coming. We had only joked about it, and hadn't set up the specifics after Drama, like I had wanted to. I hadn't called her to confirm either, and had no idea if Nelson had. Sweat dripped down my forehead as I waited.

Miguel opened the door and laughed in my face. "Oh man," he said, "I'll get Rosa."

Why didn't I think to call? I wondered, mentally kicking myself for being a space cadet.

The TV was blaring in the darkness of the living room and I could barely make out the silhouettes of the Enrique, Juan, and Mr. Gomez. Thankfully, none of them really looked up from the screen at me. They were all too engrossed in their man movie.

A light switched on in the hallway, and Miguel returned to the others. Rosa followed, decked out in the most beautiful dress I had ever seen. I really can't describe it, other than to say it was red and she looked amazing. Relief washed over me as I realized she was actually dressed and ready to go.

"Hello," I said, as she approached me.

"I'm waiting for my date," she announced briskly.

"What?"

"You left."

"You were supposed to stay home, if I got abducted, remember?"

"Yeah, well, you left and someone else asked."

"Are you serious?"

"No," she laughed, taking my arm.

"What?"

"I'm just messing with you, Seth. You ready?"

A voice called to us from the kitchen. "Wait! I have to get a picture!"

Mrs. Gomez appeared with a camera. The flash went off before I even had time to register that Rosa was going with me after all. I was still trying to figure out who the other guy was as the second flash went off. She was such a convincing actress. We were halfway out the door when I finally felt confident I was still her date.

"Have a great time, kids," Mrs. Gomez called after us.

I handed Rosa the box with her corsage. "It's for your wrist."

"Thanks." She stopped and pinned something on my lapel. "This is for you."

I glanced down at a small white rose with sprigs of green and white stuff. It matched the corsage Mom had picked out exactly. Then I looked back into her big, brown eyes with those amazing eyelashes, and I felt like I was finally home. Something inside me took over, and I picked up Rosa's hand and kissed it, like Zorro.

"Seth!" she squeaked, blushing. "Knock it off!"

"Yes, ma'am," I said, taking her hand in mine and leading her to the limo.

Before we got in, Rosa stopped and asked, "So, where have you been, really?"

"I'll show you later tonight," I promised and kept her hand in mine as we climbed into our seat.

All through dinner at the fancy restaurant, Rosa tried to get me to talk.

"So where were you?" she said, holding up her menu to hide our faces.

"Later," I whispered.

As she finished the main course, she dropped her linen napkin on the ground. We both leaned down to get it, and she whispered, "You weren't with your mom, were you?"

"Later."

On the way back out to the limo she slowed her pace,

taking my hand to slow me as well.

"You didn't really do what you said you were going to do, did you?" she muttered.

"Later," I smiled, helping her into her seat.

"Whatever, Carter."

I did my best to keep my mouth shut as we danced and got our pictures. She kept giving me weird looks, as if she were going to explode if I didn't tell her immediately. After a while, she started answering for me, "I know, I know... later." And I'd just smile and nod.

After the dance, I asked Nelson to drop us off near the abandoned lot at the end of the cul-de-sac.

"Are you sure you don't want to come with us and watch Pride and Prejudice?" Nelson asked one last time.

"Nah, we need a little time alone," I said, winking at him. "I'm just gonna walk her home."

"Oh," he smiled approvingly, and then pulled me in close and whispered, "call me and tell me everything later."

"Will do," I lied.

The limo drove away, leaving us alone in the moonlight. Rosa cocked her head to one side and scrunched up her nose as she smiled at me. "So what's this about?"

"I just want to show you where I've been."

"Here, in an empty lot?" she asked, taking one step closer to me, a shiver running through her. She bobbed up and down to keep warm, so I took off my coat jacket and put it around her shoulders. She slipped her arms inside. "Thanks."

I took her hand and walked her over to the middle of the field.

"Activate code 1162," I said, hoping Dirk was actually still there, charged up, and ready to go.

"Voice command affirmative, dude," he piped up. "Activating guest driver."

An obsidian space craft appeared out of nowhere, and although it was dark, the blues and purples still reflected delicately in the light of the lamp across the street. I hadn't realized how much the craft had transformed from red sports car to its beetle-like space ship form, but was grateful that it had appeared in that condition. It was much more effective. Rosa grabbed onto my arm. "Oh crap—you were right!"

"Of course I was right," I said, savoring every moment of the look on her shocked little face. "You wanna go for a ride?"

"I don't know…I guess. I mean, you can't drive a car yet and you're going to take me for a ride in that?"

I smiled and led her to her seat, then ran around to the driver's seat.

"Dude, you left me hangin' out with nothin' to do!" Dirk announced.

"Sorry, Dirk," I said, trying not to let him throw me off my game.

"My owner is going to kill you when she finds you, dude," he threatened. "Literally kill you."

For about two seconds, his threat actually had me worried, until I realized he hadn't run away or gone back to her, so that meant he was still operating under my orders. "Dirk, I order you to protect me, hide me, keep me hidden."

"Fine."

"You will do that?"

"Yes."

"Good."

"Is this like a genie in a lamp thing?" Rosa piped in.

"Something like that," I smiled.

"So where to?" Dirk asked, in a bored voice.

"How 'bout an orbit around the Earth tonight?"

"Excellent choice, sir." He was being sarcastic.

"And not too fast; we'd like to enjoy the view. But try to keep it down to two hours."

"Copy, dude!" he said with mock enthusiasm. Of all the annoying personalities to have on a ship, Dirk had to be the worst. I wondered if he had been traded to the Kashmaari on purpose – their most annoying model given to their nastiest customers.

The ship hummed, and Rosa reached instinctively for her seatbelt. I smiled to myself and swiveled my seat around to face her. The ship lifted up off the ground.

"This is a spaceship?" Rosa asked in disbelief.

"Among other things." I said.

We caught a current up into the atmosphere and fell into orbit. After a moment of quiet introspection, she finally whispered, "It's so beautiful."

She was right. I remembered my astonishment when I had first seen the Earth that way. It was heartwarming to share it with Rosa and watch her similar speechlessness. After a moment, I called up a little classical music to drown out the silence.

Somewhere over Africa I got up the courage to reach for Rosa's hand again. When we reached India, I was almost ready to try kissing her, but something held me back. I really didn't want to ruin the small-child-mesmerized-by-the-beauty-of-Christmas-tree-lights look on her face. Rachmaninoff's second symphony orchestrated her amazing view of the world, and tears glistened in her perfect eyes, dropping gently from her long eyelashes onto her cheeks. I knew she was enjoying herself despite the fact that she was bawling because of the wide smile she wore. Mom did that kind of thing – smile and cry simultaneously – all the time.

Somewhere over the Pacific, Rosa suddenly hit me on the shoulder and cried out, "Seth! You're such a jerk!"

"What?" I asked, holding up my hands to ward off her attack.

"I'm never going to be able to go on a date again!" she explained, dropping her hand in her lap. I wanted to hold it again but resisted the urge to grab for it.

"How can anyone ever top this?" she asked.

I shrugged.

She imitated a deep voice, "Uh, Rosa, do you want to go out?" Then she answered, "Oh, I dunno. Do you have a spaceship, because Seth Carter does and it is awesome, so bowling or a movie might be a little L-A-M-E if you ask me."

"Oh, sorry."

"Uh-huh," she said, leaning toward me. "So, are you back for good, or just for tonight?"

"What do you mean?" I reached for her hand and began to rub her fingers.

"Seth, you have a spaceship!" she pulled it free again. "You've been gone for days. Why are you even here? And when are you going back?" She folded her arms, and I realized she wanted answers. I'd kinda grown used to everyone not talking about what was really going on.

"I don't know," I said. "I went to up to space with an engineer who turned out to be my grandfather."

"The alien in the radio?"

"Yup."

"Well, I feel slightly better about that."

"Don't," I said, "I didn't know he was my grandfather. I just wanted to go because my mom left my dad."

"So instead of getting drunk or breaking something..."

"I got abducted."

"Go on," she said, with the same smirk.

I started in on my experiences in OS, but suddenly remembered the CBC had given me liquid to wipe my memory if I ever tried to reveal our secrets to the enemy, but the more I talked, the more I realized that in a million years, Rosa Gomez could never be an enemy and the whole story just flowed out. It was wonderful to tell someone about Krad and Jim-bo, even the trick they played on me.

"That's the only thing I hate about being an Air Force brat," she agreed. "The 'play dumb pranks on the new kid' thing everyone does each time we get transferred sucks."

"It's pretty stupid," I agreed.

"But at least the one on Krad served a purpose. Most of the pranks played on me have just been mean-spirited. At least they wanted you to experience the mask so you could come up with something better."

"True." I smiled and told her about the Brain thought transference and the designs we had come up with. Then I mentioned the Kashmaar and Connie's letter of explanation.

"So, wait," Rosa interrupted, "your dad sent up your ex-girlfriend to come and get you?"

"Well, not Meike," I said, "but maybe the Kashmaar who was using her... wearing her, I guess. And I don't know if it was my Dad, because his Kashmaar-assistant hasn't come knocking on our door to get her ship back. What I really can't figure out is why the Kashmaari want me so badly."

"Seriously?" Rosa smiled. "Isn't it obvious?"

"What do you mean?"

"The Kashmaari are controlling your Dad by threatening you."

"Whoa… maybe… wow, you think that's it? They're controlling Dad by using me as leverage?"

"How else could they get him to cooperate?"

"Cooperate with what exactly?"

"Maybe they have the U.S. Government's cooperation to be here and use humans for their corporeal experiments?" I could see the wheels in Rosa's head spinning hard as she brainstormed.

"Why would the Air Force cooperate with aliens who are destroying people's lives?" I asked.

"Maybe they have no choice?" Rosa said. "Maybe the Kashmaari are threatening them or trying to control them, which is why they need you. They need you to control your dad, to get to use humans without interference from the government."

"It makes sense, but I don't think my dad is that much of a pussy. At least, I hope not."

I kept telling myself that Dad was innocent and didn't know what a Kashmaar was. I wanted to believe that he didn't know that his assistant was an alien, but deep down, I knew I had been lying to myself.

Rosa had grown quiet and was staring out the window. She whispered. "I think it's my fault he knew you went to space."

"Yours?"

"Yes," she said, dropping my hand and meeting my gaze. "I told your dad all about the radio static and wind chimes after you went missing Sunday night. I came over to your house to visit you after school on Monday, but he said you had run away. I told him you were trying to get abducted, and probably had gone to see that woman from the internet. I was worried about you, Seth. I didn't know what to do, so I told him everything. Later he told me you had run off with your mom, but I didn't really believe him like Nelson and everyone else did, because he didn't look shocked or bothered about anything."

I didn't know what to say. I was still working on the concept that my father was working with the Kashmaari.

"I had no idea that this would happen," Rosa continued. "I was just worried about you."

"You didn't know," I reassured her. "You didn't know my Dad would send a nightmare to come for me."

"But did he send it?"

"I don't know."

I hoped not.

An annoying beep, like a quiet alarm, sounded at that moment. I glanced around to figure out where it was coming from.

"What is that?" Rosa asked, pointing out her window.

What looked like a florescent, lime green missile was heading straight for us. My reflexes took over instantly.

"Go manual driver," I ordered, grabbing the steering column and maneuvering our ship out of the way. Instead of falling out of our seats, I felt an invisible force restraining me as we plummeted downward. It was like being back in Nellie's game simulation. We managed to avoid the trajectory of the green light, but it quickly redirected its course.

"Uh oh, Dude, it looks like you've been busted!" Dirk announced. "My owner wants me back."

"That's your owner?" Rosa asked.

"Pretty sure... but Kashmaari all look alike without skins," he said matter of factly. "Could be someone she works with."

"That's a Kashmaar?" Rosa was straining to get a good look at the thing trying to ram us.

"Yup, and she's pretty P.O.'d if you ask me," Dirk assessed. He was really starting to bug me.

I pushed the column forward as far as it could go, but no matter how well I maneuvered, the green light seemed right on top of us, relentless in its pursuit. I called up the weapons screen and flew back around to launch a few fire balls at it. There was an instantaneous explosion, and for a moment I thought I may have done some damage, but then, the Kashmaar floated out of the blazing fireball, completely unscathed. It was still heading straight for us. The only thing I could do was brace myself for impact.

Chapter 22

ALTAAR

I felt Rosa tense up next to me as we watched the disembodied Kashmaar speed toward us.

"That was the thing possessing Meike?" she asked, shuddering as she grabbed onto my arm.

I nodded and tried one more time to escape the impact, pushing the steering column hard right and as fast as we could accelerate, but the Kashmaar broke into lightning speed and in moments tore its way into our vessel. It came to a full stop, floating eerily and silently in the air right between us. Dark flecks of black were marbled through its eerie, translucent form. I swatted at it to see if there was any way to fight it. In response, it slammed its hand right through Rosa's head. She screamed out in pain and slumped down in her seat, knocked out cold.

I grabbed for her, catching her up onto my lap. She seemed alright, except for the fact that one brush of the Kashmaar's hand had completely incapacitated her and left her unconscious.

The Kashmaar hissed and crackled as it addressed me, its voice screeching like nails on metal, "Surrender or she dies."

"I surrender." No question.

Its voice really creeped me out, almost like I was listening to a murderer trying to seduce the darkest part of my soul into some heinous submission, and its tone was too loud and blared all over, like headphones that play in your brain, way beyond your ears.

"Where to, Altaar?" Dirk piped up.

"Home."

"Copy that."

Luckily, the ship headed back towards North America. I cradled Rosa's head against my chest, listening to her short, irregular breath and trying to figure out a way to keep us both alive. I was mad at myself for putting her in jeopardy in the first place. I felt like such an idiot and hated it.

The Kashmaar was hissing and crackling right next to me which made it difficult to concentrate. Its glowing green light reflected brightly off the cabin of the ship. The only good thing about being that close to it was that I was able to discover my plasma whip design would probably work and that they Kashmaar would be contained easily in the handle. We had built it to house a specter with a slight density. Even though the Kashmaar was disembodied, it still had minor tangibility.

I looked out over the uninhabited desert beneath us and tried to decide what to do. There was only one Kashmaar at that moment. Who knew how many there would be once we landed? It was the best time to try to escape, and yet, I had never felt so powerless. There was no way to stop it. It was the third time I was up against a Kashmaar. The previous two times, I managed to escape because of Dad and Boone.

I decided to try reasoning to check its intelligence.

"What do you want with me?"

The Kashmaar sailed in front of me and stared coldly into my eyes. Its form hissed as it looked me over. Having the sparks of its body so close to my face made me flinch inadvertently, like holding a sparkler near my eyes on the fourth of July.

"You have your ship," I continued. "We're even."

It shook gently and let out what sounded like a rusty laugh when it answered. "You have no idea what *even* is, Seth."

"Why do you care what I do?"

The Kashmaar sailed through me, sending a wave of ice cold pain shooting throughout my body. It felt like someone had slashed through my midsection with an icicle. The frigid burn lingered as the Kashmaar separated itself from me and stopped in the center of the dashboard.

"I don't care about you, Seth," it said, crackling like a fire as it spoke. "You are insignificant, and I would have killed you in the desert when I found you because of your insolence."

"My insolence?"

"You were warned to stay on Earth," it hissed.

"You didn't tell me to stay here."

"You disobeyed your father's warning."

"WHY DO YOU CARE?" I screamed.

The Kashmaar raged and hissed its answer inside my head, crashing through my body again and again, as if it were slashing me repeatedly with a knife, "YOUR FATHER CARES ABOUT YOU! HE NEEDS YOU AND WE NEED HIM."

I struggled to remain defiant and indifferent, so that it would stay angry and keep sharing. A migraine registered in my frontal lobe as it exited my body the third time and I was left with nauseated chills and what felt like a fever. I shuddered, which made the Kashmaar hiss with laughter.

"Why do you need him?" I asked.

Unfortunately, that question put the Kashmaar on guard. It stopped raging and started ordering me around again.

"Listen carefully so that you understand this time, Seth," it said, slamming another fist through Rosa's head which made her yell out as if she were having a night terror. "Are you listening to me?"

"I'm listening."

"I will kill anything you love to make you stay put on Earth, including this girl... your mother... your friends. You stay on Earth with your father, and stop trying to escape or I will hurt all the things you love."

"They aren't things," I corrected, "They are human beings with lives and feelings."

It crashed through me again, this time leaving an ice cold burn which was excruciating. It took everything I had not to shout out in pain as it lingered and wiggled inside of me. When it finally left my body and the pain subsided, all I wanted to do was sleep. I held Rosa closer to me, hoping she would wake up as I jostled her, but she remained unconscious, a grimace lingering on her face, as if the nightmare in her head were still going on.

Our exchange had been excruciation, but it gave me all the information I needed. Kashmaari could not reason. They could only see what they desired and became angry if they didn't get what they wanted, like a narcissistic and selfish children. It would eventually be their downfall. Even though the CBC claimed neutrality, the Kashmaari should never have infiltrated the base of such an advanced group. What they failed to realize was that they may have awakened a sleeping giant to get me back. All I could do was hope the CBC was a little more logical and would decide they could not continue to tolerate acts of war against their engineers, and that I was still considered one of them. I saw nothing else that would get us out of the situation.

Lights appeared in the distance below, and as we came closer, I saw a few sparse bunkers and lit up landing strips. Once I saw the dried up salt bed, I knew we were heading to Groom Lake Air Force Base, Area 51, and almost chuckled at the irony. Of course there was an alien cover up there. But they weren't exactly the aliens anyone would have suspected, and perhaps the government was doing everyone a favor by hiding them.

We slowed as we descended and flew over the sparse, abandoned-looking buildings and a few F-22s. Even though our speed was decreasing, it looked like we were about to crash into the landing field. I braced myself for the impact, but then we sailed through the ground and down into a cavern beneath it. What had looked to be a landing strip was actually an optical illusion hiding a giant docking hangar of a space station.

We landed next to a row of familiar obsidian CBC ships. The hangar was dimly lit by cobalt lanterns which left blue shadows on the walls. I could barely make out a control tower full of green lights which must have come from the Kashmaari directing the traffic.

Dirk's doors opened, and he immediately powered off.

"Come," the Kashmaar hissed, and sailed out into the hangar, disappearing quickly into the darkness. It left a faint, green light in its wake.

I gathered Rosa up into my arms and followed it, as commanded.

"Halt!" a different voice called to me. Out of the darkness walked a man with an M-16 in his hands, still dressed in his white CBC uniform. As he approached, I could smell the oranges. It was Boone.

"Come with me," the Kashmaar-Boone said, its voice metal and strained.

I hesitated.

"Now," it said, brandishing its weapon and pointing it at Rosa.

I followed him into the darkness from where he had materialized, carrying Rosa in my arms. We walked out of the hangar and into what seemed to be the main room of the secret base. There weren't any windows or doors, but the ceiling was partly translucent and showed the stars. There were super-sophisticated, high tech cubicles, computer screens, and large monitors set up throughout the room. The center area housed the largest monitor and several leather sofas positioned to view it. Air Force personnel and disembodied Kashmaari bustled around the spacious room consulting various radar screens and computers.

"This way," the Boone Kashmaar ordered.

I tore my eyes away from the secret Kashmaari operation right in the middle of a U.S. Air Force base and followed the Boone-Kashmaar down a darkened corridor. We reached the end and entered a room with crappy old couches and a water cooler like one would expect to find in a small-town municipal airport. Right in the middle of one of the couches sat my father.

"Dad!" I yelled, running to him.

"Seth!" he got up and helped me set Rosa onto a couch.

He hugged me and looked into my eyes. I wanted to cry. Was he one of them? Was I hugging the enemy?

"Seth, don't worry," he said, "everything's gonna be all right. Just do what they tell you."

"Dad do you know what they are? What they do?" I couldn't help asking.

"Shhh," Dad hushed me and shot me the 'he's right there listening to you, idiot' look that I knew I deserved at that moment, but I didn't care. I was pissed that he suggested we just play along. His own father, Boone, was a bodyslave, and it didn't even seem to faze him.

The Kashmaar possessing Boone set his M-16 down on the coffee table and took a seat. It picked up a magazine from the coffee table and scanned its pages. Dad sat me down next to Rosa and then sat down on my other side. He put a hand firmly on my leg as a warning not to do anything stupid, and when I looked over at him he shot me his "don't even think about it" look.

We waited in silence for something to happen. Finally, the door opened and in walked Dad's assistant as beautiful as ever, smelling of freshly-squeezed orange juice. She sat down next to the Boone-Kashmaar and grabbed the magazine out of its hands, dropping it back down on the table, then handed him his gun.

I didn't say anything.

"You've got your vehicle back, Altaar," Dad prompted, gently.

"Yes, and you have your son, Samuel," the metallic voice hissed back at him. "Was it worth all that trouble, I wonder?"

"Please let him go." He was trying to make the whole 'pleading for my life'as casual as possible, but his expression was pained and anxious. If she really was using me to control Dad, then I'd have to say it was worth the trouble of going to Moon Base and infiltrating the CBC. He pretty much looked like he would do anything she wanted in order to keep me safe.

She looked hard at my father for several long seconds.

"Let him go," he urged again.

"Yes, I will let him go," she said, the sound of metal twisting with her lies. "Seth, you may go home to your father's house."

That's it? "I'll stay, if you let Boone return unharmed to the CBC."

"No," she countered. "He is much too useful to us where he is."

"What do you care?" I was exasperated. "Why does my adoption to the CBC matter?"

Ignoring my question, she recited, "Space is a cold, dark place full of crazy, unfriendly things, Seth. It's best just to stay here on Earth. I'm warning you. Stay on Earth."

"No," I said.

She glanced around the room, obviously trying to avoid telling me anything and upset that I wasn't taking a hint. Then, her gaze fell on Rosa, curled up on the couch.

"It would be such a pity if something were to happen to your pretty little prom date." she stood and walked toward her.

I stood up tall next to her advance and folded my arms.

"Such pretty eyelashes she has…such a pity…" Altaar continued, then suddenly spat a green logie out of her mouth, which hit Rosa in the face, waking her up.

Another scream escaped Rosa as she opened her eyes in terror. I knelt down next to her, throwing my arms around her in a protective embrace, trying to calm her as anyone would need if they had awakened from a nightmare. Dad did nothing. Altaar walked out the door, never looking back. The Boone-Kashmaar, who had been watching our exchange, picked up its magazine again, and leafed through the pages.

Dad finally broke the silence, "I'll drive you both home."

"That's it?" I asked.

"Yup," Dad said, getting up off the couch.

Chapter 23
THE CARWASH

I kept my arm around Rosa as we walked. She seemed partially catatonic, like she was sleepwalking. I couldn't decide if she was awake or not and kept arguing with myself whether to just pick her up and carry her, or help her walk it off. Eventually, I realized that I made her limp along because I didn't want my dad to see me holding her. Not that I was embarrassed, but because I knew they were using Rosa as leverage to get me to play along, and the sooner I could dump her, the sooner she would be safe. There was no way I was ever going to put her into danger again. Not caring about her was the only way I could protect her. As soon as I lost interest in Rosa, they would lose interest in her. It was going to suck, but I was going to have to do it.

As Dad led us through the darkened corridors of the hidden Kashmaari base, it seemed like we were going deeper and deeper into the earth, and farther and farther away from daylight or familiar technology and architecture. Kashmaari don't need lighting, apparently, since they are giant fireflies anyway, and, their lack of bodies meant that they don't need doors, either. The space grew darker, danker, and more cavern like as we descended.

We walked passed a laboratory that had the whole mad-scientist thing going on. Air force personnel in masks were watch dogged by Kashmaari as they worked silently in the lab. As far as I could tell from the orange grove smell, it was where they created the assimilation shots that I had given Meike.

The area adjacent was full of people. I could only imagine that they were waiting to be used as skins. They didn't seem to be aware of what was going on, but only stared blankly at me as I passed. They waited like flies caught in a web. I winced at the thought of a spider coming home to claim its victim, and remembered the feeling of ice slashing through my chest. Rosa shuddered, and I held her a little tighter.

We stopped in front of an odd-looking door at the end of a walkway. I had a suspicious label on it that read, "Janitor." When Dad opened it, we stepped through and onto the platform of a small subway station.

"Get in," Dad ordered, pushing us toward the nearest subway car.

I helped Rosa into her seat, then sat down next to her. Dad took a seat across from us. After a few moments, the subway car lurched forward. We accelerated so quickly that I almost fell off my seat. I put an arm up against Rosa's arm to keep her in place. She wasn't very coherent, and barely seemed to notice anything that was going on.

"How long is she gonna be this way?" I demanded.

Dad scowled, then took a flask from his pocket. "Try to get her to drink this," he ordered.

I took the flask and held it to Rosa's lips. She drank the contents right away, as if she hadn't had a drink in days. After she finished, she laid her head on my shoulder and fell back asleep. It hadn't seemed to help at all. I was angry at myself for still trusting my Dad.

"She'll be fine now," he said. "By the time we get her home, it will be like nothing ever happened... good as new. Promise."

He flashed me the first smile of the evening, but I was pissed. "Why are you negotiating with the Kashmaari?"

Dad shook his head slightly, pointed to his ear, then asked, "How was the dance?"

I didn't want to play his game, so I turned my gaze to Rosa, who was sleeping against my shoulder. He sighed and fell silent again.

In minutes, we had reached our destination. I scooped Rosa up into my arms and we exited the car into the other end of the subway station. An armed Air Force soldier stood guard at the station's doorway, and he saluted as we walked passed. Dad led the way to an underground parking lot where we found his SUV. I climbed into the back seat with Rosa, who was snoring lightly. At least she wasn't in a coma or having a nightmare. I buckled her in and rested her head on my shoulder once more. Her hand soon found its way into mine, and she smiled contentedly in her sleep.

Dad started the car and peeled out of the parking garage and past the front gate. As we drove off the base, I realized that it had been no ordinary subway. It had taken Roxy, Nelson and me hours to make our way and back to Area 51, but we had shuttled from Area 51 to Nellis in minutes. The guard waved as we drove passed and off base. In a matter of minutes we arrived in front of casa Gomez. Rosa opened her eyes, as if on cue, and smiled up at me.

"You all right?" I asked.

"Yeah... sorry I fell asleep."

She was disoriented and almost gasped when she saw my Dad chaperoning us.

"Where's Nelson?" she whispered.

"Probably at his house watching a movie?" I guessed, wondering why it was even relevant.

"I don't remember your dad picking us up," she mumbled. "Weird."

"What do you remember?"

"Nelson dropped us off at a cul-de-sac and you were gonna show me something... and here we are back at my house."

I think my jaw about dropped into my lap. My dad shot me a warning look.

"I must have fallen asleep," she continued as we climbed out of the backseat and walked to her doorstep. "I'm so embarrassed. I was up half the night finishing a book I really got into. I'm sorry, Seth."

"Okay...," I nodded. I couldn't believe what I was

hearing. She forgot everything.

We reached the porch and, as she stepped on to it and faced me, our noses almost touched. She was waiting for me to kiss her, but I was too confused to do anything.

"You don't remember anything that happened after the dance?" I asked.

"No," she apologized, "I'm so sorry."

"Ah… okay… so, you're okay?" I asked.

She yawned and moved in closer. "Yup, just tired, I guess."

"Okay…," I nodded.

She moved in closer to my face. I pulled her into a hug and held onto her for a while, trying to figure out what to do. Her memory had been erased. She hugged me back, stroking my hair and neck. I was happy she didn't remember Altaar's brutality, but I felt so alone. I had just lost my best friend.

"Night," I said quickly, and broke away.

"Yeah, good night," she nodded, a look of disappointment on her face. "Uh… thanks."

I nodded and backed away toward Dad's SUV. I watched Rosa walk into her house and shut the door, and breathed out a sigh. I hopped into the passenger seat next to my dad, pulled the car door shut and turned to him expectantly. But, he shook his head again, started the car, and pulled away from the curb. We drove in silence, to a dilapidated part of town and pulled into an old, abandoned-looking carwash.

"Just thought we'd get a wash," he said, as he rolled down his window and pushed a few buttons on the dead console next to us. It sprang to life and emitted a series of loud beeps as we drove slowly forward.

The stop sign flashed and Dad put the SUV into park, turned off the engine, and twisted around in his seat to face me. "This was built by the CIA. The Kashmaari are always listening to us, but as far as we know, this carwash jams their signals. We will be good to talk in here for the next five minutes or so. You better ask those questions fast."

"Does Mom know?"

"No."

"What just happened to Rosa?"

"I flushed her memory of anything to do with tonight or the strange events leading up to it." He said it as if people did things like that every day. It was the drink he had me give her. I never should have trusted him.

"You flushed her memory," I repeated his words in an attempt to show him how horrible he sounded. The soak cycle began. It was loud enough that we had to yell to be heard.

"It's for the best," he asserted. "She doesn't need to deal with this, and neither do you. I need you to forget about this. Don't try to do anything or we are all dead."

"What about Boone?"

"What about Boone?" he countered.

"You aren't going to help your own father get out of being a bodyslave?"

Dad almost shuddered when I used the word. His face was troubled for a few seconds, but after a few calm down breaths he answered, "That man abandoned me for space, and when I finally went looking for him, all I found were the Kashmaari. Then, he took my son from me. Do you really think I need to help him?"

"Dad, nobody should be possessed by those things."

"He's been trying to get to you for years, so I don't think I care where he ends up. And don't think I'm not mad at you for taking off with him."

Pink, blue, and yellow foam squirted at us from every direction. I watched the colors leak down the side of my window. Then, the rinse cycle kicked on, and water blasted us from all directions.

"Boone didn't tell me I was his grandson, sir," I admitted.

"You mean you just went off with some random guy? I assumed you went with him because you knew who he was! What if your little abduction went bad? Did you even think about that?"

I hollered back at him, "Don't you dare lecture me about thinking things through! Did you ever think about the fact that you are working with killers? They ruin people's lives!"

The water stopped and the sound of giant fans hummed loudly all around us. The sign signaled us to pull forward and dry off.

"I'm not the bad guy here," he said.

"Did you authorize the Kashmaari to take Meike?" I asked, not really wanting to know the answer.

"They were trying to choose between Roxy and Meike based on our previous conversations. I begged them not to use either one – just to take a strike force up to the base, but they were convinced that a maneuver like that would have erased the memory of the CBC guy they were working with."

"Topher." The green liquid.

We drove forward to the fans. "Topher was suspicious, but he didn't ask too many questions of us. He just wanted his wife back."

"And you told him where Connie was," I said.

The fans blasted warm air on our car—and I could barely hear him over the noise. We were in deep, and I had no idea what to do about it. Grandpa was just as bad as Dad, who would do nothing to help me find out about Connie on base. We could have avoided the whole incident if he had been willing to help Topher out. Connie was right. I couldn't trust anyone.

"Look, Seth, I love you no matter what. I love Mom more than anything. I have to work with the Kashmaari or they will destroy us… destroy America."

"That's bull…"

He cut me off, "No. We are in serious trouble here. These creatures have done horrible things in order to get the government's cooperation."

"What do they want?"

"They want people. That's it. They want a joy ride… bodyslaves, and they don't want us trying to stop their fun."

"That's it?"

"We don't know enough about them to really tell what's

going on. The ones who are here at Nellis and Groom Lake are horrible, but all they seem to want is our cooperation. They just want to use a few bodies."

"Can't you stop them?"

"We're trying, Seth," he said, "We've got guys on this, but they seem impenetrable. I think they know we're trying to stop them, so they threaten us... the people we love, to beat us into submission. Your grandfather has to have known I was in trouble, and he has never once come to help me. His organization has to have something that could help us."

"They might now," I nodded. "I can contact them."

Dad's whole demeanor grew angry again, "Seth, I absolutely forbid you to try anything. The only thing we can do is cooperate and sacrifice a few skins along the way. I'm not letting them kill you or Mom. We just need to play along and we can stay alive. Now, I need you to do what I tell you from now on. Don't go looking to get back to the CBC or Space. I'm not swiping your memory because you need to understand what's going on this time around. Just fly under the radar and keep out of trouble."

"But Grandpa," I protested. "They'll kill him."

"Look, Seth, he and Nellie took off for space and never looked back. They invited me to come with them, but I didn't want to leave my mother behind, and she flat out would not come. Then, it was too late. They never came back for me. Not once."

"Oh," I said.

"Look, Seth, stay on Earth. Graduate from high school. Live your life, here. I need you to join the military and get into intelligence work as soon as you can. Come work with me, so you can be safe. The Kashmaari will leave you alone if you choose to work with them."

"Dad, I won't negotiate with the Kashmaari. We can beat them!"

"No, way, Seth," Dad said. "Now shut up and stay out of trouble."

The fans turned off, terminating our conversation. Dad turned back to the steering wheel, and flipped on the radio. Instead of driving through another round of the carwash to discuss a plan of attack, we listened to music the whole way home. I was livid. My dad was a total sell-out. He was cooperating with the Kashmaari to save our lives. And what was worse, my grandfather, Boone, wasn't much better. Instead of helping the cause of the civil rights movement, he ran away from Earth and joined the CBC, an organization which only cared about its own self preservation.

Where did I fit in? Sell out or non-confrontational? Were those my only options? Altaar had threatened Rosa, and my grandfather was a bodyslave. The only way I was ever going to get my life back was to fight. The last option – my option – was to stop the Kashmaari, or die trying. I was a space soldier and a defender of the helpless. It was time to act.

Chapter 24
PROTOTYPES

The moment we got home, I went straight to my room. As soon as I heard Dad settle into bed, I pulled out my walkie talkie to call Jim-bo. He didn't answer for the first few attempts. Finally, after an hour of whispering "BAV 1, this is BAH 1, Over," into the receiver, I heard some static.

"I read you BAH 1," a voice chuckled.

"Jim-bo," I almost choked up as spoke his name, "I need your help as soon as you can get here."

"I'm there, man," he said.

"How many hours will it take you to reach me?"

"No, Seth, I'm there." The receiver went dead.

As far as I could tell, Mom and Dad were still asleep, so I crept downstairs to look outside. Nellie and Jim-bo were actually standing on my back patio, white CBC jumpsuits and all. They were waiting to pick me up, like Nelson and Roxy did every morning for school, or Rosa and Miguel did to go to the park.

I didn't speak, only nodded, and they seemed to understand that the Kashmaari were listening like Dad had indicated in the car wash. Nellie took my hand and dragged me out to the obsidian spacecraft parked in the back yard next to Mom's rock garden. It was barely visible in the darkness, although the back porch light reflected feebly off its blue and purple hues.

I followed Nellie inside, and claimed shotgun. She sat at the wheel and Jim-bo took up the seat behind us.

"Where do we get Boone?" she asked.

"I thought the CBC didn't get involved," I said.

"Shut up." I could tell by the look she gave me that it wasn't a good time to mess with her.

"He's at Area 51," I said. "That Kashmaar got him and is wearing him."

She nodded. "Figured that when he didn't come back to base."

She started the engine and we took off over Vegas heading for the northwest desert. I found it interesting that she preferred to drive manually. She was an excellent pilot.

"What happened to Meike?" I asked.

"She's fine," Nellie said. "She doesn't remember anything, but she might feel like she has mono for a while... which is a typical after affect."

"How did you know to get here so soon?" I asked.

"When Boone didn't come back, I went to Krad to consult Jim-bo. He's always up for a fight. He told me about your whip invention and we decided to head straight here to see if we could do anything. We hoped you'd contact us when you needed back up and you felt you were safe to do so."

"I'm not safe to do anything," I said, carefully.

"Well, they can't listen to us in here," Jim-bo said. "So spill."

I started on an explanation of everything that happened to me since leaving Moon Base, but had only reached the part about Altaar knocking Rosa out with one punch through the head when Nellie interrupted.

"Better make us extra elusive, Jacques," she said.

"Oui, my dear one," a Frenchman's voice answered.

"Dear one?" I smirked.

Nellie shrugged and beamed some of my bio suits onto the three of us.

"I added a feature to your design," Jim-bo said, and pointed to a small, rectangular button on the arm. "This will make you invisible – chameleon style. You can use it to enter the compound undetected and, hopefully, locate Boone. It will give us some time to take them by surprise."

He handed me a prototype of our plasma whip. It was exactly as I imagined it. A small, glass cylinder encased in a metal frame. It had an ergonomic handle that formed itself to my grip.

Jim-bo began his instruction, although I already pretty much knew how it worked, "You ignite the blaze by pushing that black button on the side, then lash the tail through the person who's possessed. It will glide through the body and bind itself to the Kashmaar. When you pull back, the Kashmaar will be torn out of the person. Then you push that same black button to retract both the Kashmaar and the blaze back into the chamber. Theoretically, the handle will also hold up to one thousand Kashmaari, so feel free to whip through anything that gets in your way. You can even lash out at anything tangible as well. It should sting someone pretty bad – enough to hold them at bay." He held up the side of his arm to show me a nasty gash, obviously from a test run.

"It's a good day to die," he smiled, knowing exactly what I was thinking.

Nellie shot him an annoyed look. He shrugged.

"I took the liberty of hacking into Constantine's mainframe to get whatever specs they had on Kashmaari."

"Van Helsing, dude?"

"Yeah, and I'm glad I did. He's done a ton of research and has recorded it all. I'm almost ninety-nine percent sure this will work."

"And if it doesn't?" I asked.

He smiled.

"If these things don't work, we're all dead," Nellie huffed.

"We are anyway," I decided.

"It better work, Jim-bo," Nellie sighed.

I examined the whip closely, trying not to think about what would happen if I it failed. "Where are you guys gonna be?"

"Creating a diversion." Nellie said with a smile.

"I'm with you, Seth," Jim-bo said, holding up another plasma whip. "I'll get your back."

"No. I'm the only one going in there. You need to stay

out of it so that you can build the next prototype and save my butt if this doesn't work."

"Oh… right. I hadn't really thought of that, but yeah. Good idea."

I was annoyed that he didn't put up more of a fight. He probably knew that he was sending me to my death. I supposed there was always a chance that Dad would come to my rescue again, but I seriously doubted it. At least Jim-bo would be around to build a few more whips if I failed. And it seemed like the Constantine guy would help with any future endeavors. At least I hoped so.

Our plan turned out something like this: go to Area 51, keep invisible, grab Boone and Sistah, and get out as fast as possible. I added a silent goal to take out as many Kashmaari as possible while I was down there. If I failed, plan B was: die honorably.

A few minutes later we had reached the base. I directed Nellie toward the same landing strip where Dirk had landed, and I switched my bio suit to invisible mode. My entire body disappeared, all except for the cylinder in my hand. I grabbed a bio suit for Boone, and switched it over to invisible mode as well.

"We can communicate through Jacques and your suit," Nellie directed. "Try to find Boone and Sistah, then meet us at the sign at the gates."

She meant the sign that authorized the use of lethal force for trespassers that I had thought was so cool back when Nelson and I visited with Roxy. Now it held a whole new meaning for me: I was as good as dead.

"Meet at the sign, got it," I mumbled. My mind raced as I reviewed all the things I was supposed to do.

"I've located the opening to the underground Base," Jim-bo indicated a screen which showed the hangar in the ground. "As soon as you break the ground barrier, that alarm will go, Nell."

"Here we go," she nodded, plummeting the ship into the middle of the landing strip. We descended into the earth and the hangar appeared around us. Jacques' door flew open and I practically fell out and ran right past a guard, who couldn't see me because of the suit. He smelled like oranges. I was half-tempted to try out the whip, but I needed to find Boone before starting anything.

Alarms were going off all over the place, and there was a rush of personnel toward Nellie's craft which was invisible, but certainly loud enough to locate. I heard Jacques lift off and tear through the barrier ceiling, followed immediately by half a dozen other crafts.

"BAH 1," Jim-bo's voice sounded in my ear through the mask of the bio suit. "We are away and under pursuit by enemy aircraft."

"Copy that," I whispered out of the side of my mouth. "Will contact when able."

I walked out of the hangar and into the large room full of personnel and Kashmaari without a problem. No one noticed me stepping quickly and quietly around the edge of the room. I had slid the little cylinder of the whip up my sleeve to keep it hidden and wrapped Boone's suit around the rest of it.

I had decided to head for the room with the couches, where Dad had picked me up, first. Just as I located the doorway, another alarm sounded. I glanced back to the monitors in the main room. They showed Nellie's ship, now visible, circling around in the air, firing back on the CBC-type, obsidian aircraft that had followed her out of the hangar.

The commotion that followed was perfect cover for me. I threaded my way quickly through the mass of people and disembodied Kashmaari and reached the couch room unnoticed. The Boone-Kashmaar sat on a green paisley couch with a high back and striped cushions, casually reading a magazine, a drink from the water cooler in its hand. I guess the first time around, I'd been too scared to notice how ugly the couches really were.

"Is someone there?" it asked, standing up.

It stared straight through me at the open door, and I remembered that I was still invisible. All that wouldn't matter if I hesitated too long, however, so I marched straight toward it, pressing the black button on the cylinder as I went. The lash of the whip shot out of the glass and metal in my hands, and the Boone-Kashmaar lunged toward it. His movement startled me, and I pulled back prematurely. The whip cracked in the air, missing him by two feet, sizzling as it hit the floor.

Both of us stared for a second at the scorch mark it had left when it hit, and then the Boone-Kashmaar rushed at me. I stumbled backward, forgetting for a moment that I still was invisible. I ducked behind the water cooler, and it put its hand out and closed on the air where I had been standing. I stepped around quietly and took aim again.

The whip lashed through Boone's skin, pulling the green wisps of the Kashmaar's spirit through the flesh as I retracted it. A metallic howl sounded inside of Boone's body, and I pulled harder. Then, the lash tightened like a fish when the hook is set. I pushed the black button again, sucking both lash and Kashmaar into the chamber. Boone crumpled to the ground.

I waited for a few anxious moments to see if the Kashmaar would be able to escape the chamber, but it stayed put. I exhaled and ran to Boone to check his pulse. He was unconscious, but he was alive. It was hard to shove his body into the invisible bio suit, especially since I kept fumbling for fear we'd be discovered.

"BAH 1," I said out loud, "I have him. Where are you?"

"We're right over your hangar and about to get blown out of the sky," Jim-bo announced delightedly.

"So much for preserving your life to build the next prototype," I said.

"Did the whip work?" he asked.

"Clockwork," I said.

"Is his suit on?" Nellie interrupted.

I zipped up the last of it making him disappear completely, and said, "Yes, although, now I can't see him. This is going to be tough."

"Hang on; I'm sending in the tear gas to cause some confusion…maybe disorient everyone," Nellie announced.

What sounded like bombs came crashing down on the ceiling and almost immediately, smoke poured into the room. As the gas colored the air around us, I was suddenly grateful for the seaweed oxygen I had been breathing. I sighed, threw Boone's arm over my shoulder, and hoisted him to his feet, half walking, half dragging him out into the smoke-filled hallway. I could hear yells and coughing all around.

A disembodied Kashmaar wandered directly into our path. Shifting Boone to one side so that I could aim the cylinder, I pushed the button again and cracked the whip out in its direction. This time the blaze hit the target dead center, lashing itself around the Kashmaar's mid-section. I pushed retract as quickly as possible, sucking it back into the base, the painful metallic screams trailing behind.

Boone stirred and staggered against me, then grunted with the effort of trying to force himself upright and onto his own two feet. I kept a fist firmly on him. With the bio-suit making him invisible, I couldn't afford to lose physical contact.

"We've got to find Sistah," I coaxed him. "Which way?"

"I don't know who you are." His voice was weak.

"I'm your grandson, Seth," I said.

"Oh," he said, still sounding confused.

"We're invisible in order to escape from the Kashmaari."

"I don't know what you are saying."

"Boone, do you know where you are?"

There was silence. He pulled away from my grasp, but I clenched down on him hard. "Don't try to break free. I don't want to lose hold of you."

"Okay," he mumbled. "Who did you say you were again?"

"Seth."

"And what are we doing here?"

"Escaping."

"Whatever you say, son." He was perplexed, but at least he was cooperating.

"Can you walk?" I asked, helping him find his footing.

"Yeah," he muttered. "I can't see my feet, though."

"Just try."

We staggered back to the main room where several Air Force personnel lay writhing on the floor, gasping for breath. Above them, a group of disembodied Kashmaari sailed in the air, like ghosts. I brandished the whip and lashed through five of them, pulling them back into the chamber just as the last one started in the direction of the whip. But we had still drawn too much attention to ourselves. They couldn't see us, but they knew we were there. I spun around.

Eight more of them were heading straight for us. I managed to lash four and capture them, as the remaining four sailed past the blaze and circled back around. One tried to fly straight through my path, but I managed to repel it with the whip, catching its leg as it struggled to get away. I fumbled at the button to retract and then turned just in time to the final three right before they reached us.

"Yes!" I whispered, allowing myself a small moment of triumph. It was short lived, however, because in my excitement, I had let go of Boone. When I reached for him, he wasn't there.

"Boone," I hissed, whirling around and stumbling over an unconscious body on the ground in front of me.

There was no answer. It was futile to fumble around, hoping I would bump into him.

"Crap, guys, I lost Boone," I said into the communicator, but Nellie and Jim-bo were silent as well. I took a deep breath. My only chance was to make myself visible and hope he was coherent and capable enough to find me.

My hand shook as I reached down for the cloaking button on my bio suit. It was one thing to enter a Kashmaari liar in stealth mode. It was quite another to be caught in the flesh. What choice did I have? I punched the button and watched my limbs and torso materialize around me.

"Please be awake, Boone," I muttered under my breath. "Please find me."

The Kashmaari found me first.

I saw them out of the corner of my eye. At least twenty, lime-green fire beings converged all at once. I steeled myself, concentrated on avenging Rosa, Boone, Dad, and Connie. All the anger I felt smashed through the whip and into the fray. There wasn't any time to analyze my situation or their positions, I just went ballistic. I was sweating and my muscles ached, but I kept slashing at the electric storm of green spirits spiraling at me. I slashed and thrashed, circling around and around, trying my best to keep them from entering me.

Finally, I was down to four, then three, then two, and then it was over. Everything was silent except for the giant screens, ablaze with the dog fight between Nellie and the Kashmaari aircraft. She wove in and out of the crossfire as the sun peaked over the horizon behind her. In spite of their impressive attack, my Aunt Nellie had outclassed and outgunned every last one of the Area 51 defense air craft. As if reading my thoughts, they launched a counter attack and suddenly an onslaught of green Kashmaari flew right for the ship like missiles. They penetrated the ship and then disappeared.

"Guys, are you okay?" I asked. Silence, and then, finally, a crackle over the communicator. I could hear the bomb blasts all around them.

"This whip really works," Jim-bo answered back, completely shocked. "Like bees to honey... Seth... they keep coming and never know what hits them. Let's just hope this containment chamber you came up with holds 'em."

"You're the one who built it man... can't wait to find out how we're gonna dispose of them."

"Me neither," Jim-bo countered. "We haven't really thought about what to do with them... have we?"

"Let's pray they hold," Nellie said, "We'll beam them to hell once we get out of this. Now get Boone out of there! Over and out."

"Yes... well, the problem is, I lost Boone," I said, quickly explaining what had happened.

There was a stunned silence, then Nellie cursed under her breath.

Jim-bo interrupted her, "He's still got the suit on and is invisible?"

"Yes," I said, "but he's really weak.

"Get out of there," Jim-bo ordered. I could hear his

whip slash through the air.

"I can't just leave him here. That was the point of the whole mission."

"There's still a chance," Jim-bo reasoned, calmly, "He's invisible. Maybe he just needed a quiet corner to recover. Just hide yourself and get out of there."

"If I disappear, there's no way he'll be able to follow me out," I said.

They both started yelling at me, trying to get me to hide myself and leave. I promptly decided to go against orders and keep visible in order to distract the Kashmaari from finding Boone, and help him find me if he could.

I headed down another corridor and found Sistah parked in the hangar beyond. Three airmen were writhing on the floor next to her, gasping and coughing from the gas, as three Kashmaari rose in lime-green spirals out of their bodies. I held out my whip and cracked it through the air, grasping up two of the three and sucking them into the chamber. The other Kashmaar was too quick, though, and dashed out of the way. It caught sight of the cylinder and rushed at it as if it wanted to burst through me. I stumbled backward and dropped the cylinder, forgetting myself in my desperation to escape its onslaught.

My getaway was too slow and I could feel its cold, icy touch pouring through my suit and into my skin.

"This suit is supposed to be Kashmaar proof," I mumbled, and felt myself going numb.

"Something had to go wrong," Jim-bo said. "Better the suit than the whip, right?"

I didn't reply.

"Seth," Nellie yelled, "Are you alright?"

I couldn't answer. I was frozen and in burning, excruciating pain. I wanted to vomit my insides all out and die immediately. Suddenly a flash of warmth sailed through me and something tugged hard at my waist. Someone or something else had grabbed the plasma whip and managed to catch the Kashmaar through my midsection. It writhed and screamed as it fought desperately not to be sucked into the chamber, but with a final hollow howl, the lime-green

FIONA OSTLER

wisps disappeared out through my skin. I whirled around. The whip clattered down to the floor, and I heard the sound of something heavy falling to the ground.

Ignoring the queasiness in my stomach, I scooped the whip up in one hand and felt around the floor with the other.

"Boone?" I asked.

My hand reached what felt like a shoulder as he wheezed out, "Nice contraption."

I pushed the button on his suit, revealing him.

"Thanks," I said. He was tired and anxious. He still seemed disoriented. How could he forget me?

"BAH 1," Jim-bo's anxious voice interrupted. "Are you..."

"We're good, BAV 1," I cut him off, "meet us at the rendezvous point."

"You've got Boone and Sistah?"

"That's a roger."

"Awesome."

Boone sat up and leaned in the direction of Sistah up on the platform. I waited for Boone to take over, but he just smiled.

"Go ahead," I said.

"Go ahead, what?" he answered.

"Say activate." I pointed to Sistah.

"Activate."

"Voice command correct," Sistah said, coming to life, "Hey there, Sugar, good to hear your voice again."

"You have a space ship?" he asked.

"Boone, it's Sistah."

He said nothing. He was so bewildered, just like Connie had been, that I suddenly knew what happened. The moment the Kashmaar enemy claimed Boone as a bodyslave the CBC green juice had jettisoned his memory. He didn't know anything that was going on, but had managed to save me anyway, in true Carter style.

"Come on, Boone," I said, leading him over to Sistah, and helping him into the passenger seat. "Let's get you to safety."

"Thanks for helping me, young man," he said. "I don't understand what it going on, though."

"I know," I said. "But thank you for trusting me, and saving me back there."

He nodded.

I activated guest driver and ordered Sistah to keep hidden and take us to the front gate.

"Sure thing, Sugar Two," Sistah cooed, making me smile.

We flew up out of the base and circled, invisible, through and past the dogfight toward the gate. I had no desire to fire on Air Force planes, even if they were working with the Kashmaari. I had a pretty good idea they were flying against their will.

"BAV 1, do you need assistance?" I asked reluctantly, but all I heard was static.

Jacques landed on the strip closest to the mountain range, all the ships circling fast around it, firing everything they had.

"Nellie?" I called, desperately. "Jim-bo..."

I was suddenly worried that they had been taken over by Kashmaari and that I was witnessing their execution. Sistah landed by the trespassing sign, still invisible, and her doors hissed open. The guard who was supposed to be on duty was gone, obviously trying to find out what was going on. I watched in horror as the gunfire rained down on Nellie and Jim-bo. Several military personnel ran toward Jacques with their guns.

"We've got to save her," I said, panicking, but a moment later, Jacques exploded in a brilliant burst of pyrotechnics, sending the guards falling over themselves to scramble away from the fire and shrapnel flying through the air.

"Relax, Seth," someone said from behind my seat. I looked back and in a moment Nellie appeared, dressed in her own bio suit. Jim-bo came in behind her, grinning widely.

"That last touch was mine," he said. "I'll build you another Frenchman, Nel."

"Why'd you blow it up?" I asked.

"Give them something to do while we get you home," Nellie answered.

Chapter 25

GOODBYE

Minutes later, Sistah touched down in my back yard. Nellie had finally calmed down about Boone's memory loss, after Jim-bo promised her that he'd be able to figure out how to get him back to normal. All he could remember was his life before the CBC. They were all so caught up in Boone, that they didn't really address the fact that I might need a little help as well. I couldn't believe that they were just taking me home. I half-hoped that we were stopping by to pick up Mom and Dad, but I knew that they were dropping me off.

"Seth," Nellie said, "I owe you one."

"Boone saved me on Moon Base so that I could get back to Earth and you took Meike home," I said. "I'd say we're even. Besides, I couldn't let my own grandfather become a permanent Kashmaari bodyslave."

She nodded, understanding that I knew about both of them. Jim-bo tensed up next to me, but didn't offer an explanation of blowing anyone's cover back on Krad.

"I'm sorry that we didn't tell you," she said.

"Why didn't you?"

"He wasn't sure how you felt about him," she admitted. "He abandoned your dad, Seth. He left him here when he didn't want to come with us. That doesn't necessarily make him the good guy. He was worried that you hated him."

I nodded and looked at Boone. He hadn't understood the exchange at all. I smiled and said, "I don't hate you, Boone."

"Okay," he said, returning my smile. It was his turn to try to keep up with the conversation.

Nellie said, "Well, you better get in there, or your I-was-asleep-the-whole-time cover is blown."

"I don't want to stay on Earth anymore," I said.

"The CBC won't take you back," Nellie said.

"And they'll take Boone back?"

"They don't know he was with the Kashmaari, but they do know that you are the reason one came to our base," she said, completely tearing up our emotional peace treaty with her well-reasoned argument for abandoning me.

"Seth could come back to Krad with me," Jim-bo offered.

She shook her head. "They'd know."

My fist clenched tightly around the plasma whip. "Why doesn't the CBC ever do anything nice for anyone?" I couldn't hold back my anger anymore. "We need help!"

"They just don't like to get involved." Nellie said.

"They just don't like to get involved?" I echoed. "Will they help Dad, now that they know the Kashmaari have gone after Boone and Connie?"

"They won't Seth. I'm sorry."

"Will you?"

There was an even longer pause. Nellie cleared her throat, uncomfortably. She was a flying ace, a warrior, and it looked like she wasn't interested in getting involved, now that she had Boone back. I punched my fist as hard as I could into the seat, and nearly broke my hand. Ships that fly beyond the speed of light are pretty much built to last. The ache throbbed through my knuckles and down into my wrist.

"Will you help us?" I asked them, again.

"I'll need to talk some things over with Constantine," she said, finally.

"The scientist who first discovered them?"

"He'll know what to do, Seth," Jim-bo reassured me and held out his hand for the plasma whip I was still clutching in my hands. "And you need to leave that with me. If any of them escape, you're a dead man."

I handed the whip over reluctantly and felt my heart sink, wondering how long it would take for them to find

Constantine and get back to me.

Nellie beamed off our bio suits and started fidgeting with her Brain. She changed her hair from dreads to long, flowing extensions.

"I guess we'll keep in touch," Boone offered, giving me a half hug with his arm.

"Call me," Jim-bo said, trying to give me a reassuring smile, but I could tell he was not happy about leaving me behind.

"You better get in before your Dad wakes up," Nellie ordered.

There was nothing left to say. I nodded, and backed out of Sistah. A hollow tone of regret chased me as I walked across the lawn toward my house. The faint sound of wind chimes floated back toward me as I felt Sistah lift off the ground behind me and disappear into the dawn.

The morning birds had finished choir practice. Their calls faded into the sounds of a typical morning in my Vegas suburb, but underneath all of it, I could still hear the faint tinkle of the wind chimes sounding from the back porch rafters. It left some hope in me that I would get to go back up to space soon.

And next time, I thought to myself as I walked through the back door into my house, *I'm taking Rosa Gomez with me.*

As I crept into the kitchen, I was startled to find Dad waiting for me at the kitchen table. His face wore an odd expression, almost as if he were getting ready to yell at me for something stupid I had done, but part of him didn't want to. I opened my mouth to say something, but that's when I caught it – a faint whiff of freshly-squeezed orange juice wafting toward us from the kitchen. I froze, staring at Dad, then looked down at the table in front of him. He was holding a flask in one hand and a gun in the other. I tried to keep calm and think of a way out as I took up the seat opposite him.

"Drink up," he said. His face twisted in agony at what he was commanding me to do.

"Dad," I pleaded.

He held a finger to his lips, and pushed the flask toward me.

I shrugged, looking away.

He cocked his gun.

There was no way I was going to lose everything like this. Then out of the shadows, Altaar walked up behind me and Dad pointed the gun at my head.

I picked up the flask and held it to my lips, the absurd irony becoming clear in my mind. There really was a cover up at Area 51, and, after finally getting abducted, I was about to forget everything.

Altaar cleared her throat behind me, and I felt her reach for my arm. My dad stared at me, trying hard not to flinch as her fingers touched me. I laughed ever so slightly, tipped the flask up, and drained it into my mouth.

"Now swallow," Dad said, and I did.

Everything faded to black.

Fiona Ostler is happily-ever-after married and raising four amazing children. She moonlights as an author in an attempt to not go crazy in her role as a domestic goddess and is pleased that her readers keep wanting more of her books. While one of her biggest fantasies in life is to fly a UFO, she'd also be happy hunting for buried treasure. Fiona is also the author of Guardian: Gold Rush (the first in a three part series). You can find out more about Fiona at fionaostler.com and on Facebook.

Made in the USA
Charleston, SC
16 December 2013